"Distinct bite-sized mysteries inspired by Virginia's regions, history, and all manner of murder."

—**Mary Burton, *New York Times* Best-Selling Author**

"*Virginia is for Murders, Volume III*, is an eclectic collection of stories by Virginia writers, all featuring Virginia locales. Themes run the gamut from blackmail to greed, love to revenge. So grab a can of salted peanuts, a bourbon with branch water, and settle in for a satisfying tour of the state for lovers, and sometimes . . . murder."

—**Bradley Harper, Award-Winning Author of**
A Knife in the Fog

"A flat-out terrific read with an amazing sense of place, this absorbing anthology covers the Virginia waterfront, literally and figuratively. From nefarious happenings in tourist havens to awful things done for the sake of antiquities and ancestors, to throwbacks to a history that isn't really past, these sharply plotted and beautifully written stories are a mystery lover's perfect trip to Virginia."

—**Kathleen Marple Kalb, Author of the Ella Shane**
Mystery Series

"A plethora of murder and mayhem abounds in this delightful collection of sixteen short stories set in Virginia."

—**Marilyn Levinson/Allison Brook, Author of the**
Haunted Library Series

"The *Virginia is for Mysteries III* authors have hit it out of the ballpark with more tales of murder and mayhem as they transport readers across Virginia's rich but deadly landscape. Enjoyably satisfying quick reads with something for everyone."

—Allie Marie, Award-Winning Author of True Color Series and more

"Such a treat! Don't miss this terrific short-story tour of this fascinating and historic state—but be very afraid! In historic hotels, oceanfront estates, and boozy bars, you'll discover blackmail, revenge, sinister conspiracies, and landmarks made for murder. It's a twisty and suspenseful trip that will keep you turning pages as fast as you can!"

—Hank Phillippi Ryan, *USA Today* Best-Selling Author, Winner of Mary Higgins Clark and Anthony Award, and Five-Time Agatha Award winner

"A cornucopia of short stories with something for every mystery lover's taste. Grab your copy, then gobble up the mayhem. Set in Virginia, this collection is perfect for armchair travelers to learn about the history and diversity of the Old Dominion while trying to solve sixteen murderous crimes."

—Fiona Quinn, *USA Today* Best-Selling Author

"Secrets, murder, and revenge bubble just under the genteel façade of brilliantly drawn Virginia settings in this page-turning collection. Settle in and prepare for a wild ride through the Old Dominion's darker side—there's something here for every mystery fan."

—LynDee Walker, National Best-Selling Author of the Nichelle Clarke Series

"Everyone knows that Virginia is for lovers. They also may have heard about its significant history and beautiful geography. Who would have anticipated all these elements together in a single book? Whether it's business or personal, the stories in this anthology show the remarkable diversity of inhabitants and environment that makes Virginia so special. I truly enjoyed the virtual journey as much as trying to figure out who did it or what's about to happen. This book would be a terrific beach read or a great volume to snuggle up with in winter. Get your favorite drink, relax, and immerse yourself in the mystery of Virginia!"

—Paula Gail Benson, Short Fiction Author

Virginia is for Mysteries: Volume III

by Teresa Inge, Kristin Kisska, Yvonne Saxon,
Frances Aylor, Jayne Ormerod, Heather Weidner,
Michael Rigg, Maggie King, Smita Harish Jain,
Sheryl Jordan, Vivian Lawry, Maria Hudgins,
Rosemary Shomaker, Max Jason Peterson,
Judith Fowler

ISBN 978-1-64663-517-7

Published by

köehlerbooks™

3705 Shore Drive
Virginia Beach, VA 23455
800-435-4811
www.koehlerbooks.com

Virginia is for Mysteries

VOLUME III

An Anthology of Mysteries Set in and Around Virginia

Teresa Inge — Kristin Kisska — Yvonne Saxon
Frances Aylor — Jayne Ormerod — Heather Weidner
Michael Rigg — Maggie King — Smita Harish Jain
Sheryl Jordan — Vivian Lawry — Maria Hudgins
Rosemary Shomaker — Max Jason Peterson
Judith Fowler

VIRGINIA BEACH
CAPE CHARLES

Introduction

The idea for the third installment of *Virginia is for Mysteries* came about when anthology coordinators Teresa Inge and Heather Weidner discussed the idea of sharing more of Virginia's unique and deadly landscape at Malice Domestic.

Virginia is for Mysteries features fifteen established authors. Their stories transport readers across Virginia's rich landscape, filled with landmarks, crime, and murder. The book is a follow up to the *Virginia is for Mysteries, Volume I* and *II* anthologies published by Koehler Books in 2014 and 2016.

Teresa Inge and Heather Weidner
Anthology Coordinators

TABLE OF CONTENTS

Virginia is for Mysteries: Volume III
Story Locations

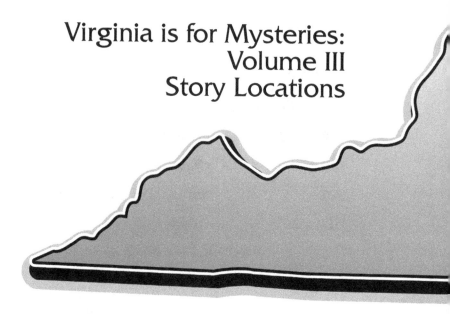

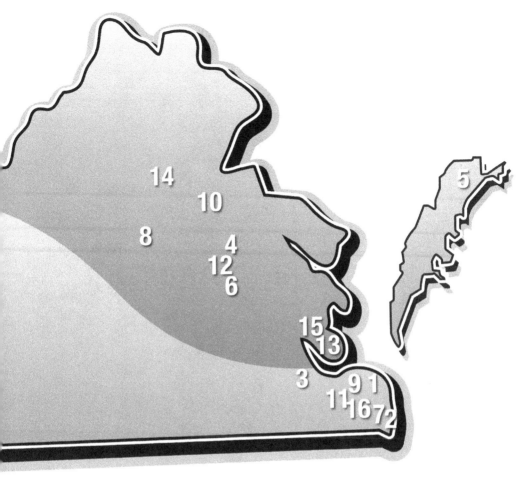

KISS, MAKEUP & MURDER

BY TERESA INGE

"WELCOME TO THE CAVALIER. My name is Connar Randolph, owner of the hotel." Connar smiled as she greeted her guests at the registration desk. "Please let me or my staff know if you need any assistance during your stay in Virginia Beach."

A blond man in a stylish pink shirt and white shorts strolled across the checkerboard floor toward her. "Tell me, can I get a bottle of your straight bourbon whiskey in my room to beat this stifling heat?"

Connar recognized the man as wealthy playboy Gavin Heath. "Yes, Mr. Heath. I'll ask the porter to place a bottle of our signature bourbon in your room." She paused. "Oh . . . and we have an indoor pool to cool off, or the beach is just steps away near our private beach club."

He gave his infamous boyish grin and touched Connar's hand. "Please, call me Gavin."

Flushed, she smoothed her tailored, navy-blue suit and shifted her stance on her heels.

"Nice place." Gavin nodded toward the elegant chandelier suspended over the vintage lobby. Light bounced off the light fixture from the ceiling to the floor, showering spectacular crystals of luminosity throughout the room. "Unusual for a babe such as yourself to own such an extravagant hotel. I assume there's no Mr. Randolph?"

Connar was not surprised at Gavin's flamboyance. She had seen him in the media, partying with celebrities and wealthy socialites around the globe. "The hotel opened in 1927 under the ownership of my great-grandmother, Helena Randolph.

Helena and my grandmother Maggie Randolph operated it until my parents took it over. I took ownership three years ago after they passed away. Is there anything else I can do for you Mr . . . uh, Gavin?"

"No. That's all."

Connar summoned the porter and instructed him to bring bourbon to Gavin's room. "This is Max. He'll take good care of you."

"Follow me." Max placed Gavin's bags on a cart and walked toward the elevator.

As Connar waved to Gavin, she contemplated other demands he would put on her staff. She prided herself on taking good care of her guests with the same high standards her parents had insisted on for more than fifty years. Guests had returned annually to experience the hotel's charm and personal service. But Gavin had emitted a high-maintenance, hard-to-please vibe. In a word, *trouble*.

And the last thing Connar needed was a troublesome guest, adding to the burden of running an aging building that costs millions to restore to its elegant grace. If it weren't for the rich Virginia Beach legacy and historical listing on the National Register of Historic Places, she would have had to close the doors years ago.

A disturbance near the lobby stairs caught Connar's attention.

"For the last time, grab my purse!" Barbara Harrington of Harrington Cosmetics shouted to her assistant, Marlo Van Allen.

Already toting four cosmetic bags, Marlo grabbed the purse, which was the size of a small suitcase. She waved her hand toward Rex Adler, Barbara's much younger fourth husband, who stood on the marble stairway in deep conversation with Connar's niece, Kathleen Randolph.

Connar walked toward the stairs. "Let me help you, Marlo."

"Thank you, Connar."

"Anything for our returning guests." Connar grabbed the purse and motioned for Kathleen to return to her hostess stand in the Becca Restaurant and Garden.

Rex squeezed Kathleen's hand and made his way toward Barbara.

Kathleen had worked for Connar during the past three years.

Connar had kept her on staff even though her work performance left a lot to be desired. Too much partying with Virginia Beach's elite crowd made Kathleen late for work or tired on the job. But Connar felt an obligation to her brother John's only daughter. The two siblings had worked together until his passing, at which point Connar had become the sole owner of the Cavalier. She held little hope that Kathleen would ever be mature enough to take over.

After Max returned from helping Gavin, Connar motioned him to join her at the bottom of the stairs. "Please escort Barbara Harrington to the presidential suite."

"Right this way, Mrs. Harrington." Max set her remaining bags on the cart.

"And Mr. Adler," Rex added, making the point that he expected to be recognized as Barbara's husband.

Connar nodded, vowing to do everything she could to help Barbara during her visits to the Cavalier. What were the odds that marriage would survive? Rex needed attention that Barbara couldn't provide. At sixty-two, she traveled frequently to manage her makeup line, New Age Foundation. She was the reigning cosmetics queen and had to keep pedaling her line to pay for her three ex-husbands' extravagant lifestyles.

Connar made her way to the outdoor garden to check on reservations. It was busy. Waitstaff served cocktails and lunch to guests. Since the renovation, the clientele had changed to a more upscale, diverse—but demanding—crowd. Once seated, they expected their cocktails to be promptly in hand.

She approached Kathleen at the hostess stand. "Looks like another late-lunch crowd."

"Yeah. We've had two bridal showers, four birthdays, and of course tourists and locals," Kathleen said.

Connar glanced across the garden. "The new wrought iron chairs are beautiful with the shiplap dining tables."

"It's very chic. Plus, guests love the ocean view backdrop from the top of the hill while dining outside," Kathleen added.

"How many guests are dinning this evening?"

Kathleen viewed the reservations. "Eighty."

"Great. By the way, dear, don't forget the no-fraternizing-with-guests rule."

"What do you mean?" Kathleen frowned.

"Mr. Adler is Mrs. Harrington's new husband."

"Oh, you mean Rex? We're old friends." Kathleen winked.

Connar glanced at her watch. "We'll continue this conversation later." She had just enough time to finish her staff rounds before meeting Barbara, Rex, and Marlo in the grand salon for a cocktail then dinner at the Hunt Room. "See you later."

After finishing her last round in the Becca, Connar headed to her room as staff prepared for the dinner hour.

She showered and dressed in a chic, silhouette dress for the evening's festivities. Connar sat in a lavish French-country armchair that had been gifted to her by a visiting diplomat trying to win her affection. But she wasn't interested in being a diplomat's wife and attending never-ending cocktail parties. Her future husband would be by her side at the Cavalier. Just like her parents.

She brushed her blond hair and glanced out the window, enjoying her penthouse view. Her parents had converted three rooms as their living quarters to raise their family. Barbara Harrington might have the presidential suite, but Connar had the larger accommodations.

She exited the elevator and entered the grand salon. Barbara stood at the bar with Gavin. Further down, Rex, Kathleen, and Marlo sat in cozy sofas, chatting and sipping cocktails. "Evening," Connar said. "You two know each other?"

"We met earlier." Gavin winked.

"We're fast friends," Barbara slurred. She frowned when noticing Rex with Kathleen.

Connar had never seen Barbara drunk.

A server approached. "Something to drink, Connar?"

"A glass of rosé, please."

After getting their drinks, Connar, Barbara, and Gavin joined the group on the sofas.

Barbara plopped down next to Rex, who sat dangerously close to Kathleen.

Connar sat on the opposite couch, Gavin by her side.

Marlo sat in a wing chair, facing the group.

"I take it Max delivered your whiskey earlier?" Connar asked Gavin.

He lifted his glass.

Rex placed his hand on Barbara's knee. She pushed it away, spilling her drink.

"You drunken fool!" Rex grabbed a napkin and wiped the liquid off his expensive shoes.

"Well, if you didn't act like a tomcat, I wouldn't have to drink."

Connar frowned at Kathleen. She'd already warned her niece not to socialize with Rex. Now she was causing trouble. She changed the subject to keep the argument from escalating.

"How has your stay been so far?"

"Fabulous," Marlo said. "Your staff is outstanding."

"I concur," Gavin added. "Accommodations are elegant, and the bourbon is top notch."

Connar smiled. "Glad to hear it." She grabbed her phone. "Our table is ready." The group exited the salon and headed to the Hunt Room located on the lower floor of the hotel. The Hunt Room infused Southern cuisine with hand-crafted cocktails that showcased the bourbon made at the onsite distillery.

Once seated in the rustic restaurant, the group ordered food and beverages. The alcohol flowed. Rex focused his attention on Kathleen. Barbara became more belligerent toward her husband.

Connar pulled Kathleen to the side. "I need you to say goodnight to the group."

"Why?" Kathleen crossed her arms.

"Your relationship with Rex is upsetting Barbara, and Barbara is our guest."

"But we're friends. Plus, he invited me to join the festivities tonight."

"I understand. But until this is resolved between them, it's for the best."

Kathleen said goodnight.

Marlo and Rex escorted a staggering Barbara to the presidential suite.

That left Gavin to finish his bourbon and Connar to handle the dinner bill.

"If there isn't anything else, enjoy your evening." Connar placed the receipt in her clutch.

"Uh . . . there is one thing?"

Connar faced Gavin. "What is that?"

"I would love a private tour of the rooftop. I hear the view is fantastic."

Connar hesitated. "The rooftop is closed for renovation."

He lowered his head and voice. "I see."

Always wanting to keep her guests happy, she relented. "I can do a tour this once. Follow me."

She led Gavin to the elevator to the top floor and pushed the rooftop door open. It should have been locked. Connar made a mental note to have maintenance repair it. She held the door open as they scaled the small steps leading to the rooftop. A salty breeze greeted them.

"Watch your step. Construction materials are on the far side of the roof." Connar motioned toward a pile of bricks and wood.

"The rolling hills are stunning, especially since the rest of the landscape is so flat." He pointed toward the front lawn of the grand hotel and leaned against the low wall.

"It's part of the original landscape. I come up here to think things out."

"It must be lonely not having someone to share it with." Gavin moved closer. He rubbed her arm, then lifted her chin and kissed her. "I would love to get to know you better."

———————

The next morning, Connar awoke to a beautiful June day. She sat up in bed, stretched her arms, and remembered Gavin's gentle touch last night. But she could not discount his attraction toward Barbara nor his playboy ways.

First on today's agenda was to welcome new guests, check in with her staff, and call Barbara. She showered and made her way to the lobby.

"Morning, Connar." Max pushed a cart filled with luggage. "This way folks," he said to a family of four.

Connar smiled as she walked to registration to greet guests and to prepare the agenda for her staff meeting.

Her staff meeting passed quickly with no hitches. Connar let out a slight sigh and grabbed a quick sandwich and nibbled on it while dialing Barbara's room.

After four long rings, she heard a slurred, "Hello."

"Good afternoon, Barbara. I just wanted to see how you were doing."

"Oh, Connar, I'm so sorry for last night. Or at least what I remember. Why don't you pop by before dinner for our chat time. I've got a new line that you just have to see."

After doing afternoon rounds, Connar dressed in a burgundy, off-the-shoulder jumpsuit. She had the beauty and body to attract any wealthy suitor, including Gavin, who had extended an invitation to dinner.

As she walked to the presidential suite, she stopped in her tracks. The door to the rooftop stood ajar. She crossed through the entryway to secure the door but noticed Gavin leaving Barbara's room. She stepped back, hoping he wouldn't notice her.

After her visit with Barbara, Connar entered the Becca restaurant and approached Kathleen at the hostess stand.

"Right this way. Gavin is seated at a corner table." Kathleen led her aunt toward Gavin. He radiated money in a crisp black shirt and white pants. Connar understood why women were attracted to his good looks and wealth. Heir to a diamond fortune, Connar doubted Gavin had ever worked a day in his life.

Gavin stood as Connar sat. "Good evening, sugar."

Connar smiled. She would not describe herself as sweet.

"Your waiter will be right with you," Kathleen said.

"Beauty runs in the family." Gavin smiled at Kathleen. His hand brushed hers as he took the menu from her.

"I see you're breaking your fraternizing rule," Kathleen whispered to Connar and walked away.

Connar frowned and then glanced at Gavin. If he heard Kathleen, he didn't react to her comment.

"Good evening, Connar and Mr. Heath. What will we be drinking tonight?" The waiter placed a napkin in Connar's lap.

"The lady will have a glass of your best rosé, and I'll take another bourbon." Gavin winked at the waiter.

"I'll be right back with your drinks."

"How did you know what I like to drink?" Connar asked.

"I asked the waiter. Plus, you drank rosé last night."

"I think you're trying to impress me."

"I'm the one who is impressed." Gavin gazed into her eyes.

"Rosé for the lady." The waiter placed the glass in front of Connar. "And bourbon for the gentleman. Would you like to order any appetizers before dinner?"

"Give us a few minutes," Gavin said.

Connar sipped her wine. "Thank you for inviting me to dinner."

"It's my pleasure to finally dine alone with the stunning Connar Randolph."

"What brings you to Virginia Beach?"

"Business, and of course the pleasure of visiting the fabulous Cavalier."

Connar noticed Kathleen escorting Marlo into the restaurant. Barbara's assistant was alone, which was unusual. The two were almost inseparable.

Gavin moved closer. "Tell me, why isn't there a Mr. Randolph, since you are such a beautiful woman?"

"I haven't met him yet." Connar sipped her wine.

"*Help, help!* Is there a doctor in the house?"

Connar turned to see Max running into the restaurant, hands waving.

"I'm a doctor." A distinguished man in a blue shirt yelled from his table.

"Please follow me. It's Barbara Harrington," Max shouted.

Connar jumped from her seat and followed Max and the doctor to the elevator, then up to the rooftop. There on the floor lay Barbara Harrington in a blood-stained, gray silk dress, the same one she'd worn earlier when Connar visited her room. A wood board lay beside her.

The doctor knelt beside Barbara and checked her pulse. He shook his head.

———— 🎎 ————

After the medical examiner left the Cavalier, Connar stood in the lobby trying to take it all in. A man in a suit approached her. "I'm Detective Jax Murphy. I need to ask you a few questions."

Connar nodded.

"Since Barbara Harrington appears to have a blow to the back of the head, can you tell me what happened?"

"I don't know. I was having dinner with a guest."

"And?"

"I heard screams and rushed to the rooftop. That's when I saw her on the floor."

"Do you know how she got there?"

"No."

"According to the porter, you had drinks earlier with Mrs. Harrington in her room, which is across from the rooftop door. Can you elaborate?"

Connar wondered why Max mentioned this to the detective. "It's a tradition for Barbara and me to have a cocktail together when she arrives."

"Did you notice anything unusual during your visit?"

Connar paused. Not wanting to reveal the bombshell that Barbara dropped about her plans to divorce Rex due to his constant philandering, she cleared her throat. "No," she lied.

"That's all the questions I have for now. Please stay close to the hotel in case I have anything further."

How did Barbara get on the rooftop? Was the door unlocked, as Connar had found it when giving Gavin a tour? If Gavin knew about the unlocked rooftop, could he have killed Barbara? But why? Had the two been having an affair? If so, maybe Rex had found out and killed Barbara. Although Barbara was probably worth more to him alive than dead, it's possible he would fare better if she were dead rather than divorced.

So many questions . . .

Connar glanced toward the hostess stand to check on Kathleen. But her niece wasn't at her station. Connar summoned Max to the lobby.

"Can I help you, Ma'am?"

"Where is Kathleen?"

"She had to take care of something on the boardwalk. Said she would be back soon."

Connar tapped her lip. "How about Rex Adler?"

"I believe he mentioned taking a walk on the boardwalk."

"I need you to go and find out what they're doing. But don't let them see you."

"In my uniform?"

"Take your jacket off and then go. But hurry."

Max left the hotel.

Connar took the elevator to the top floor and made her way to the presidential suite. She used her master key to unlock the door. While inside, she inspected the room for anything unusual. She glanced at a paper tucked under the desk pad. A letter from another cosmetic firm, addressed to Marlo, thanked her for her interest, but declined a deal to partner on a new cosmetics line. Connar's heart raced.

"I see you found the paper," a voice sneered from behind.

Startled, Connar turned to face Marlo standing in the doorway. "What does this mean?"

"It means I was double-crossed."

"I don't understand."

"Since I helped Barbara create the New Age Foundation and never got credit for it, I figured I could do the same with another cosmetics line. But they didn't believe me and informed Barbara I was trying to cause trouble."

Connar looked at Marlo. "What happened when Barbara found out?"

"After you left the suite today, she confronted me and said I was fired. We argued, and I hit her in the head with a vase. I thought she was dead, but somehow, she stumbled to the rooftop door and up the stairs. I killed her with a wood board, and now I have to kill you, too."

Marlo moved closer, slipped her hands around Connar's neck, and began to squeeze.

Connar couldn't breathe and felt her eyes bulge from her head. She ran her hand across the desk and wrapped her hand around a cosmetic jar as tight as she could and slammed it in Marlo's eye.

Marlo reared back, snarling.

She grabbed Connar's jumpsuit and yanked her to the ground. Connar fell against the door and landed outside the suite, her head smacking against the ground. Marlo jumped on her back, pressing her face against the floor.

Connar writhed on the floor, but Marlo had her pinned. She started to go limp just as pressure suddenly eased. Connar rolled away, scrambling to her feet, watching as Max wrestled with Marlo.

The detective emerged from the elevator and raced to help Max. Soon Marlo was in handcuffs. And none too happy about it.

Max approached Connar. "You okay?"

"Yes. Thank you, Max. You saved my life." She turned to the detective. "But what are you doing here?"

Before he could respond, Max interrupted. "With Mrs. Harrington murdered, I suspected Kathleen and Rex, as I think you did, too," Max said.

Connar nodded.

"But when I spotted them together on the Boardwalk, they looked more like a young couple in love, not people who had just killed a woman. There was only one person left with a motive. Marlo. So, I alerted the detective."

Detective Murphy yanked Marlo to her feet and whisked her to the elevator.

— 🎀 —

Two weeks later, Connar stepped into the lobby. Max, now promoted to manager, motioned to a porter to carry the arriving guests' bags. Connar stepped closer to Max. "Tell me. Did maintenance repair the rooftop door?"

"Yes. It kept sticking, but it's fixed now."

"Great." Connar glanced at Kathleen at the registration desk. She felt a bit of remorse for even thinking of Kathleen and Rex as murderers. Thankfully, that relationship had been short-lived. Not because it wasn't true love, but because Gavin had given Rex a substantial one-time payment to get lost.

She also felt a bit of guilt for considering Gavin as a suspect. After all, she had witnessed him coming out of Barbara's room shortly before her death. She hadn't thought the two had anything in common. Connar had later learned Gavin had signed a contract with Barbara to invest in the cosmetics business. He stood to make even more millions.

For now, he'd extended his stay at the Cavalier. Who knew where that might lead?

Max handed Connar a note as she turned to head to her office. *Will be back next month. Hope to see you for dinner. Gavin.*

VENDETTA BY THE SEA

By Kristin Kisska

CLAUDETTE

AFTER KNOCKING ON THE door of Triona's beach house, I adjust the wide brim of my straw sunhat and sunglasses. The girls' getaway vacation was my idea, and I can't wait. What better way to co-celebrate our fortieth birthday year? Umbrella cocktails. Sundresses. Tans. The beach. It'll be just like our high school graduation trip so many years ago.

What's taking those bitches so long?

A woosh of ocean air whips around me. This time I pound a little harder and longer, taking care not to chip my beach-themed manicure—hot pink with painted sun umbrellas on both ring fingers. After getting a late start and all the traffic delays, I need to party. "Hey, open up. Where are you guys?"

Metal clicks and slides, then the door creaks open.

"Oh!" Within seconds, my longest girlfriends ever—Triona, Shelby, and Malia—welcome me inside. But I'm a girl on a mission. Within seconds, I dump my travel bag by the door, kick off my strappy heels, swipe a glass of rosé, and then march straight past them to the spiral staircase.

"I don't care what all y'all do this week, but that rooftop platform is all mine!"

While the girls follow me like ducklings, Triona informs us the deck is called a widow's walk. Whatever. As long as I can sip cocktails on this wraparound balcony and admire waves crashing on endless stretches of Sandbridge Beach, I'll be happy.

Yes, this is precisely what I needed. The years haven't been too kind to me, with both my divorces and one dead-end job after another. Screw that insanity. I came to settle the score with these three friends.

"Ready to party, bitches?"

— 👧 —

TRIONA

"How much did this beach house set you back?" When Claudette burst into my beach house yesterday evening like a pink tornado, she embodied the drama queen she'd always been. Though I hadn't seen her in person since the day I left our high school beach week twenty-one years ago, she hasn't changed. Well, besides her puffed up lips.

"Good to see you, too. Claudette." I might as well have been the conch shell decorating my kitchen counter. I'd been dreading this vacation for the last three months, ever since I gave in to Claudette's relentless begging.

Don't get me wrong, I adore Shelby and Malia. We've rendezvoused every year since graduation, despite living in different areas of Virginia. It took a lot of convincing to get them on board with this vacation. Claudette promised me that she'd make amends, that everyone deserves a second chance. I caved.

This morning, I stand alone atop my widow's walk still dressed in my PJs, drinking coffee, and watching the sunrise. Footsteps on the spiral staircase give me enough warning to mask my grimace with a smile.

"Good morning, Claudette."

"Do you think this bathing suit is too matronly?" Claudette emerges from below, then parades across my balcony in her bikini and platform stilettos as if she were on a Ms. America runway. What little fabric she wears strains under her ample bronzed cleavage and booty. No tan lines for her.

"No worries on the granny front. Did you sleep well?" Looks like another perfect summer day in the making. Gorgeous, but endlessly irritating with Claudette in tow. "A pot of coffee is ready in the kitchen if you'd like some."

"Oh, my gawd. I forgot how high up we are!" Claudette backs away from the balcony ledge as she thrusts her hand over her heart. Not that I buy her faux concern.

At all.

Claudette certainly didn't have a fear of heights twenty-one years ago when she cornered me on the balcony ten floors up from the Boardwalk. She and I were the only two still in our Virginia Beach high-rise hotel room. Malia and Shelby weren't there to witness Claudette berating me.

"I saw you last night, Triona. Don't think I don't know what you were up to." Claudette had poked my sternum with her finger.

"What are you talking about?"

"At the crab shack party." Her jaw jutted as she stepped closer to me. "I saw you flirting with Jake."

"He was between me and the bar. I was just trying to get around him to order a drink."

"Jake is mine."

"Fine. You can have him! He's a meathead, Claudette. I'm not even sure they handed him his diploma at graduation. Besides, I'm leaving for college, why would I want— Oh!"

Crap! My pulse hammered as vertigo had overtaken my sense of stability. Somehow, Claudette had pinned me against the balcony railing, with my head and torso leaning over the side while I clung to the metal bars with both hands. I remember her eyes flaring with hatred as she snapped my shell necklace and held it over the edge. One by one, each shell fragment slipped from the string, free falling a hundred feet to the ground.

"If you even look at him one more time, Triona, you're dead." She had pressed her body against mine, the metal rail biting into my ribs. Then she backed off, marched inside our hotel room, and rode down the elevator to meet Malia and Shelby in the lobby.

Instead of following her, I had slid down to my knees, crawled inside the sliding glass door, and curled up on the floor to catch my breath. I massaged my naked throat. Had the railing not held fast, I'd have ended up splat on the ground below.

Now, just thinking about that day makes me want to shove her over my widow's walk railing, micro-bikini and all. Instead, I escape to my kitchen under the guise of refilling my coffee mug. Claudette asks for some as well. I'll chalk up a win if I don't give in to temptation and spike it with bleach.

For twenty-one freaking years, I'd made a point to never ever be in her presence again. Then I caved. I was expecting an apology—fat chance.

When will Shelby and Malia wake up and help diffuse her crazy?

I wish Claudette were dead.

— 🎎 —

SHELBY

Crap! Claudette's high-pitched squeal wakes me from my one blissful escape from memories.

Rolling over in my bed, I cover my ears and eyes with the pillow, willing myself to fall back asleep . . . and for Claudette to fall off the balcony above my room. How did Triona talk us into inviting this walking nightmare into our annual girlfriends' beach vacation?

Last night had been uglier than I expected. If Triona hadn't begged me to stay, I'd have already packed my bags and driven back to Fairfax. Don't get me wrong, I'd give up anything—even my photography career—for Triona and Malia, but this week may exceed my limits. You'd think after all these years, Claudette would've grown a freaking conscience. That she can still goad me and push my buttons is something I'm not proud of.

"Shelby, you really should do something about all that weight you put on. Have you tried intermittent fasting?" Her fake Southern drawl seemed sincere, but we were all with her and knew she originally hailed from New Jersey. "Just a good diet and . . . well, maybe if you grew out your hair, wore some makeup, and went shopping for somethin' a little more feminine. I'm sure some man will take a second look at you."

"No, no. I'm not trying to find a man—" Hoping a pause in the conversation would distract her, I gulped the rest of my margarita.

"Bless your heart. You've always been so shy around the boys, but take it from me, honey. A low-cal dinner date or two will not kill you. I'm going to take you shopping this week, and we'll get you started."

"I'm married." Holding up my left hand, I flashed her the

simple platinum band on my ring finger, suspecting it was way too mundane for her flashy taste.

"Well, miracles never cease to happen, now do they." Claudette arched one eyebrow, crossed her arms, and took a slow, appraising look up and down what I knew she'd considered my stocky body. "Well, who's the lucky guy?"

"There is no guy. My wife, Melanie, has a big deadline at work, so she's back home taking care of our fur babies." I bit back my smile. As the realization hit Claudette that I was a lesbian, she nearly spilled her cocktail. I might be the first gay person she'd ever befriended.

Her neck turned patchy shades of pink, and her eyes got all shifty before she changed the topic of conversation. "So, does your *wife* eat peanuts?"

Peanuts! What an evil bitch! And to think I'd expected an apology. Certainly not another chance to be mocked about my night-from-hell during beach week.

Twenty-one years ago, the four of us had been getting ready to head out to the beach dive bar, where all the recent grads convened every night. I'd been surprised that Claudette had focused her attention on me. She'd helped me pick out a cute outfit and style my less-than-trendy hair. She even sat me down and applied my makeup—back when I actually wore makeup—and had us all do shots in my honor before heading out. And then hovered by me the whole time at the bar, laughing at my jokes, introducing me to all the students partying there, because she knew everyone. I'd been so freaking flattered by her attention.

At the bar, someone dropped a peanut in my beer. My throat started swelling, and I had a severe allergic reaction. Who would do that?

I survived. Barely. It wasn't until the next day, after being discharged from the emergency room in the wee hours of the morning, that I solved the mystery. Triona helped me search for some pain meds to help with my residual headache. That's when we stumbled on a small foil bag of salted peanuts with one corner ripped open in Claudette's makeup case. But I knew for sure when Triona found my EpiPen in the pocket of the sundress Claudette had worn the night before.

Claudette tried to kill me. Why? So she could call 9-1-1 and get all the attention at the bar for saving my life? To flirt with the paramedics when they stabbed me with an EpiPen to stop my throat from swelling? Or maybe to get a ride in the ambulance to the ER with the sirens blaring. Who knows?

Yesterday was the first time I'd seen or spoken with her since that hellish night. I won't fall for her crap this time around. I don't want her attention, nor her faux goodwill. And I sure as hell won't let her anywhere near my food or drinks during this vacation.

Now, as I crush my pillow over my head, drowning out Claudette's irritating shrieks on the widow's walk, I fight every instinct to keep hiding. Instead, I change out of my PJs into shorts and a T-shirt, then brave my way up to the balcony.

I'd never, ever knowingly leave a friend dangling. Right now, Triona could probably use reinforcements.

I wish Claudette were dead.

——— 🐾 ———

MALIA

What a glorious morning. I slept in until after sunrise; can't remember the last time I did that. Three kids under the age of ten—and all early risers—keep me on my toes at home. I'm not complaining, mind you, but I appreciate the luxury of no one waking me up before daylight with "Mommy?" A sleep-deprived girl could get addicted to a good night of sleep.

And we're all turning forty this year. Where did my thirties go? I don't feel that old, but according to the calendar, I must be. The woman staring back at me in the dresser mirror has permanent bags under her eyes. Next to me lies my shoulder-bag that includes the Cheerios, extra outfits, wipes, and Pullups I'd forgotten to unload before this beach getaway.

From above, I can hear the other three chit-chatting about heading down to the beach. After wiggling into my bathing suit, I rummage through my luggage for my flip-flops, beach towel, and sunscreen. That I don't have to stay alert and play lifeguard to three little water bugs today is downright dreamy. I may even be able to read my book. Regardless, I'll definitely be sipping all day long on cocktails.

God, I love vacationing with my girlfriends!

But I wish Claudette hadn't joined us this time. For all the times the three of us have vacationed together, we've never hidden our loathing of that bitch.

But this year, Triona must've been feeling charitable because she decided to give Claudette a chance to settle up with each of us. And she'd even managed to talk Shelby and me into it, which was nothing short of a miracle of diplomacy.

Venturing out to the living room, Shelby and I lock eyes. She looks as if she's walked through hell and back already this morning. She could use a drink, and it's not quite noon.

"Good morning! How about I mix us a batch of mojitos before we head out to the beach?" I sidle behind the kitchen counter and reach for the rum.

"Yes! Make mine a double." Triona races back into her bedroom. Moments later, she returns with her beach bag and plops on the stool opposite me as I add crushed mint to the pitcher. Triona motions over her shoulder toward Claudette with widened eyes, which only Shelby and I can see. Then, in an exaggerated voice, she adds, "No, no, Malia. These aren't strong enough. You need to add way more rum."

Aha. Triona must be trying to get Claudette drunk. So drunk that perhaps she'll fall asleep while tanning on the beach. A sleeping Claudette is way less painful than an awake one. We all learned that lesson the hard way.

"Oh. My. Gawd!" Speak of the she-devil. "Who put Malia in charge of making the cocktails? Remember that time she was pouring our shots at beach week, but got a little . . . um . . . distracted by the law? We never saw you again that night, Malia. What happened again?"

"But you—" My mixing spoon clatters onto Triona's granite countertop. How dare Claudette bring that up? It was all her doing. Manipulative little bitch!

"Now, now, Claudette." Shelby's soothing voice interrupts my stuttering and offers me a diversion to keep from answering something I might regret. Instead, I regain my composure while wiping the countertop. "You know that night was not Malia's fault."

That's putting it mildly. Didn't help that I spent that night in jail because of her.

Back then, I'd been so excited. My parents had given me as a high school graduation present my very first cell phone—one of those new flip phones that were all the rage before smartphones were invented. While pouring shots to get our night of partying started, my phone rang for the first time.

"Malia?" Claudette's voice sounded so clear through my earpiece. "Go outside. Hurry!"

"Wait, what?" I downed my shot, perhaps my third or fourth. "Why?"

"Parker is in front of the hotel on the boardwalk. You look hot tonight." Her voice changed from needling to enticing at the name of my crush for—oh, just about all four years of high school. "Go downstairs and see him. Now!"

Chills washed over my body as I closed my cell phone. Parker had never noticed me in school. Maybe now was my chance? With all of us scattering to all ends of the country for college in the next few months, it was now or never. What did I have to lose?

"Malia, take this." Claudette, still holding her phone, met me as I reached our hotel room's door and shoved a bottle at me. "I hear he likes tequila, too."

That's all I needed to hear. I raced into the hall, then down the elevator, praying I was making the right choice. The warm, salty night air embraced me. But instead of seeing Parker, I dashed straight into two tall men dressed in dark uniforms, complete with dispatch walkie-talkies and weapons, alert for any kind of trouble.

Especially the underage drinking variety.

I hid the bottle behind my back, but it was too late. Faster than you can be read your Miranda rights, I was in the back of a squad car heading to the Virginia Beach jail and making my one phone call.

All because of Claudette. Well, no. I was definitely guilty— drinking underage and in possession of a bottle of liquor. But I would never have been caught, charged, and prosecuted without her manipulative little sting operation. And I'd fallen for it.

As mortifying as it was to call my parents that night, what was worse was losing my college scholarship because of my new criminal record. Without that funding, I dropped out and attended community college to work and save tuition money. My dreams went down the drain along with every last drop of tequila that I threw up in that jail cell's sink.

The judge found me guilty. It stayed on my record for five years and kept me from getting jobs and loans. I still cringe every time someone runs a background check on me.

My life would've been so different if only I hadn't answered my cell phone. If only I hadn't been stupid enough to chase a boy who never knew I existed. If only Claudette hadn't railroaded me.

And here she is—a lifetime later—standing in the middle of Triona's beach house, teasing me about making cocktails. No apology. No remorse. And with several ex-husbands and ex-careers under her belt, she hasn't matured a minute. The world would be a better place without her in it.

After pouring my mojito concoction into three highball glasses, I hesitate before pouring the fourth. How can I keep pretending that I don't hate the very air Claudette breathes? The same air I happen to be inhaling right now. Every cell in my body screams to chuck the contents of my pitcher in her face. Though tempted, I resist. I'm sure Triona would understand, but I don't want to cause a big sticky mess all over her beach house's floor. Instead, I finish pouring.

Claudette grabs a mojito and catwalks into her bedroom. No appreciation. Only entitlement.

God, I wish she were dead.

Holding a finger over her mouth, Shelby motions for me to follow her, tiptoeing up the spiral staircase to the widow's walk. Triona, already there, pauses while moving a chair against the balcony railing. Shelby, wearing rubber gloves, pours a can of salted Virginia peanuts, scattering them on the seat of the chair.

We all exchange silent nods—agreement. Time to activate our backup plan. STAT.

CLAUDETTE

Sipping the mojito I swiped from idiot Malia, I saunter back into my bedroom to glam-up for the beach. No one rocks a forty-year-old body like I do, not that I'd admit my age to anyone on the planet. I even faked my birthdate on my driver's license, so everyone thinks I'm thirty-one. I'd make time stop if I could.

The body and face reflected in my mirror are utter perfection. I'm the envy of every *The Real Housewives of Wherever* fangirl.

Bronze tan with no tan lines. *Check.*

A thigh-gap to die for. *Check.*

Peroxide blond hair with no roots or grays showing. *Check.*

Lacquered one-inch nails and perfect pedi. *Check.*

Triona had always been jealous of my boyfriends in high school. She could never get a date for any dance or event. So, when I saw Triona flirting with my boyfriend, Jake, at the bar at beach week, I had to teach her a lesson. If only I'd had these dagger nails during beach week, Triona would've fallen off that balcony, and it would've looked like an accident.

Sculpted body, surgically enhanced as much as my alimony checks would allow. *Check.*

No peanut allergies here. And to think Shelby fell for my little peanut joke at beach week. It doesn't get more stupid than that girl. I'd found out her tie-breaker vote as class president kept me from being crowned prom queen. She'd deserved to die that night.

After adjusting my itty-bitty black bikini, I turn this way and that. Not a stretchmark or ripple to be seen. *Check.*

But I already knew that. I had Malia's husband inspect every last inch of me yesterday before I drove up here. He gave his stamp of approval (several times). Malia was the only competition I ever had looks-wise. What she never knew is that while she was in the slammer that night during spring break, I hooked up with her crush, Parker. *Oops.* Looks like I can still take what I want from her.

Little do they know, I crashed my high school frenemies' annual get-together with an agenda. I'll finally finish what I started all those years ago. Triona, Shelby, and Malia won't get the best of me. Not this time. Soon, they'll all be dead. They each deserve it.

When my cell phone rings, I answer it. Malia.

"Where are y'all? Let's get the party started, bitches!" I amp up my best cheerleader voice.

"We're down at the beach, setting up chairs. We are surrounded by hot guys! If you go up to the widow's walk, you can probably see us."

—— 🧑 ——

TRIONA

Shoreside, Shelby, Malia, and I have set up our umbrella way down the beach from our house. It's a good thing Claudette was taking her sweet old time packing her beach bag.

"Can you see us?" Malia's voice is sugary sweet while she holds her cell phone in one hand and exaggerates waving with the other up at our building. "Nope. Further south. By the lifeguard stand. Trust me, Claudette, you're gonna love this eye candy."

Listening to this one-sided conversation, I envision Claudette, dressed in her micro-bikini and stiletto heels, lured by our bait.

"No, no. They are young, tan, and ripped." Malia rolls her eyes but waves her arm harder. Shelby covers her mouth to keep her laughter in check. But not me. My gaze is focused on my widow's walk in the distance. "Yes, of course, we're on the beach! You can hear the waves crashing behind me. Keep looking south."

"Trust me, we have the primo spot." Malia motions to us to wave as well. "We're kind of far away, but we can see you. Maybe if you stand on the chair, you can see us waving."

In the distance, high up on the beach house's lookout tower, the shadow of a woman rises above the balcony railing, waves both arms. Having slipped on the loose peanuts we'd scattered, she teeters in midair, then flutters down out of our field of view.

Malia hangs up her cell phone. We all take a moment of silence for closure, the sounds of water crashing on the shore, then receding. Sunshine sparkles on the Sandbridge waves, making it look like diamonds are dancing on the water.

"Like I promised you both, Claudette had to choose. Apologize or payback. May she rest in peace." Winking, I reach my cocktail toward Shelby and Malia, who join me in a toast. Our smiles grow stronger by the second. "Well, bitches, let's get this party started."

DIRTY BUSINESS

By Yvonne Saxon

CARRYING FOUR MEDIUM PIE pumpkins in your arms in the rain in the dark across a soggy graveyard isn't easy, especially when you're terrified of getting caught for taking them from the farm stand. But it's not stealing if you left some money, right?

I'd never felt so guilty in my life, but I'd had to have those pumpkins! This late in November, they were probably the last uncanned pumpkins in Virginia. I knew they were the last in Smithfield.

My shoes squishing, I hurried down the side of St. Luke's Historic Church, Virginia's oldest church, adding trespassing at a National Landmark to not quite breaking and entering. Nothing at the farm stand was broken, really, and I left extra money with a nice note on the pumpkin crate. It was so dark, and I was concentrating so hard on my footing that I looked up in barely enough time to avoid plowing into a cast-iron fence. *Wait, am I going the wrong way?* Walking faster, my head up now, I struggled to maintain my grip on the now-slick pumpkins. A passing car's headlights illuminated the trees and ancient headstones around me. Had I seen a metallic glint? That would be the poles for the canopy I had seen earlier. I wished for more cars.

How much farther? Damp and cold, I began to fume. I *should* be dry and warm in the house on the golf course we rented for Thanksgiving tomorrow. I *should* be baking pies right now with Phil's family in the kitchen, laughing, talking, impressing them with my Southern hospitality. But no. Phil had to go out of state on one last business trip before the holiday, leaving me with an—

Whatever hit me was hard, sharp-edged, and sent me sprawling down into a muddy pit. My pumpkins! I heard a plop and a splat before everything went dark.

— 👧 —

YESTERDAY

I slammed the trunk of the car shut. Everything for Thanksgiving dinner was stuffed inside, and I mean everything. Perishable food in coolers? *Check.* Twenty-two pound not-quite-thawed-yet turkey? *Check.* Pots, pans, and cooking utensils? *Check.* Dishes, flatware, glasses, tablecloths, and centerpieces? *Check.* Everything else except the proverbial kitchen sink? *Check.* I was inordinately proud of myself for being so organized. I couldn't wait to get to the vacation house we'd rented. Evie, my roommate from college, lived in Smithfield, and we were meeting for dinner and then going to the rental, making a girl's night out of it. She was staying over to help me cook tonight and Wednesday. Phil and I always traveled up North to be with his family, but this year the whole bunch was coming to Virginia, and I was determined to show them what a traditional Southern Thanksgiving was all about.

Phil's call came in as I entered the Smithfield town limits.

"Getting everything ready to leave tomorrow?" he asked.

"Tomorrow? You mean today, silly. The car's packed full, and I'm already in Smithfield looking for the rental," I told him.

"No, Val," he said, "we don't have the rental until tomorrow after lunch."

"No, Phil," I said, "we have the house starting today until Saturday. We *paid* for the house from today until Saturday."

"Then what about the text the agent sent Sunday?"

"What text? I never got a text."

"The one that said there was a problem with the stove, and it would take them an extra day to get a new one. They said it would be installed and ready to go by Wednesday morning."

"Wednesday morning? What am I going to do with all this food until—wait a minute, when you called to tell me you arrived safely and were at the hotel Sunday night, you never said anything about waiting an extra day."

"It must have slipped my mind."

A polite tap on the horn from the car behind me prevented me from saying things to her husband a wife might later regret. I accelerated through the green light and took the first entrance I saw into a parking lot.

"You'll just have to go back home and come back tomorrow, Val."

"Are you kidding me, Phil? Drive all the way back, unload, repack in the morning, drive back here, unpack—"

"Val, my next meeting is about to start, so—"

"Cook all the side dishes, welcome and entertain your family—"

"I have to go now."

"There's got to be a way to work this out, Phil."

"Take it up with the rental agent—what was her name—Charlene something?"

"I'll see you tomorrow," I said through gritted teeth.

"Uh, yeah."

"What?"

"Umm, nothing. It'll wait."

While I waited for Charlene to contact me, I got out of the car and looked around. I had pulled into the St. Luke's Historic Church and Museum parking lot. Open for tours. *Why not?* I'd take a preview, and if it was as interesting as it looked, it would be a great place to bring Phil's family on the weekend. I paid the admission fee in the gift shop and wandered down the trail to the old brick church. *I'll still get into the house today,* I told myself. Evie and I would still have fun preparing everything. My coolers were highly rated; I wasn't worried about the food. Yet.

The late afternoon sun shining through the wall of stained glass painted the front of the church in jewel tones. I tiptoed forward, in awe, and for some moments bathed myself in a shaft of blue, then purple, then blue again.

Hearing voices at the door, I stepped quickly toward it, but no one came in. Maybe I wasn't supposed to be in here yet. I peeked out into the open brick foyer. Nobody there.

"Hurry. Get that in the pit and cover it up," a man's voice said. "The tour's about to start."

"What'd you find out?" another voice, a woman's.

"They're closing down tomorrow at sunset and staying closed through next week," he said.

"Please tell me there's a funeral," she said. "I'll check the roster. I can set up and say I looked at it wrong."

"We'll have to come back tonight," he said.

"How can we—"

"Just go. Here they come."

What had I just overheard? I stepped into the empty foyer. And what were they trying to hide?

The tour was interesting. I took photos of the old church, the beautiful grounds, and the old gravestones. I hoped the tour guide didn't see me checking my phone every few minutes. *Why hasn't Charlene called?* Our guide pointed toward the oldest graves, the ones from the 1700s, and began telling us that a little farther out, around the perimeter of the church, at least one hundred unmarked graves were discovered in 2017, using ground-penetrating radar.

"Could they be older than the 1767 one?" a guest asked.

"It's possible they could predate the earliest marked grave we have here," the tour guide said.

"Could they contain a lot of artifacts like the ones they're digging up in Jamestown?" someone else asked.

"That's also possible," he said, "but unlike the archaeological exploration that's been going on in Jamestown, there are no plans to dig here."

My phone buzzed. I grabbed it and hurried away from the group. "Hello?"

"This is your final notice to lower your interest rates—" I clicked off.

Because I was on the other side of the church from the group now, I could see a canopy set up in the area the guide had said contained the unmarked graves. It didn't look like a set up for a funeral, so I went closer.

I could see several people standing over a table shaking wooden boxes full of dirt, and dirt was falling out of the bottom, the same way flour did when I sifted it for a cake. I got closer, using the zoom feature on my phone's camera, and got some good shots. Objects started to appear in the boxes. *Is that silver?* I came closer still.

"Hello?" You'd have thought I blasted an air horn, the way they jumped. One girl almost dropped her box on the green indoor-outdoor carpet that covered the ground. "Is it okay for me to watch?" I asked.

"Sure." A tall man with a goatee and glasses wiped his hands on his khakis and came over to shake my hand. "I'm Mark, and I'm in charge of the educational programs here. This is Carrie, my associate." He pointed at a woman who waved. "And grad students Ty, Alyssa, and Josh."

I stood speechless for a minute. The voice. *His* voice was the one I'd heard earlier at the church. "Oh, hi. This looks exciting," I said quickly. "Are you doing a dig here?"

"No," Mark said, "we do a hands-on archaeology program for elementary students, and we're practicing for a school field trip presentation on Tuesday after the Thanksgiving holiday."

"So, the kids get to sift?" I pointed to the box that Ty was shaking, uncovering what looked like coins and a pipe.

"Yes," Carrie said, stepping in between me and my view of Ty's box. "We're teaching the school kids the basic practices of archaeology. We want to show them how careful you have to be when working with artifacts."

"Are these items real?" I asked.

"They're fakes, reproductions, but it's to make the kids feel as if they're really archaeologists," Mark said, smiling.

My phone rang again, so I thanked them and hurried away. It was the agent, finally!

I called Evie immediately after the tour ended. "Oh Evie! This Thanksgiving is going to be a disaster!" I wailed.

"What's going on? No, wait . . . first, where are you?"

"I'm in the parking lot at the old St. Luke's Historic Church with all the food for Thursday in the trunk, and I can't get into the rental until tomorrow afternoon because the stove won't be delivered until tomorrow and Phil and his family are all coming in around suppertime tomorrow and—"

"Whoa!" Evie said. "You're at St. Luke's?"

"Yes."

"Turn right onto Benn's Church Boulevard and enter the next church parking lot that you see. I'm here helping to pack Thanksgiving boxes. I'll be outside in five."

Just knowing that Evie was there to talk through this mess with me made me feel better. I got in the car and pulled in at the church as Evie walked into the parking lot. We hugged and I may have cried a little.

"You say you've got the food in the trunk?"

I opened it and showed her.

"Yeah, that's a lot of stuff." She thought a minute. "Follow me to my house. We'll get the perishables into my fridge. You can call Phil, and then we'll go to dinner and come up with a plan."

— 🎭 —

On the way to the restaurant, I asked Evie if we could drive by the rental. Why we were sneaking up to the back of the house where the kitchen window was, I don't know. It's not like anyone could see us in the dark. I used the flashlight on my phone to see inside. There was a gap where the big combo stovetop-grill-oven should have been. "I *sooo* wanted to cook on that," I said. Then I noticed the black marks on the wall above, the plastic sheeting on the floor, and the paint cans. "Why didn't Charlene tell me there was a fire?"

"Maybe the painters went to supper and are coming back to work on it all night," Evie said, trying to make me feel better.

"Yeah, by tomorrow afternoon they should have it done," I said, also trying to make me feel better.

Evie gestured at me with her pasta-laden fork. "Here's a thought. We can use the church kitchen where I was putting together the Thanksgiving dinner boxes. It's big, it's got stainless steel counters, and best of all, it's got a working stove." She popped the spaghetti into her mouth.

"They won't mind?"

"Great group of people," she said, chewing. "And since we *both* are volunteering to help again in the morning, *and* are volunteering to clean up, I'm sure they won't mind. After all, they have to get home and get their own Thanksgiving meals started."

"That is the best thing I've heard all day," I told her.

"Now tell me more about that tour you took. I can tell when you're holding something back," Evie prodded.

I looked around the restaurant, then leaned in toward her. "I need to tell you about the voices."

"You're hearing voices now?"

"Stop. There were two people, but I couldn't see them, and they were talking about covering things up and coming back tonight to finish. And then, at that tent where the grad students were sifting dirt? One of the voices I heard was the director's, and the other one belonged to a woman named Carrie. Weird thing is, they were being really nice and all, but I got the distinct impression they didn't want me there."

"Is that all? There can be a lot of explanations for what you heard."

"There could, except for these." I pulled up the pictures I'd taken on my phone and handed it to her.

Evie's jaw dropped. After a full minute, she recovered enough to say, "Did they see you taking pictures?"

"I don't think so."

"Good."

"Do those look like fake artifacts to you, Evie?"

She rolled her eyes, which was all the answer I needed from one of the former curators of artifacts with the Jamestown Rediscovery project.

"Evie?"

"Yes, Val?"

"Want to drive by St. Luke's on the way home? Just for fun?"

We couldn't get as close as we wanted, pointy-topped fences being in the way and all, but we could see activity underneath that canopy. The sides had been draped, but a little light shone at the bottom. We'd have to try again in the light.

Wednesday morning dawned bright and chilly. I had a lot of fun helping Evie and the others put together the food boxes for the church to give out. As soon as everyone else left, I poured Evie and myself another cup of coffee, and we sketched out our battle plan for the day.

"What do you want to do first?" Evie asked.

"Go back to St. Luke's and find out what's going on under that canopy," I said.

"Oh, I know what's going on—"

"You think they're digging up the unmarked graves and taking what they find?"

She bit her lip, thinking. "Not exactly. Would you say there was a lot of dirt under that canopy?"

I pulled up my photos again, and we scrutinized them. "The only dirt you can see is what's in the sifting boxes and that cardboard box in the back."

"Are you sure they didn't see you taking pictures, Val?" She sounded worried. Then she slapped the counter and said, "But first things first. This Thanksgiving dinner won't cook itself."

We started with the side dishes, stirring and chopping, mixing and baking, and in less than two hours we had them all ready. I'd only have to heat them to bubbling tomorrow.

"How about the pies next?"

Evie agreed. I started rooting through the bags and pulled out apples, pecans, spices, flour, and sugar. "Evie, where are my pie pumpkins?"

"What pie pumpkins?"

"The orange round things with stems?" I joked. "We didn't leave them at the house, did we?"

"No, I brought everything from the house and out of the car. I haven't seen any pumpkins. I assumed you brought canned."

"You know me better than that. I need real pumpkins for Phil's family. They're always looking down their noses—" I stopped. I wanted to cry. Nothing that I had planned for this family Thanksgiving was working out.

"You can use sweet potatoes. You've got loads of them, and they're just as traditional as pumpkin pie," Evie said quietly, once again trying to make me feel better.

My phone rang. It was Phil. I put it on speaker so Evie could hear.

"There's been a delay, and I've been rerouted to Boston. I'm getting a rental car, driving to Mom and Dad's, and we'll all be coming in around noon tomorrow."

"Oh, no! Well, we'll have Thanksgiving dinner at two then. And Phil—"

He'd already hung up. But I wasn't as disappointed as I might have been. "Evie? When do we have to be out of here?"

"We can stay 'til tomorrow if we need to. Why?"

"I need to find pie pumpkins and . . . we need to find those artifacts."

Evie gave me a long look. "I made some calls early this morning. The items in your photos are showing up for sale on antiquities websites already. There's even an auction set for Saturday. Collectors will pay big money for a piece of history. That's why it's so dangerous, Val. That's why I put you off earlier. I don't think it's safe for you to get involved."

"Just one more look, Evie. We know they'll be there till closing today. If we can see what they do with those boxes, then I'll come back and cook all night if I have to. Who knows? Maybe I'll find my own prize—a pumpkin on the side of the road." I smiled.

We headed straight for the side of the church where I'd seen the canopy yesterday. There was nothing there. No canopy, no table, no students, no sifting trays, no artifacts. Only a sunken patch of grass, about the size and shape of a screen door, showed that anything had been there at all. I walked over and looked at it. "It's all gone. There's no way we'll find the artifacts now."

Evie started kicking at grass clumps with her shoe. "Don't give up yet."

I joined her, using the toe of my shoe like a wedge. A corner of a piece of sod stuck up. Evie pushed her toe underneath it too and we rolled it back. Dirt had been replaced and tamped down. She sighed and told me to take some pictures of the area anyway. They might come back here again later.

"Stop," Evie said. "Someone's coming."

Ty, the grad student, was walking our way. I waved and smiled.

"I was really disappointed that you all weren't working today," I told him.

"We are, but not here. We're over there 'til dark." He pointed. But all I saw were canopy poles.

"Well, thanks," Evie said. "Have a happy Thanksgiving!" She took my arm and led me back to the car.

"What was that about?"

"Ty saw us taking pictures, and that's not good."

Back in the church kitchen, we schemed and argued while we worked fast, peeling apples, chopping pecans, making fillings and pastry for the pies. *Only the turkey will be cooked tomorrow,* I thought, *and the genuine Smithfield ham Evie surprised me with earlier.*

It was almost dusk when we put the pies in the oven, set timers on our phones, and ran for takeout. On the way back, I saw a farm stand on the side of the road with sweet potatoes, collard greens, pecans, and a few small pumpkins.

"Evie, Evie, stop! Let me out. I'm getting those pumpkins."

"There's nobody there. Plus, it's getting dark and it's starting to rain. Besides, what are you going to put them in?"

"Well, I'm not messing up my purse. I can carry them."

"You are absolutely craz—"

The phone timers' beeping interrupted her.

"Just pull over and let me out. You go get the pies out of the oven. We're on the back side of St. Luke's, and I can see the church kitchen from here. I'll be there in ten minutes."

"Don't you dare go through St. Luke's, you hear me?"

Buzzing. Something was buzzing. And flashing. I opened my eyes and saw dirt all around me. A grave! The buzzing and flashing stopped. What hit me? My knee throbbed when I pushed up to a sitting position. Dazed, I patted the mud around me for the pumpkins. Two were right beside me, another one was split open, and the last was in pieces. The buzzing and flashing started again. *My phone!* It lay on top of some boxes and pallets. *Boxes!* I opened them, seeing artifacts that would go at auction for, how much had Evie said? Well, a lot. Marc's voice sounded above me. I covered my phone.

"Which one did you hit?" Marc said.

"I don't know," Carrie responded, "but she's out cold."

"Go get the ladder and the hand truck to carry the boxes," Marc said. "I'll drive the dirt truck over here. Make sure to get her phone out of there, too. Those pictures will put us in jail."

"It seems a shame to put all that rich dirt back before we have a chance to sift through it," Carrie said. Then it got quiet.

It's amazing how the threat of imminent death can energize you. I counted to five after it got quiet, and then I stood on the boxes and catapulted myself out of there, making sure I held on to my purse, stuffed to bursting with two good pumpkins. Yes, I did hit the ground running and might have made it all the way through the cemetery to the road and the other church kitchen, had Charlene, the rental agent, not called just then. The noise caught Carrie's attention. I heard her yelling for Marc to "get her." I couldn't run any faster, and I could hear the truck gaining on me. Only the low brick wall surrounding the cemetery was in my way now. I threw myself over it, landed on my hands and knees, pushed up, and ran hard for the road leading to the back of the church. Behind me, gravel was pinging off headstones. Marc must be flooring it to get back to the entrance and out on the road. His truck engine roared behind me.

"Val, get in!" Evie yelled, driving beside me with the passenger door open. I threw myself in. Marc's truck was right on top of us now. We rounded the corner on two wheels and skidded to a stop at the church's back doors. Marc bounced his truck over the curb, aiming for us. We were trapped.

"Give me the phone. All I want is the pictures," he said, getting out of the truck.

"No."

He pulled a shovel from the truck bed and started toward me. "Give me the phone."

"Okay." I reached in my purse.

He seemed surprised by the pumpkin flying toward him. Knocked him flat.

While the police processed the scene and took our statements, they let me prepare my one pumpkin pie. Evie, a former curator of artifacts at the Jamestown dig, volunteered to testify against Marc and Carrie, whom they caught leaving the cemetery.

The pumpkin pie was cooling when Phil called. They weren't going to make it after all. He had called Charlene earlier, and she was refunding all the money because of the trouble with the house. I put on a pot of coffee, grabbed the homemade whipped cream, and served pie to the officers. They deserved it.

DEIDRA, DOG DETECTIVE

By Frances Aylor

THE COSTUME WAS HOT. And heavy. And in the lengthening shadows of early evening, it was almost impossible to see where she was going. Even in the brightest daylight she could only see straight ahead, with no peripheral vision. She always needed her handler, Morton, to be nearby, to say "There's a kid to your left," or "A little girl is right in front of you," so she didn't stumble over the screaming children who surrounded her each day, eager for a photo.

Wandering around as Deidra the Dog Detective, the chocolate curly-haired labradoodle made famous in the children's hit movie, wasn't what Diane planned for her second summer season at Kings Dominion, the giant theme park in Doswell, Virginia. She had auditioned to be a star performer, to sing and dance and wear a beautiful costume while applauded by adoring fans.

Always wanting to be a dancer, she had studied ballet since being a toddler, learning to point her toe and spin in a circle without falling on her bottom, which sounded easy now but was no small feat for a three-year-old. She had stuck with her dance classes throughout elementary, middle, and high school, hours and hours of jazz and tap and pointe, recital after recital, until now, as a rising high school senior, she felt ready to take center stage.

She made it through several rounds of auditions, concentrating on squaring her shoulders and keeping her back straight, on maintaining eye contact and smiling at her audience, on projecting energy and enthusiasm, all those things that had been drilled into her over the years. But in the end, it wasn't enough. Becky Anderson, a college sophomore majoring in theater and dance, prevailed. Becky, who could hit high C without straining her vocal cords. Becky, who had long blond hair that made her perfect to play the role of the fairy princess.

After Diane spent a few weeks in her role as Deidra, no one even remembered her real name. Everyone called her *Deidra*, whether she was wearing her costume or not. Diane was now invisible, her identity totally obliterated by a fictional labradoodle.

Becky spent her days in an air-conditioned auditorium, spinning gracefully across the stage. Deidra sweated outside in the ninety-plus heat of a Virginia summer, wearing a giant furry head with long droopy ears and beady black eyes. Her paws were so big and bulky that she couldn't even feel it when kids pulled on her fingers or jumped on her toes.

Becky sang and danced with Larry, the hot guy who was sure to be a Hollywood legend once he graduated from college and headed West. Deidra spent her shift with Morton, the geeky handler who insisted on wrapping his arm around her waist as he accompanied her through the theme park to the kiddie playground. Morton always seemed to disappear whenever Deidra needed him the most, to climb steps or to navigate a narrow pathway. Then he would turn up, laughing hysterically, when she tripped or bumped into a low-hanging branch.

Her job was to bounce and prance and wave at the children as they rushed from the swings to the boats and all the rides in between. At least they didn't make her catch a ball in her mouth or turn backflips, like Deidra had done in the movie. She swayed from side to side, her pink tongue flapping out below a gigantic rose-colored nose, while she tried not to think about how long it was until her next break.

Today's shift had been worse than usual. After sweating for hours in the hot sun, with the smell of grilling hot dogs and cotton candy and funnel cake so thick inside her costume that she could barely breathe, she collided with a little boy who had just staggered off the spinning Whirlybird. He grabbed for her legs and puked onto her wavy fur, the contents of his stomach spewing out in gut-twisting heaves. The stench of vomit hovered in the humid air, and the kids around him, already dizzy from the ride, soon caught the barf bug and started hurling their guts out all over the steaming asphalt. Morton caught her elbow and pointed her toward the dressing rooms.

"You need to get out of that costume," he said. "I'll be right behind you. I have to do some cleanup here first."

Deidra stumbled past the Space Buggies and across the footbridge into Candy Apple Grove, keeping the sounds of the giant Anaconda and Intimidator roller coasters to her left. She had followed this path a hundred times before, but somehow, with the smells of puke and hot dogs and funnel cake, with the sounds of screaming riders on the roller coasters, with the fading light of early evening, she got confused. Unsure of exactly where she was, she followed a path through the trees, getting into more undergrowth and darker shadow, unable to see anything except what was directly ahead.

Suddenly, she tripped. As she fell, she spouted four-letter words that her parents never suspected were in her vocabulary. Now she was screwed. It was tough enough to maneuver in this costume when she was standing upright. It was almost impossible when she was sprawled on the ground like that old lady in the TV commercials, the one who whined that she'd fallen and couldn't get up.

The labradoodle head had gotten twisted, and all she could see was fuzz. She grasped it with awkward hands and shifted the eye holes to the front, trying to figure out what she had tumbled over—a log maybe, or some trash tossed onto the pathway. Squinting in the fading light, she first saw ballerina slippers. Then smooth tights. Then layers of pale tulle at the base of a sparkly leotard.

Deidra's heart pounded as she breathed in short gulps. She recognized this costume. She would have given anything all summer to wear it. Except not right now, of course. Not with blood splattered on the soft nylon of the fairy wings.

She scrambled backwards, then maneuvered into a downward dog yoga pose, her head low and her butt poked up in the air, to walk herself to her feet. She was desperate to get away from Becky, who was slumped on the ground with her head smashed against a tree. Deidra wobbled toward the roller coasters, her screams muffled behind the wagging tongue of her giant head.

Morton stopped her right before she tumbled into the Lazy River. "Deidra, what are you doing?"

"Get this off of me." She tugged at her head with floppy hands as tears ran down her throat. "I'm choking."

"Not here," Morton said. "Not where the guests can see you." He pulled her behind a building and eased her out of the labradoodle head. "What's wrong?"

"It's Becky," she said. "Back there. I think she's dead."

Morton's radio crackled as he called for help. Soon several security guards rushed up. Deidra pointed back toward the trees as she told her story. "Show us," they said.

Deidra wasn't sure she could find Becky's body a second time. The world looked so different when she could see the sky above and the ground beneath her feet. She stared straight ahead, focusing only on things at eye level, trying to remember landmarks from when she stumbled down this path the first time, confused and lost.

And then she saw her, Becky's mangled head still against the tree, her sparkly costume stained with blood. A security guard caught Deidra as she fainted.

———— 👧 ————

When Deidra opened her eyes, she saw the blue flashing lights of police cars. "Are you all right?" a policeman asked.

She slowly sat up. "Where's Becky?"

He nodded to the right. "Over there."

"Is she okay?" Deidra hoped she'd been mistaken, that Becky had only been knocked unconscious.

"No, I'm sorry." His dark eyes stared down at her. "Can you tell me what happened?"

"I tripped over her," Deidra said. "I had the costume on, and I couldn't see her, lying down there on the ground."

"Did you see who attacked her?"

"No. No one was out here. Just Becky and me."

He put his hand under her elbow. "We're gathering all her coworkers in the auditorium, to see if anyone knows what happened. Can you stand up?"

She nodded. "But can I please get out of this costume? Some kid puked all over me. I stink."

He gestured to a female officer who didn't look that much older than Deidra. "Tiffany, can you take this young woman to get some clean clothes? But keep the costume as evidence. It's got blood on it."

Tiffany and Deidra walked to the changing room, where Tiffany took pictures of the costume from every angle. Deidra slipped into shorts and a T-shirt and then handed the costume to Tiffany, who stuffed it into an evidence bag. "Do you know of anyone who would want to hurt Becky?" Tiffany asked. "Anyone who was angry with her? Jealous, maybe?"

Deidra hesitated. She hadn't even tried to hide her disappointment when Becky beat her out for the fairy princess role. Deidra had vented to her family. To Caleb, her best friend, who carpooled with her to Kings Dominion. To Grace, who worked at the funnel cake stand, and to Ashley, who ran the baby bumper car ride. But she wasn't going to confess that to Tiffany.

"She did have an argument earlier today," Deidra said. "Seemed pretty angry."

Tiffany jotted down the information. "Who with?"

Deidra shrugged. "They were backstage. I didn't see them."

"Male or female?"

"A male, I think. I didn't recognize the voice."

"Did you hear what they said?"

"Becky said something like, 'You have to stop.' I couldn't hear the guy. He mumbled."

Tiffany looked up. "Do you know what she was talking about?"

"No. Sorry."

Tiffany stood up as her radio squawked. "We need to move to the auditorium now." She handed Deidra a business card. "Please call me if you think of anything else."

There were many familiar faces in the auditorium—characters, performers, other employees who Becky had contact with. She loved the park, and even when she wasn't on stage as the fairy princess, Becky spent a lot of time there checking out the rides, wandering through the gift shop, playing arcade games.

Deidra took a seat near the back. Her friend Caleb slipped in beside her. "I heard you found her," he said. "Was it horrible?"

Caleb had been one of Deidra's best buddies since eighth grade. They tossed frog legs at each other in bio lab. They memorized the preamble to the Declaration of Independence and the benefits of New Deal programs while studying for AP history exams. They celebrated the end of junior year by sneaking a bottle of vodka from Deidra's house and taking off through the woods on their dirt bikes. Deidra gradually realized her attraction to him was more than friendship, but she was too nervous to tell him, afraid she'd scare him off.

Deidra shivered. "Yes. Her head was bashed in, and there was blood everywhere."

"That's tough." Caleb awkwardly patted her shoulder. "They have any idea who did it?"

"I don't think so." She sniffed, rubbing her nose on her sleeve. "They're still sifting through all that stuff at the crime scene."

Caleb glanced up at the stage, where a policeman thumped his fingers against a microphone, testing to see if it was turned on. "Why do you think they brought all of us in here? Do they think one of us killed her?"

"God, I hope not." To Deidra, working at Kings Dominion was a lot like high school, with the same frustrations and anger and hurt feelings. The popular kids hung together. The second stringers kept their heads down and focused on getting through the day. Deidra didn't think any of them had a reason to kill Becky. "I think they're trying to figure out if anyone saw what happened."

"Your attention, please." The policeman winced at the screech from his mic. "I'm sure you've all heard that there was a terrible incident today. A young woman was killed."

Caleb drummed his fingers against his thigh. "Her name was Becky," he muttered. "They should know that."

Deidra knew Caleb was fond of Becky. She had often seen them laughing together at the shooting arcade where Caleb worked. The prizes were stuffed animals, from miniature bears and lions to giant elephants and unicorns, and Becky's locker was full of them. Even on days when her aim wasn't so good, Caleb would pull down one of the bigger animals to give to her. Deidra warned him to stop. "If they catch you giving away prizes, you'll lose your job."

The policeman strutted across the stage, enjoying his moment in the spotlight. A few inches forward and he would topple off the edge. "If any of you know anything about this, we'd like you to come to the front and tell us."

Caleb snickered. "Like that's gonna happen," he said. "Does he really think somebody's gonna walk down there and snitch on anyone?"

Grace from the funnel cake concession, sitting several rows ahead, raised her hand. "What about all the visitors in the park? Are you questioning them too? Or have you already decided one of us did it?"

"Wow, she should have kept her mouth shut," Deidra said. "She probably just became suspect number one."

The policeman nodded to another officer, who started moving up the aisle toward Grace. "We're questioning everyone," he said. "But you folks knew her. You worked with her every day. Odds are you know something about this crime, even if you don't realize it yet."

Deidra jumped as someone tapped her on the shoulder. Tiffany, the officer who had interviewed her a few minutes ago, leaned down and whispered, "Can you come back here with me? I have a few more questions."

Deidra took a deep breath. *She's found out*, she thought. *She knows I was angry that Becky got the lead part instead of me. She thinks I killed her.*

Deidra clutched Caleb's wrist. "Don't leave without me."

"Not much chance of that. You drove carpool today." He leaned closer. "Be careful what you tell them."

Deidra nodded. Outside the auditorium, she and Tiffany sat at a nearby picnic table. "I wonder if you could identify this." Tiffany handed Deidra a sealed plastic bag. "Have you seen it before?"

It was a ballpoint pen, yellow with black writing on the side—*Alice Annie's Tasty Treats*.

Deidra nodded. "Yes. We all have them. Morton's been handing them out today. They're a promotion for his grandmother's bakery in Ashland."

Tiffany pulled out her notebook. "Who's Morton?"

"He's my handler. He walks around with me when I'm in costume. We can't see very well when we're suited up, so it's not safe for us to wander through the theme park on our own. Too easy to step on the little kids."

"So, a lot of the employees had one of these pens?" She seemed disappointed. No doubt she'd thought it was a significant clue. "Not just Morton?"

Deidra nodded. "The employees. Park guests. Morton's been giving them out like trick-or-treat candy. Why?"

"We found this near Becky's body."

"You think her killer dropped it?"

"I don't know. Could it be yours? Could it have fallen out when you tripped over her?"

"Nope. None of the animated characters can carry anything personal with us. Wouldn't fit the image if our cell phones suddenly started ringing. It couldn't have been Becky's, either. She didn't have any pockets in her costume."

Tiffany reached for the plastic bag. "Tell me more about Morton."

Deidra shrugged. "He's in college. This is his first summer working here."

"Does he do a good job as your handler?"

"The guy's a creep," Deidra said. "He's always putting his hands on me. But then he disappears when I get close to stuff. He thinks it's hysterical when I trip over baby strollers."

"He was with you today?" Tiffany asked.

"Yes. In the kiddie playground."

"But he wasn't with you when you found Becky?"

"No. After that kid on the Whirlybird puked all over me, Morton told me to go change. Said he was going to stay behind to help with cleanup."

Tiffany thought for a moment. "What did Becky think of Morton? Were they friends?"

"Are you kidding? Nobody's friends with Morton. He's a perv. Keeps peeking into the girls' changing rooms. We've all caught him doing it. Becky threatened to turn him in if he didn't quit."

Tiffany flipped back through her notebook. "Could Morton

have been the one Becky was arguing with? When she said, 'You have to stop'?"

Deidra chewed her lip. "I don't know. Could be."

"Did she report him to someone?" Tiffany asked. "A supervisor? Human resources?"

"I doubt it. She did tell Larry, and he smacked him around a bit."

Tiffany brightened at this new lead. "Who's Larry?"

"Her costar in the show. The handsome prince."

"Becky got Larry to beat Morton up?"

Deidra shook her head. "Not beat him up, exactly. I mean, Larry didn't break any bones or knock out any teeth or anything. But after that, Morton knew he'd better leave Becky alone."

"Morton was angry about that?"

"Wouldn't you be? It happened right out in front of everybody. Nobody would talk to Morton for days after that. He was mad at Becky. Mad at Larry. Mad at everybody for laughing at him."

Tiffany tapped her pen against her teeth. "Tell me about Larry."

"He's hot. And he knows it. But he's possessive, you know? Didn't want Becky to talk to anyone else. Morton wasn't the first guy he tangled with this summer."

"Who else?"

"Anybody he thought Becky was spending too much time with. He even got rough with Becky when he thought she'd been too friendly with some of the guys. She had bruises on her arms that were tough to cover up with makeup." Deidra scuffed her feet against the asphalt. "When can I go home? My shift's over, and I don't get paid for sitting around doing nothing."

"Sorry. We're still talking to folks, so I may have some more questions for you."

"Are you allowed to do this?" Deidra asked. "Interview us, without our parents here? A lot of us are under eighteen, you know."

"You haven't been accused of anything," Tiffany said. "We're chatting here, gathering information." She paused. "Do you want me to call your parents?"

"No. But I want to get out of here. This whole thing has freaked me out."

Tiffany and Deidra returned to the auditorium. Deidra slid back into her seat beside Caleb. They heard a loud argument up front. Morton stood up, a policeman on each side, resisting as they dragged him down the aisle. "Deidra," he called out as he passed her, "tell them I was with you. You know I didn't do this. This is a huge mistake."

"What's that about?" Caleb asked, turning to watch as they led Morton from the building.

"The police found one of Morton's pens next to the body," Deidra said. "You know, from his grandma's bakery."

"They think Morton did this?"

"Looks like it."

They next heard a shout from the opposite side of the room. Two policemen stood behind Larry, pushing him toward the exit.

"The police asked me about Larry, too," Deidra said. "I told them what a hothead he was. How he roughed up anyone who showed too much interest in Becky." She giggled as she ruffled Caleb's bangs. "How's your head, by the way? That lump gone down yet?"

"Oh, shut up." Embarrassed, he smoothed his hair. "Pretty much. A little sore, is all."

"I told them he'd attacked Becky. Grabbed her so hard she had bruises."

Caleb's eyebrows shot up. "When did that happen?"

"You didn't know about that?"

"No." He twisted toward her, his eyes crinkling in disbelief. "You made that up, didn't you?"

She settled back in her seat. "I've given this whole thing a lot of thought." She was Deidre the Dog Detective, after all. Solving crime, cornering the bad guys, was what she did. "I don't think anyone meant to kill Becky." She crossed her legs and wrapped her hands around her knee. "It was probably an accident."

"How you figure?" Caleb asked.

"Well, maybe somebody went out in the woods with her just to talk, you know? Lots of the guys here had a crush on her. She was talented. Beautiful. Made everybody feel special. Hey, if I'd been a guy, I would have been after her myself."

"You think?"

Deidra nodded. "The thing is, if Becky thought some guy was hitting on her too much, if he followed her around, gave her little trinkets—stuffed animals and stuff—she would probably have told Larry. And if Larry came after this guy, warned him off, maybe even knocked him upside the head, he would have been super angry. Angry enough to follow Becky into the woods to talk it over."

"Really?" Caleb chewed his thumbnail.

"She probably told this guy to buzz off. And that if he didn't, she'd send Larry after him again. And who would want that? I mean, think about what happened to poor Morton. He was humiliated. Anybody would be."

Caleb bounced his fist on the arm of his seat. "Morton got a tough break."

"Could be." Deidra toyed with the bracelet that Caleb had given her for her sixteenth birthday. "Anyway, I figure the two of them worked it out. Becky figured everything was settled and ran back toward the stage, because her next show was ready to start. It was shady in the woods by then. Getting dark. Hard to see. She probably took off and ran right into that tree. Banged her head up against it hard."

"You think it happened like that?" His voice squeaked, and he cleared his throat.

"Pretty sure. Then what could he do? She was already dead. If he stuck around, or if he called for help, people might get the wrong idea. Think he'd murdered her or something. When like I said, the whole thing was probably just an accident."

"An accident," Caleb repeated slowly. "Who do you think the guy was?"

"Who knows? Morton? Larry? Some other dude who'd been hanging around her all summer?" She tented her fingers together. "The thing I don't understand is, why do guys always go after the girl they can't have? You know, the beauty queen who's not interested in them? The one with the jealous boyfriend? When probably there's a girl nearby who's been a good friend, always there for him during the rough times, ready to stand with him against the world. Who's been waiting for him to realize how she feels about him? Waiting for him to reach out for her?"

"Diane," he said, biting his lip.

He was the only one at the park who called her by her real name. She loved him for that.

"Hey, do you still have the pen that Morton gave you today?" she asked.

He patted his pockets. "Nope. Must have fallen out somewhere."

"That's what I figured." She handed him a pen. "Here, take this one. In case they ask you about it."

"Diane, I never meant—" His eyes teared.

She dug in her pocket for a tissue. "It's okay. Things happen." Diane leaned closer and kissed his cheek. "But the next time I come to your shooting gallery, I expect to win a prize. One of those pink elephants. A great big one."

He rolled the pen back and forth between his palms, then carefully tucked it into his shirt pocket. "Sure thing."

SORRY, WRONG NUMBER

By Jayne Ormerod

"OH, MY FREAKIN' GAWD!"

A dead body floated up next to my kayak, gray face lifted heavenward and supported by a faded orange lifejacket. Eyes staring, empty and lifeless. Lips as blue as the berries I sprinkled on my oatmeal every morning. The tide kept pushing him against my vessel, adding more wobble to my bobble on the open water. Not a good feeling.

My hands, fingers splayed, fluttered like ten little hummingbirds next to my face. The screams kept coming, soft at first but then with increasing intensity, until I had the presence of mind to form words.

"Carolyn," I screeched to my kayaking companion, about twenty oar lengths ahead of me in the Assateague Channel. "Get back here!"

I tried not to look, but some invisible force pulled my gaze downward. Having never seen a body that hadn't been tidied up by a mortician, I wasn't prepared for the bloating resulting from of time spent in chilly water. The site made my stomach queasy, and yet I couldn't look away.

Help me! he seemed to plead. *But he's beyond help, now, isn't he?*

Carolyn paddled up next to me, peeked over my shoulder and screamed. Right into my good ear.

"Stop it," I said.

She started to back her kayak away, but I grabbed her paddle and pulled her in close, on the far side from the body. She tended to react a bit more emotionally than me. "Okay, we need to stay calm. Really calm. Deep breaths." The last thing I needed was for her to freak out, stand up, and tip her kayak. Then I'd have to save her. That is, if I didn't freak out first. Deep breath.

"He's already dead," I said. "No need to worry about saving him. What we do need to worry about is reporting him." I pulled my cell phone out of its waterproof pouch attached to my hip. Shaking fingers added to the challenge of pecking out numbers, but I managed to reach the Coast Guard. They asked questions I didn't have answers to.

"What is your location?"

I didn't see a channel marker anywhere. We'd drifted off course. I could see land both east and west—Chincoteague and Assateague Islands. So, we weren't totally lost at sea. Yet.

"Can you describe the body?"

Um, pale and dead. What more do they need to know?

"Are there signs of trauma?"

I refused to look close enough to make an assessment.

"Can you tow the body to shore?"

That one I did answer. "No." I was not about to hook him to my one-person kayak and paddle him back to *terra firma*. And now that I thought about it, I had no paddle. I must have dropped it when I put my hands to my face and screamed.

The Coast Guard operator sighed. "It'll be thirty- to forty-five minutes until we can get to you. Can you stay with him?"

"Like, follow as he floats around?" The tone in my voice let it be known that was not a possibility. With nerves stretched to their snapping point, I wanted—needed—to get to shore to avoid a major meltdown. Followed by a good stiff shot of tequila.

"Ma'am?"

"What?" I sniped. I'm not proud of myself when that voice comes out, but under the circumstances—

"Tide's coming in. Currents are going to change. We don't want to lose sight of the floater."

Floater? The technical term?

"It's important to get some sort of ID so that, in the event you get separated from the body, we can match him to the report. Will you please take a photo and text it to me?"

"Do you get a lot of them? Floaters, I mean?"

"More than most people realize. Please send me the photo as soon as you can. Not this number, it's a landline. I'll give you my cell phone number."

Not having anything to write with, I said the number aloud to Carolyn and she repeated it back to me three times. *Got it.*

Snapping a photo of a subject I did not want to look at while it floated away tested my inner strength. And my sensitive stomach. Add to that shaking hands, a tippy kayak, and a friend gripping my knee until I'd lost all feeling down to my toes. Please forgive me for not taking a perfectly framed and properly lighted photo from the most advantageous angle.

I sent the photo to the number Carolyn recited.

A few seconds later, my phoned dinged. Incoming text. Expecting a thank you for doing my civic duty, I was surprised to find a terse message, WHAT THE HELL IS THAT?

Umm, what you requested?

I suppressed my snippiness and refrained from responding.

I looked more closely at the phone number. "Carolyn, what was that number again?"

She recited it. "Why?"

"Well, it seems I texted to five-five instead of six-five." Understandable, given my thumb's nervous tremors. "Recipient is not too happy."

Proper etiquette for accidently texting an up-close-and-personal photo of an ashen, bloated, dead man's face to someone who wasn't expecting it? I don't believe Emily Post ever addressed that. After giving it serious thought, I texted back, SORRY, WRONG NUMBER.

Oh, my freakin' gawd.

Snuggled into a back corner at the ChincoTiki Bar and Grille, Carolyn and I relived the awful events of the afternoon. Who'd a thunk that floaters were a common occurrence? Makes you want to stay out of the water for the rest of your life.

After three tangy margaritas, we found humor in our day's adventure. I mean, can you imagine receiving a text like that?

Between listening to the music and sipping our drinks, one of us would say, "What the hell is that?" and we'd both dissolve into hysterical giggles. If you can't laugh at life's absurdities, why bother living?

We ordered another round, along with two baskets of the daily special, fried freshly caught sea scallops and fries.

"What a day this turned out to be, huh?" I said.

We clinked glasses.

So much for an afternoon retracing the infamous route of the annual pony swim between Assateague and Chincoteague Islands. Ponies ran wild on Assateague, survivors of shipwrecks from the 1700s. To maintain the health of both the herd and the island, once a year ponies are rounded up, herded across the channel by Saltwater Cowboys, and then auctioned off to lucky buyers who traveled hundreds of miles to participate. It's a huge deal here on Chincoteague Island, made famous by Marguerite Henry's book, *Misty of Chincoteague*.

Visiting the islands had been on my bucket list since before I knew what a bucket list was. Inviting Carolyn was a no-brainer. After all, our shared love of Ms. Henry's books had been the basis for our lifelong friendship. Not being a big fan of crowds, nor having a desire to buy a pony, the swim event didn't hold much interest. Hence our early October visit. Fall foliage and ponies—two birds with one horseshoe.

We'd driven in from Roanoke, Virginia, last night. Today we'd hiked the Assateague Island trails, spotting a dozen wild ponies galloping along the shore, their manes and tails blowing in the wind. That was a thrill of a lifetime. Got some good snaps of that. Couldn't wait to blow up a few to hang on my office wall.

Retracing the pony swim in kayaks had been Carolyn's idea. Looked good on paper. And we know how that turned out.

My phone rang. I answered without checking the number, as I always do. It's a sales-agent thing. Every unknown number is a potential new client.

"Who's this?" a gruff voice demanded.

"Margaret Gunderson. To whom do I have the pleasure of speaking?"

"Where did you get that picture of Tuffy?"

"Tuffy? Who's Tuffy?" The band had kicked their second set into extra-loud mode, making it hard to hear the caller. Or maybe it was the margaritas muffling my hearing.

"You texted a picture earlier today."

Oh, the wrong number. "You meant the floater?" I cringed at the word, but if that's the technical term, then sobeit.

"Yeah, the floater. Where'd ya find 'im?"

"In the Assateague Channel." Wait. A thought. "Are you a family member?" If so, the shock of receiving that photo would be quadrupled. Maybe a hundred-tupled. But what are the odds of that?

"Yeah, we're family all right." The call disconnected.

Oh, what a horrible mistake my shaking fingers had made. But you can't unsend a text any more than you can unring a bell. "Well," I said to Carolyn as I placed my cell phone on the table. "Our John Doe has a name." I sipped my margarita and then licked my lips. "Tuffy."

"Oh." Carolyn sat back in her seat.

"And he has family."

Her hands shredded the paper napkin on the table. "That kind of makes it real, huh?"

I nodded. "That was one of his family members on the phone."

"Tuffy, huh? Did you get a last name?"

I shook my head.

The band played "Brown-Eyed Girl." The crowd sang/shouted along. I tuned it all out while thinking about the life and death of Tuffy. "We should maybe have given him last rites or something."

"We're not ordained clergy. I don't think it would have counted."

"Maybe offered up a prayer?"

Carolyn put her hand on mine. "I don't think your old standby blessing, 'Over the lips and past the gums, look out stomach here it comes' would have been appropriate."

She had a point. My last real conversation with God had been in seventh grade. I wouldn't even know where to begin praying over a dead body.

Carolyn patted my hand. "I think it's enough we stayed with

Tuffy until the Coast Guard arrived. Now here's a thought. Are you in a hurry to get back tomorrow?"

"Not really. Why?"

"I was thinking maybe we'd stick around, pay respects to his family." She swiped trails of tears off her cheeks.

"That sounds like a good idea."

"Good. We'll stop at that bakery on Main Street and pick up a little something to take to them."

That's the difference between Carolyn and me. She finds comfort in food and tears. I, on the other hand, am more likely to find comfort in wine and beers.

Except for tonight. We both searched for comfort in margaritas.

Way too bright but not real early the next morning, we settled into our seats at the Sandfiddler Café. Lots of black coffee and two pieces of dry rye toast and I felt marginally less hungover.

Mellie, our waitress, came by for refills. "Y'all hear about the floater yesterday?"

"Not only did we hear about it," Carolyn said around a mouthful of blueberry pancakes, "we're the ones who found it."

"Get outta town," Mellie said. She pulled up a chair. "Details, please."

Carolyn filled her in.

Mellie nodded throughout, then added the little information she had. "Paper said he pro'lly got hit in the head when his sailboat's boom swung around and smacked him, knocking him overboard. Hate to say it, but that happens all the time."

"He didn't drown?" I asked.

Mellie pulled a pen from behind her ear and ran it through her fingers. "My son-in-law's in the Coast Guard. He said the life jacket did its job. Man died from a blow to the head."

Note to self: Always wear a life jacket when on the water. And duck when the sailboat's boom swings around.

"The curious thing, though," Mellie continued, leaning forward and resting her arms on our table. "My son-in-law said there weren't no missing waterman reported, no missing boat neither." She tapped the pencil against the wood table. *Tap. Tap. Tap.* "Makes you wonder, huh?"

"Wonder what?" I asked.

Tap. Tap. Tap. "If maybe it hadn't been an accident, if you know what I mean."

Oh, how I wish I hadn't known what she meant.

— 🎎 —

We left the cafe, and, thanks to Mellie, we had in our possession a rumpled edition of the *Island Tattler*. Carolyn read from it as we walked. "Look here." She shoved the paper under my nose and pointed. "We got credit for finding the body."

Sure enough. I read aloud, "On Wednesday, kayakers Margaret Gunderson and Carolyn Prewitt of Roanoke, Virginia, discovered the body of Chincoteague resident Shamus 'Tuffy' O'Malley floating on the calm but cool waters of Assateague Channel."

"Now we know his full name."

I scanned the rest of the short article. Absolutely no suspicion of foul play, according to the police.

While reassuring, I wasn't all the way convinced. Without actually wanting to stick my nose in where it didn't belong, a plan formed in my head.

We made our way up Main Street. Small storefronts tucked into century-old buildings lined both sides of the narrow street. The theme of the shops covered the gamut from nautical to artisan, with a gentle sprinkling of pony-themed shops and general souvenir stores. Chincoteague was a quintessential coastal town. Not exactly the murder capital of the world. Probably not even the jaywalking capital of the world. So, what exactly had happened to Tuffy O'Malley?

"You still want to share condolences with the family?" I asked Carolyn.

"You betcha," Carolyn replied, equally curious. "We can't go empty-handed, though."

We skedaddled back to Sandfiddler, this time leaving with a nicely boxed and very aromatic pineapple coconut pound cake and a local address for Tuffy.

Six blocks later we arrived at a ramshackle Victorian home surrounded by a white picket fence that had seen better days. A sign hung crookedly from a front post. *Rooms to rent. Meals Provided.* A boarding house? Did those still even still exist?

Carolyn rang the bell.

A tall, thin, dare I say scrawny woman answered the door. Couldn't be a day over thirty, but the faded green housecoat she wore aged her two decades. "How can I help you?" She pushed her glasses up higher on her nose.

"We came to express our condolences to Shamus O'Malley's family," Carolyn said. "Are you his sister?"

She slipped her hands into the pockets of her housedress. "Not hardly. Only met the man once. He's one of Nana's borders."

"Do you, perchance, have an address for his family?" Carolyn asked. "We're the ones who found the body."

"Oh, my," the woman said. "That must have been awful. Come in. Come in. We'll ask Nana if she knows anything about him." She stepped aside and motioned for us to enter. "My name is Lizzie, by the way."

Carolyn and I introduced ourselves.

It seemed beyond rude to enter someone's home holding a cakebox and not offering it over. Lizzie accepted graciously. We'd have to stop and get another for Tuffy's family.

Lizzie looked down at her housecoat. "Please don't think I dress this way all the time. I showed up to take Nana to lunch and she handed me this dress and told me to get to work cleaning out Tuffy's room." The woman laughed.

We laughed, too. More like a polite chuckle of solidarity on my part. Many a trip to visit my mother had included onerous chores, which I think, but can't prove, she saved up for me.

Nana was the opposite of Lizzie—a living, breathing, plump apple doll. She stood peeling potatoes at an old farm sink in a kitchen that was genuine 1960s. People paid big money to achieve this sense of farmhouse nostalgia. But all the money in the world can't hide the scent of authenticity.

Nana wiped her hands on her apron and sat us all around a small, scarred, wooden kitchen table.

We explained our mission while sharing the pound cake.

Every bit as good as it smelled. Could have used a scoop of vanilla ice cream, but 10:17 a.m. was too early for ice cream, wasn't it?

We chatted, mostly about Chincoteague, past, present, and future. Neither Nana nor Lizzie had much to say about Tuffy, other than he'd moved in six months ago to work a temporary job over at Wallops Island. He kept to himself, never mentioning family.

"Ya know," Lizzie said as she escorted us to the front door, "a stranger visited the other day. Nana was out at her mahjongg game. I'd stopped by to drop off groceries and saw a man race out the front door. He wore a dark suit, darker glasses. A football type who wasn't aging well."

"Did he say anything to you?" I asked.

"I was still in my car. He didn't see me. But before he got into his truck, he turned and looked up at the front of the house." Lizzie hesitated. "He yelled, 'Revenge is a dish best served cold, suckha.'" She shrugged. "At the time I thought he was yelling toward one of the other boarders' windows—Stan has some sketchy friends—but the more I think about it, he was looking directly at Tuffy's window."

The theme to *The Godfather* played in my head.

— 🎎 —

Something they didn't cover in ethics training: Does civic duty require a person to report suspicions of a mob hit to the police?

Carolyn and I held a whispered conversation on that very topic while we strolled to our Airbnb.

Or could all of this be a result of our overactive imaginations? Looking for trouble where there wasn't any? Always an option.

Let's examine the facts. No boat found, no waterman reported missing, a "wiseguy" type character shouting a godfather-branded warning to Tuffy, even though Tuffy wasn't there to hear it. Why weren't the police all over this?

We decided to reach out to the family member who'd called last night. Once we confirmed the guy was genetic family or mob bonded, we could proceed accordingly.

"Hmm," I said as I scrolled through my phone looking for the number. "That call came from a different number than the one I accidently texted the floater's photo to."

"So?"

"So, how did the family member know about the photo?" A puzzler, for sure. Only one way to find out. I tapped the number on my screen.

The gruff voice from last night answered. "Who's dis?"

"This is Margaret Gunderson. You called me concerning Tuffy's picture."

Only silence from the other end.

"My friend and I wanted to express our condolences on the passing of your family member. How were you two related?"

More silence. Somebody wasn't holding up his end of the conversation.

"I'm sure it's too early to have arranged the details of the funeral, but you have my number. I'd appreciate a text with the information. We'd like to attend."

Still no response. *Am I even still connected?* I glanced at my screen. *Yup.* Phone call in progress. "Um, can I ask you a question?" I expected silence and that's what I got. "How did you get my number?"

"We got our ways, lady."

Yeah, that sent my heartbeat racing. The words were bad enough, but the threatening tone in his voice . . . wow.

He disconnected.

"Well?" Carolyn asked.

"I suggest we load up the car and leave town." I didn't want to worry her, so I played it cool.

We returned to the Airbnb, packed our things, and loaded the car.

Traffic was light on VA-175 out of Chincoteague, a peaceful drive along a two-lane road, water on one side, marshland on the other. Weather remained comfortable and overcast, a perfect fall day for cruisin' in my sporty Beemer M240, a gift to myself after reaching a long-eluded sales goal. "California Dreamin' " played on the 70s station, and we sang along. With every mile we put between ourselves and the island, I allowed myself to relax a tiny skooch.

A big, black Cadillac Escalade pulled up on my left, even though we travelled in a no-passing zone.

My hands grabbed the wheel. I eased off the accelerator.

The Escalade slowed to match my speed.

"He wants you to pull over," Carolyn said.

I glanced to my left. A man in the passenger seat waved his meaty hand, motioning me to the side of the road.

"You probably left your gas cap open again," Carolyn suggested.

I don't know what she meant by "again." I'd never left my gas cap off in my life. But if it gave her solace in thinking that, then who was I to argue?

I steered my car off to the generous berm. Two scenarios scrolled through my head—either the FBI wanting information, or a mobster wanting to make sure we didn't talk. Ever! Fingers crossed for option one.

We rolled to a stop, out of the way of traffic, which was disconcertingly light.

The Escalade pulled in front, then backed up until their bumper kissed mine.

Carolyn used her cell phone to snap a photo of the car. "I'm gonna record this." She tapped the screen a few times and then slipped it under her seat. With hands tucked under her thighs and black Keds tapping out a beat against the carpet, she sat in her seat, a menacing scowl on her face. "What's gonna happen to us?"

"Nothing," I said. *I hope*, I added in my head.

The Escalade's passenger door opened. A bulky man oozed out. He wore a slick dark track suit and even darker glasses, which he removed as he strolled to my side of the car. He didn't have the FBI vibe, but not the mafia-hitman vibe either.

I sat there, confused and trembling. My hands, wrapped around the steering wheel at the ten and two position, were as bloodless as Tuffy's face when he'd knocked into my kayak. A panic attack threatened to take over my bodily functions and turn my mind to pudding.

The man stopped at my window, giving me an up close-and-personal look at his abdomen. His hand reached around, and his sausage fingers unzipped his nylon jacket. He pulled the flap back just enough to show me the menacing black gun holstered to his hip.

He tapped on my window with his beefy knuckle and then motioned me to lower it.

I complied, although my head vibrated so violently it blurred my vision. The stink of fear wafted upwards from my armpits.

"I'm gonna need to see your phone." The voice from the phone call.

"Ummm." And I'd judged *him* on his poor conversation skills.

My fingers fumbled as I unzipped my purse and extracted my lifeline to all matters business and family. I handed it out the window, but it slipped through my sweat-soaked hands and it clattered to the ground.

He bent and picked it up.

"How did you find us?" Carolyn called from the passenger seat. Her voice had a nervous twinge. I could relate.

"We got our ways, lady." He wound up like a major league pitcher and tossed my phone into the marsh. "You'll be smart not to mention this to anyone."

He ambled, bear-like, back into the Escalade and off he went.

———⚉———

"You won't believe the latest." Carolyn reached for another parmesan crisp.

We were sitting on the back deck of my mountain cottage overlooking the Blue Ridge mountains, about as far away as we could get from Chincoteague Island without crossing the state line. Carolyn stopped by occasionally to update me on the case regarding the murder of Sean "Tuffy" O'Malley. For some morbid reason, she kept close tabs on the investigation. Says it was only thanks to us there even was a case.

We had, of course, contacted the police and told them our story. That's the kind of thing good citizens do.

They'd pulled my cellphone records to track the phone number. They'd used Carolyn's photo of the Escalade, which offered a clear picture of the license plate. They'd listened to the recording of our roadside conversation, which hinted at their role in Tuffy's untimely demise.

"The charges against the two guys in the Escalade have been dropped to manslaughter."

"What? Your last report said it would be slam dunk for murder one." I slowed the speed of my rocking chair in order to take a sip of wine without splashing on my shirt. Merlot does not pair well with a white blouse. I'd learned that lesson the hard way.

Carolyn shook her head.

We'd known from almost the beginning of the investigation that it hadn't been a mob hit, just retribution over an unpaid bet on a college football game.

"Turns out Tuffy's death really had been an accident. They'd all gone out for a day on the water. Tuffy, not being a good swimmer, had worn his life jacket. Also, not being an experienced sailor, he didn't know to duck when the boom swung around. He took a blow to the head and landed in the water. That's what did him in."

"Just like our waitress Mellie suspected from the get-go." I used my foot to push my rocker back and forth, a gentle motion that I hoped would sooth my anxious soul. "So why a manslaughter charge then? Why not just chalk it up as an accident?"

"This is where the story turns tragic." Carolyn paused to take a sip of her wine. "Since his friends, and I use that term loosely, really were mad at him over the unpaid bet, they didn't attempt to save him. Just sailed off into the sunset. Makes it worse than premediated in my book."

Yes. It did. Ever so much worse. A man killed over a two-hundred-dollar bet. Oh, my freakin' gawd.

DERAILED

By Heather Weidner

DELANIE FITZGERALD GLANCED AT her buzzing phone and paid the guy in the drive-thru for her iced mocha. Throwing her change in her purse, she peeked at the caller ID and sighed. Chaz Smith, sleazy strip club owner and best cash-paying client for her PI firm, Falcon Investigations. She clicked the button on her Mustang's steering wheel.

"Hey, there. I haven't heard from you in a while."

"Yep. Long time no see. I need your help. This is hush-hush. Can you meet me?"

Delanie pursed her lips. "Sure. What works for you?"

"How about a half-hour or so at my office?"

"See you then."

Chaz was always dancing on the edge of impropriety, but his hidden, softer side had grown on her over the years.

She pressed the button and said, "Call Duncan's cell."

After a few rings, her partner, Duncan Reynolds, answered. He specialized in web design when he wasn't poking around the Dark Web looking for information.

"I got a call from Chaz. He wants to talk about a job."

"At least he pays in cash, and none of it's counterfeit."

Delanie grunted. "I'll see what he wants. I'll be in after that."

"It could be anything. Margaret and I'll be here."

Delanie smiled at the mention of Margaret, Duncan's faithful sidekick, a rotund, brown-and-white English bulldog who ruled the office.

She pointed the car toward the Powhite Expressway and headed downtown. About thirty minutes later, she pulled into the almost-full lot of the Treasure Chest, Richmond's finest gentlemen's club, according to Chaz.

Chaz's head of security stood with the side metal door propped open. "Good to see you." Marco smiled, showing his gold tooth. "The boss is expecting you."

"It's nice to see you, too."

She followed Marco and a faint scent of citrus down the narrow hallway past the kitchen and prep areas. The bass from the club's speakers echoed and bounced off the corridor walls. At the end of the hallway, he stopped abruptly, and Delanie almost ran into the back of him as he rapped on the door.

After a faint, "Come in," he held the door for her.

"Hey, Delanie," Chaz said from behind a black lacquered desk. He muted the almost wall-sized television and nodded at Marco, who backed out and closed the door.

"What can Falcon Investigations help you with?" Delanie took a seat in one of the guest chairs.

He paused. "I had a weird visitor this week."

Delanie furrowed her brow. She wasn't sure what constituted weird in Chaz's world, but the strip club owner did look distracted today. His normally slicked-back, blond hair stuck up in random spots like he hadn't fully combed it. His shiny gray suit with a black dress shirt, unbuttoned at the collar, looked like he slept in it.

Chaz took a sip from a Diet Pepsi can and wiped his mouth with the back of his hand. "It was totally random. This guy asks for me at the bar. He said he had a message for me and my crew."

"Your crew?"

"I had no idea what he was talking about, so I listened. He said the person who hired him knows why I have this tattoo." He touched the stylized blue teardrop at the corner of his eye. "And he needed to be persuaded not to tell anyone."

"Just the cryptic message?" Delanie asked, leaning forward.

"He pussyfooted around. The gist was he wanted fifty-K from each of us to keep quiet. He would text me next week about how to make the payments."

"Are you going to pay it? And who's in the crew?"

"No, I don't give a rat's uh . . . backside about some stupid theory of how I got my tattoo, but it does affect Trey. My buddy,

Trey Stafford. We go way back."

"The city council member?"

"And future state representative. I don't care what this dude says about me, but it could hurt Trey's chances in the election."

Delanie, antsy to figure out what Chaz wanted, squirmed in her seat. "What was the mysterious guy holding over your head?"

"A very stupid and tragic mistake," he replied. Chaz glanced at his hands. "Four of us were at the wrong place at the wrong time. It was one summer way back in the nineties. Trey and I were with Bob Prince and Larry Winters, guys we'd known forever. We were drinking at a bar downtown. Some guy and his buddy started running their mouths, and a fight that made its way out to an alley got out of hand."

"What happened?" Delanie leaned forward, being careful not to tip the chair.

"It started out as jawing. Then it was pushing and fists. Bob and one of the other guys pulled out knives."

"Then what happened?" Delanie asked.

"Everybody'd been drinking. You know, bad judgement and too much testosterone."

Delanie raised both eyebrows and waited for him to continue.

"The mouthy guy got stabbed, and his buddy ran away. He died on the sidewalk. Bob freaked out. He couldn't go to jail. He was already on probation for some other stupid stuff. Larry had an idea. He knew of a place. We threw the body in the trunk of Bob's car and dumped it. Back then, people could be made to disappear. I never heard about anyone finding the body. And if they did, no big deal. Cold case."

Delanie waited for the rest of the story, hoping there would be a change of heart or a hint of remorse.

"Then the four of us made a pact never to tell. We all got tattoos to seal the deal."

Delanie pointed to the corner of her eye and Chaz continued. "Maybe not the best choice, but I like it. It makes people wonder about my past. The guys got different designs and put theirs in other places. I was looking for some street cred. Hey, I was in my twenties."

"Who was the guy who died?" she asked.

"Don't know," Chaz said. "The other guy kept calling him Patrick."

"Have you heard from Bob or Larry lately?" Delanie asked.

Chaz shook his head. "Bob did time for distribution. I haven't seen him in years. Larry died about four years ago in a motorcycle accident."

"Where is this place?"

"You have time for a field trip?" Chaz asked.

"Sure. Nearby?"

"Closer than you think." Chaz rose and pocketed his keys and phone. "Come on. I'll drive."

Delanie hesitated.

"We'll take my Mercedes," he said.

She sighed with relief. Chaz's other vehicle was a gold Hummer wrapped in bikini-clad women that advertised the Treasure Chest. She wasn't up for a city tour in his pimp mobile.

Chaz dodged traffic on Main Street and wended his way through town to the historic Church Hill neighborhood, turning sharply into a parking lot next to a warehouse that had been repurposed as upscale condos. "How much do you know about the tunnel accident?" he asked.

"It's part of the haunted tour."

"I'm gonna stop here, so you can see one end of the tunnel. Then we'll go to the other side. Back in the 1920s, there was a cave-in that trapped workers and a train underground. They tried for days to rescue people. Finally, they decided to seal the tunnel and leave the bodies and the train inside because they were afraid of more cave-ins. Every boy in Richmond has tried to sneak in there." Chaz turned off the car and made his way to a stone arch walled up with cement blocks. A steady trickle of water seeped from between the blocks.

"This it?" Delanie asked.

Chaz pointed to the arch. "It didn't look like this back then. It was covered with graffiti and the wall had been broken. The source of thousands of dares and ghost stories."

Delanie Googled it on her phone and skimmed through pictures of the original construction and of the abandoned site.

"Come on, I'll show you the other end. That's where we, uh, explored."

They hopped back in his car and drove about a mile. Upscale condos gave way to abandoned buildings. Chaz stopped next to an aging apartment complex across the street from some new construction. An overgrown lot that sloped down a hill looked out of place in the urban setting.

"If you head down that path there, it'll take you to the other end of the tunnel." He pointed to a gap in the brambles.

Delanie shuddered at the thought of snakes and ticks on that overgrown trail full of briars and thick weeds.

"Do you still have those pictures?"

Delanie fished her phone out of her pocket.

"See that one?" Chaz pointed at her phone. "That's what it looked like. The fence was torn down, and you could see the stone arch of the tunnel entrance. If you went inside, it was flooded. The sealed end is inside the tunnel."

"That's where you all left the body?" Delanie stared at Chaz.

"Yeah. Larry said nobody would notice. Larry and Bob wrapped him in blankets. We carried him down the hill and waded in. Back then you could squeeze past the wall. We took him back a few feet and submerged him with cinderblocks and some old chain Larry found. Come on, I'll show you the spot."

She followed Chaz, who swatted at low-hanging branches and vines. He trotted down the sloping path while she gingerly stepped, trying to avoid mud, ruts, and years of abandoned tires and trash. Chaz stopped at the water's edge. It looked like a drainage area. The smell of stagnant water and decay overpowered the woodsy smell.

"See over there, it looks like the tunnel's open, but it's not."

Delanie slapped at a bug.

"The whole thing's filled with water. It's pretty deep in places."

"You didn't see the train, did you?" Delanie asked.

Chaz shook his head. "No. Just part of the old tracks. We did what we had to do that night and hightailed it out of there.

This is the first time I've been back since. We all swore never to mention it again."

"But obviously someone did."

Chaz shrugged. "Come on, let's get out of here. This place gives me the creeps." When they reached the street, he continued. "I need you to find out who blabbed. I'll have my security team send you camera footage of the guy who came in demanding the ransom."

When Chaz parked in the back of his club, he handed her an envelope. "This should cover a few weeks' worth of your time. If you need more, let me know."

"Thanks." Delanie dropped it in her purse. "Anything else you remember? Did any of the guys give you reason to believe they wouldn't have kept the secret?"

"Nah. We swore an oath."

"Anything else?"

Chaz shook his head.

"There's not much to go on. I'll get with Duncan. We'll see what we can find."

Once inside her car, Delanie called her partner. After a couple of rings, she heard, "What exciting adventure does Chaz have for us?"

"I found out how he got that teardrop tattoo. You going to be around this afternoon?"

"Yep. Why don't you bring food? Any names I can look at now? Can't wait to hear about the tattoo."

Delanie gave him the men's names. She could hear him tapping on his keyboard. "And the Church Hill Tunnel," she said.

"Whoa, that thing has spawned all kinds of legends. There have been cave-ins through the years, causing the houses on Church Hill to lean. Some locals claimed the tunnel work released an evil force on the city."

"Yep, we'll battle evil, but first, why don't you call in an order at Gotham Pizza, and I'll pick it up?"

"Deal."

About forty-five minutes later, Delanie juggled her purse and two pizza boxes. She hip-checked her car door and managed to unlock the office door without dropping anything. Falcon Investigations inhabited a small suite in the middle of a strip mall.

In the conference room, Delanie threw her purse in a nearby chair and plopped down as Duncan returned with drinks and paper plates. Margaret followed him like a shadow.

"I've been looking at all the urban legends and Richmond vampire connections." Duncan grinned from ear to ear. Geeky stuff made his eyes sparkle.

Delanie helped herself to a slice of New York-style pizza. She took a bite and wrapped the stray string of cheese around her finger.

"After the cave in, they mounted a rescue team. There were some survivors. It took days to retrieve the engineer's body. A lot of the workers were day laborers, so they don't know for sure how many others were trapped inside. Some stories say two. Others say three or four. The tunnel was precarious before the cave-in. Sink holes have damaged roads and houses at the top of the hill for years."

"Chaz took me to both ends of the tunnel."

"Y'all climbed down there?" Duncan stopped eating and stared at her.

She nodded, and he continued, "Awhile back, a reporter and some divers ventured in, and later an excavation company drilled some holes to lower cameras. Neither effort was successful. The tunnel's filled with muck. Before they sealed it, the railroad company packed it with sand to prevent further cave-ins. There are all kinds of stories of people who have heard screams and noises near the tunnel."

"According to Chaz, there's another body down there. He said back in the nineties, a fist fight turned ugly when the knives came out, and one guy died. Chaz's friends hid the body in the tunnel. And they made a pact and got tattoos to seal the deal."

"I always wondered about that teardrop. I thought he had it put there for show."

Delanie shrugged. "He didn't actually kill anyone. Chaz never heard anything else about the dead guy named Patrick. Then some man approached Chaz and his friend Trey Stafford with a threat."

"I looked up the names you gave me. Larry Winters died in a motorcycle accident. He had an ex-wife, Bev Robinson, who's lived in Oklahoma for twenty years, and a daughter named Lauren, who lives in Richmond with some guy named Wyatt Smith. Bob Prince did some time for distribution and possession. He got out three years ago. His last known address was his mother's in Ginter Park, and he works at a restaurant in Scott's Addition." Duncan took a long breath and paused. "Oh, and Trey's been in office for the last ten years. His wife is a nurse. He inherited money from his parents and sells insurance."

Duncan pulled the crust off his pizza and gave it to Margaret. "A pizza bone for you."

The English bulldog took her treasure and gnawed on it under the conference room table.

"Okay, so we can start with Bob Prince and Lauren. The leads are sparse. Oh, wait. Chaz had his security guy email me the video of the blackmailer."

After a few clicks, Duncan pulled up the video clip on his laptop. "Tall, bald guy with a bushy brown beard and glasses. I'll run it through some facial recognition sites. I'll see what I can find."

"You have that kind of software?"

"Let's just say I have access to it." Duncan winked and stared at his screen. Then he reached for more pizza. "I'll check out any reports of missing persons in the city during that time, too."

Duncan didn't have any luck with the facial scanning, so Delanie had to do her investigating the traditional way. The next afternoon, she found parking on West Leigh Street. The former industrial area had turned almost overnight into a hipster place for foodies and craft beer lovers. She wandered in the front of a nondescript seventies-style building that sported a Blue Dog Brewery logo on the glass door. Inside, floor-to-ceiling murals of Richmond sites and blue dogs covered every inch of space.

Lapis lazuli-colored pendant lights focused a soft glow on the bar, made from reclaimed wood. Delanie checked her phone. The guy behind the bar matched the photo Duncan found of Bob.

"What can I get you?" the man asked as she approached the bar.

"Do you have ginger ale?"

He frowned. "That it?"

"For now."

He set the glass down on the wooden counter hard enough to slosh some of the liquid. He grabbed a rag and wiped the spill.

"Neat place. Do you have a lunch menu?"

The lumpy guy, who had probably been muscular in his younger days, slid a laminated page to her and returned to stacking glasses.

"Can I get the three-cheese sandwich with the kettle chips?"

The guy disappeared in the back, and Delanie flipped through her emails.

About fifteen minutes later, the bartender returned with her plate and a napkin. "Let me know if you need anything else."

"Know much about the area?" she asked.

"Lived here all my life." The bartender sliced a lime with a large knife and dropped the pieces in metal trays.

"What can you tell me about the Church Hill Tunnel?"

Delanie detected a sideways glance and a pause. "It's downtown." He pointed to the door with his knife. "Why?"

"Are you Bob Prince? Friend of Chaz, Trey, and Larry?"

He stood up straight and glared at her. He paused his fruit prep and held the knife just above the lime.

Delanie lowered her voice. "Chaz had a visitor this week who brought up something from the past."

Bob sliced the fruit with more energy than necessary. The blade clanked on the counter's surface.

"I don't know what you're talking about." The man looked down and concentrated on his task.

"When was the last time you saw or talked to Chaz, Larry, or Trey?"

"Larry's dead. I haven't seen the other two in years. Our lives took different paths."

"Has anyone been to see you about the tunnel?"

"No."

Delanie held up a picture of the bearded man. "Know this guy?"

The man glanced at the photo. "You're pretty nosy."

"Chaz wants to know."

"Hundreds of people come in here."

"Still, if you see him, call me." Delanie pushed her card across the counter.

She took several bites of her sandwich. Bob moved on to tasks at the other end of the bar.

Delanie finished her lunch and left cash next to her plate. When she hopped off the stool, Bob returned and cleared the space.

"Need change?"

"I'm good. Thanks."

"Not sure what the guy wanted with Chaz, but that's not my life now. I can't help you. I don't need anyone dredging up the past."

"If you see the guy with the beard, I'd appreciate it if you'd call me."

Bob shrugged and disappeared in the back. If she didn't get any more leads, she'd come back and tail Bob when he left work.

Delanie checked her notes and decided to try Lauren Winter's work address first.

After a quick drive, Delanie pulled into the parking lot of an office building, wedged in between two used car dealers. An electronic squeal on the front door made a bleached blond look up from her computer screen.

"Hi, I'm Chrissie Edmonds, and I'm looking for Lauren Winters." Delanie glanced down at the faded brass nameplate on the receptionist's desk.

"I'm her. What do you need?"

"I'm working on a story, and I hoped to get some information if you have a few minutes to talk."

"I'm busy here. What's this about?" The younger woman made a face like she was eating pickles.

"It's about a cold case in Richmond, and I have a few questions."

The woman furrowed her overly manicured brows. "You're confused. I have no idea what you're talking about. You have the wrong person."

"I'd like to talk to you about something that happened to your father about thirty years ago."

The woman stood and slammed her hand on her desk. "I told you I was busy."

A man in a brown suit stuck his head out of an interior doorway. Lauren looked at him and shook her head. He paused and disappeared back in his office.

Delanie wondered if bluffing would work. "I think you do. This is about a body in the Church Hill Tunnel that you and Wyatt are interested in."

The woman flashed a surprised look before she rummaged around her desk. Lauren picked up an e-cigarette. "Time for a smoke break," she bellowed.

Lauren followed Delanie outside away from the door and the front window. "I don't know who you are," she hissed. "Or why you're bothering me."

"I want to know why you and your boyfriend are so concerned about a murder from the nineties."

Lauren inhaled deeply. She closed her eyes and exhaled water vapor. She stared at Delanie with a laser focus.

"Did you hear the story from your dad?"

With a pained look she said, "We're done here. You've got the wrong person. Leave me and Wyatt alone."

Lauren looked around and then back at Delanie before she rushed back in the building.

Through the window, Delanie watched Lauren punch numbers into her phone. A few minutes later, the blond flew out the door and jumped into a late model Chevy. Delanie had to floor the Mustang to keep up.

Zigzagging her way through some narrow neighborhood streets with lots of graffiti-covered fences, Lauren skidded to a stop in front of a row of townhouses. Delanie parked her car several yards away and settled in to watch the door that Lauren entered. The wood trim on the porch sported a faded redwood stain. The missing balusters made the banister look like the crooked smile of a professional hockey player.

Stakeouts were the part of the job that Delanie disliked most. Her mind tended to wander. She stretched as best she could in the seat to ward off kinks in her back.

About an hour later, the door of the townhouse opened, and a bearded guy stepped outside. Delanie looked at the picture Chaz's guy had sent. Bingo. Sometimes hunches pay off.

The man slammed the door. Delanie's pulse raced. She snapped several pictures and waited to see what the man would do. He trotted around the corner to a mom-and-pop grocery store. Deciding to wait outside, Delanie watched the front door.

About ten minutes later, the man reappeared with a paper bag and a case of beer. He walked purposefully back to the townhouse. Lauren's car still sat at the curb.

Delanie rummaged through her purse for her notebook, pen, and phone. She jumped out and jogged toward the man. "Excuse me, Wyatt Smith?"

The man glared at her.

"I'm working on a story about a dead guy in the Church Hill Tunnel. Could I ask you a few questions?"

The man grunted and turned.

"Care to make a statement about trying to extort money from a local politician? Were you hired by the other side?"

"What? No. Nobody hired us. Mind your own business if you know what's good for you." He turned to leave and then pivoted, swinging the grocery bag at her.

Delanie ducked, and Wyatt put his head down and charged her like a bull.

She grabbed his collar and shoved him with a force that surprised her. He stumbled, falling on his back in the grass. Delanie kicked him in the ribs when he reached for the bag, its contents strewn on someone's lawn. "Stay down. Maybe you and Lauren should leave the past in the past. And an anger-management course might help you."

She pushed several stray curls out of her face and turned toward her car as a small crowd gathered nearby. Some were recording the scene on their phones, while others clapped and hooted.

Delanie jumped in her car and called Chaz. "I found your blackmailer. The guy lives with Lauren Winters, Larry's daughter. His name is Wyatt Smith."

"Give me the address."

"2614 Grayland Avenue."

"I'll take care of it. Thanks for the info." Chaz disconnected the call.

Delanie sighed. She wondered what Chaz would do. With Chaz, she always felt like she was walking a thin line between doing the right thing and being loyal to her paying customer.

"Call Duncan," she told the car.

After a couple of rings, "What's up?"

"I found the blackmailer, and I had to remind him of his manners."

"So, what's next?"

"Chaz said he'd take care of it, but it feels undone. We need to leave Richmond homicide an anonymous tip. I don't like loose ends."

"I didn't have much luck narrowing down the list of missing persons in the area from thirty years ago. I didn't find any Patricks."

A week later, a local news segment caught Delanie's eye while she was on a treadmill at the gym. A reporter rattled on about heightened police and forensic activity in the area of the infamous Church Hill Tunnel. The PI smiled. Maybe Richmond PD would find the body after all.

GHOSTS OF SANDBRIDGE

By Michael Rigg

"MARGARITAVILLE." His go-to song for stress relief. So retired Navy pilot Ryan Kensington cranked up the volume in his Acura RDX. He alternated between the gas pedal and brake as his car inched along Sandbridge Road headed toward the southeastern tip of Virginia Beach.

More stress—the nagging chirp of an incoming call. *Unknown* flashed on the hands-free display. He *should* let it roll over to voicemail. But he worried that it might be Jake Sanders—his client from Richmond—using a burner, again. Ryan silenced the music.

"Kensington here. Jake, that you? Didn't recognize the number." Lawyers. So damned paranoid about someone monitoring their communications.

Jake skipped the pleasantries. "Any updates?"

"Nothing big." Now on Sandpiper Road, one of two north-south thoroughfares running through Sandbridge, a quarter-mile-wide community wedged between the Atlantic Ocean and Back Bay, Ryan stopped for pedestrians in a crosswalk. "Downloaded good intel from the deed and tax records. Haven't had a chance to analyze it. Should be to the house around four."

"Understood. Call me once you're settled."

"Will do. Kensington out." The last pedestrian cleared the crosswalk. He accelerated and increased the volume, just as "It's Five O'Clock Somewhere" began playing.

The Sanctuary, a five-story condominium complex, loomed ahead. His cue to turn. A left at White Cap Lane, then another onto Sandfiddler—the other north-south road—brought him to the driveway of Pirate's Hideaway.

The house underwhelmed. Its 1970s exterior—particularly the three stories of vinyl siding—appeared drab and tired. Except for an ancient live oak, its front yard consisted of sand, heat-stressed Bermuda grass, and weeds. Mostly weeds. Next door, to the north, stood Dolphin's Cove—an older, weather-beaten rental badly in need of renovation. A For Sale sign displayed prominently. Not an awe-inspiring pair when compared to mammoth party-castles commanding so much prime oceanfront real estate.

Ryan carried a cooler up wooden stairs to the second-floor entrance. Shimmering heat waves danced above the water, making solid objects appear fluid—almost surreal and Daliesque. His nostrils flared at the combined aromas of saltwater, sea life, and sunscreen. Overhead, seagulls serenaded his arrival. He was definitely at the beach.

Ironic. An oceanfront retreat—all expenses paid—should be a welcome escape. For Ryan? Just another falsehood in a long line of falsehoods.

Pretense. Play acting. Prevarication. All critical tools for a private investigator. But they boiled down to one thing—lying. Ryan loathed that part of his new career. Especially today, when his first conversation with a beautiful woman, and whatever followed, would be a lie.

It was all in a day's work. Nothing personal. Besides, after picking up the key to Pirate's Hideaway from Seaford Realty's rental office, he probably wouldn't see Nancy, or those stunning grey eyes, again. A brief encounter, but a definite connection. Ryan sighed. Time to rein in his libido. Get on with business.

His phone vibrated. *Damn!* Hardly past four o'clock. If the pattern held, he would receive two more texts in the next few minutes. No use stopping. Finish unloading the car, then read them all at once.

Around four-thirty, Ryan rang through to Jake. "You're on speaker."

"Okay. What's up?"

"First three texts—just as expected." Ryan scrolled through his phone. "'We know what you did.' And number two: 'We're watching'. Third—"

"Let me guess," Jake said. "Leave while you still can."

"Bingo."

"Well, they're sticking with the script. Were the texts from a local phone?"

"Three different area codes."

"Probably prepaids. Harder to trace. Like the others."

"I've got a pal with the State Police. I'll call in some markers."

"Great," Jake said. "But let's not call the locals yet. The other occupants got spooked after a couple of days. Let's see what happens."

"Okay. I guess you're paying me the big bucks to be bait." Ryan laughed.

"Sorry, man. I didn't mean—"

"Don't worry. This assignment can't be as difficult as landing on a carrier in a gale. I got this." Ryan paused. "But the worm on the hook needs to start acting the part. I'm just a guy taking advantage of a last-minute vacation on the cheap, remember?"

On the cheap. What an understatement. During July, a stay at Pirate's Hideaway should cost over ten thousand dollars per week. Actually, less than a week, beginning with check-in late afternoon Saturday and ending with a midmorning checkout the next Saturday.

But that was *before*. Before the strangeness that started Memorial Day weekend. Before the cancellations and demands for refunds as word spread that Pirate's Hideaway was haunted. Or cursed. Or whatever. The weekly tariff spiraled lower until reaching three thousand dollars—the amount Ryan had already invoiced and been paid by his client Jake, the owner.

A margarita would be great right now. But he hadn't brought tequila or other ingredients. A high-speed run for supplies tomorrow would rectify the situation. Fortunately, he'd brought along a bottle of bourbon—Knob Creek—almost as an afterthought. He poured himself two fingers on the rocks. Just what the doctor ordered.

He looked for a blender—for later. No luck. He called the Seaford rental office. An enthusiastic teenage girl promised that one of the maintenance guys would deliver one as soon as possible.

Sitting at a sturdy, composite-material picnic table on the second-floor deck, Ryan sipped his bourbon. As he sifted through data on his laptop, a pattern emerged.

"Knock, knock."

Ryan glanced over his left shoulder. Nancy.

"Sorry." She appeared half embarrassed and half ready to break out laughing. "Didn't mean to scare you."

"That's okay." He stood. "Just reading some reports."

"No answer downstairs. Figured I'd check up here."

Ryan accepted the medium-sized carton Nancy thrust at him—a blender. "That was quick."

Nancy was more attractive than he remembered. Ashen-gray hair pulled back in a bun complemented her sun-bronzed face. She didn't need cosmetics, though she must have used something to highlight her features. Her lipstick—more like lip-gloss softened by dulcet orange tones—emphasized the bright intensity in her eyes. In her mid-forties, maybe, about five years younger than Ryan. And no wedding ring. Nancy's flowery sundress, the same one she was wearing when he picked up the key, emphasized her curves.

"I expected a maintenance worker. Surprised to see—"

"Normally, I'm a real estate agent with Seaford. But on check-in day, we all pitch in. I'm meeting friends at La Playa. This is a quick detour."

"La Playa?"

"On White Cap, across Sandpiper. Baja California vibe. Best fish tacos around. Two- or three-minute walk from here."

"Right. Passed it when I drove in."

"Drop by . . . if you're not busy."

"Sounds appealing." Hint taken. Regardless, business before pleasure. "But I'll have to take a rain check."

Nancy left. Time to button up the house—Physical Security 101. Lock the windows and doors. Mark each with clear tape and thread, an old trick to reveal if anyone opened them afterward. Add extra sets of eyes—strategically placed pinhole-cameras. Finally, check his Emergency Kit—a Glock 19, pepper spray, and an expandable baton known by its brand name, ASP. Final step—lights out.

Ryan settled on an oversized couch in the darkened great room. Eleven-thirty. Enough time for a couple of hours shut-eye before the next message. He'd slept through nighttime flight ops on the carrier, so revelers setting off fireworks and laughing on the beach shouldn't present a problem.

— 🎎 —

Mini-earthquakes from his vibrating phone—signaling an incoming text—shattered his slumber. Except for fluorescent streetlamps and the glow of lights from several units at The Sanctuary, darkness and shadows predominated. No footsteps or other sounds indicating an intruder. No fireworks. No laughter. Silence.

Three-fifteen—Sunday morning. The text came later than he expected.

"We told you to leave."

More texts—from three separate numbers—arrived fifteen minutes apart, ending just before dawn. Each warned him to vacate the premises. The final message turned up the heat.

"Time's running out."

Threatening texts had scared off previous occupants, usually by Monday or Tuesday. One New Jersey family lasted until Wednesday morning. The Seaford Realty clean-up crew found an open front door and a raccoon carcass in the first-floor game room.

Police investigated but couldn't trace the messages. With no evidence of forced entry, they concluded that a sick animal had wandered through a door left ajar by negligent, or perhaps inebriated, vacationers from the Garden State.

Ryan's job—stay put. Force their hand. He sat at the kitchen table and replied to each text the same: "Kiss my ass."

He reflected on the pattern he noticed in the deed and tax records last night, before Nancy dropped off his blender. With the sun fully over the horizon, after breakfast he headed out on foot northward along Sandfiddler to verify, or disprove, his hunch about the pattern. He walked ten or twelve blocks, noting the types of houses. On the left—semi-oceanfront side—were mostly single-family homes, predominantly rentals, but many occupied by full-time residents. Almost no mega-structures. On the right—

oceanfront side—were a few single-family houses, both rentals and private occupancy. Fully a third were monstrous party-castles—each of which easily accommodated three dozen occupants.

The trend toward larger properties had escalated after the Sanctuary opened fifteen years ago. Before then, rentals generally fit an extended family—around a dozen or so adults and children. The newer, fortress-like buildings tripled the capacity, housing an extended family on each of three floors. Add superior common areas, and each unit became a self-contained mini-resort, garnering twenty-five thousand dollars—or more—per week during the summer.

Of special interest—the parcels of land involved. Despite their architectural footprint, the larger, more profitable houses only required a single lot. Dolphin's Cove needed a major upgrade—a costly proposition. Tanking Pirate's Hideaway's revenue potential could force Jake to sell, allowing a buyer to obtain both properties at a steal, raze the relics, and rebuild in their place. Two lots and two rental cash cows. More than enough reason for the intimidation tactics.

His defiant response and steadfast refusal to leave must have stymied his adversary. Time to keep him or her—or them—off balance. Force the other side to make a mistake, fumble the ball. Decision made. Now would be a great opportunity to shop for margarita ingredients. Leave Pirate's Hideaway unprotected. Perhaps they'd be foolish, explore inside, and be caught on camera. He loaded his computer and Emergency Kit into his RDX and punched the ignition button.

Texting, Round Three, started shortly thereafter. More of the same nondescript bullying. "Get out." "Go home." "Don't be a fool." His response to each: "Go to hell."

He pulled into the driveway at Pirate's Hideaway about two hours after he left on his errands. His phone buzzed—another message. "Welcome home."

Ryan's heartbeat seemed to move from his chest to his teeth and behind his cheeks. They *had* to be somewhere near. How else could they know? But where? His jaw tightened. Inside the house? Only one way to find out.

He grabbed pepper spray and his ASP—the expandable baton—

but not his Glock. No reason to escalate the situation. No physical violence yet—to humans, anyway. The spray and baton—and his fists—should be enough. Ryan took several calming breaths. This was attack-mode, and in control was the only way to be.

A tense, thorough search of the entire place revealed nothing out of the ordinary. Security measures still in place. No evidence of intrusion on the camera footage. Crisis alleviated. All in all, an emotional roller coaster. Time for a break.

— 🎭 —

La Playa was as Nancy described. Laid back. Decorated like a dive in Baja. Fish tacos with cabbage—not lettuce. Pacifico, his favorite Mexican beer. And another surprise. Nancy and two female companions in the bar, less than twenty feet away, commemorating an unspecified occasion.

Around nine-thirty, Nancy's friends departed, leaving her alone to drink and fiddle with her phone. Should he say something? Or pay his bill and escape without being noticed?

"Hey, handsome." Nancy walked slowly, weaving slightly. "Look at you in your Mommy Bahamas." She sat at Ryan's table. "I mean Tommy Alabama's." She giggled. "I've been celebrating."

"I see."

"It's my fifth anni . . . *divorcery*." She hiccupped. "My fifth-year divorce."

"Fifth anniversary of your divorce?"

"Right." Her eyes moistened. "Five years since being traded in for a newer model."

"I didn't realize."

"Yeah, he's a shyster and lobbyist in Washington and Richmond. A player. In politics and in life . . . get my drift?"

"I do. Sorry."

"Judge socked it to him, though." Nancy snickered. "Alimony. Seed money for my new life at the beach."

"Nice."

"So, what brought you to Pirate's Hideaway all by your lonesome?"

"It's complicated."

"Oh? Is there a Mrs. Pirate's Hideaway?" Nancy hiccupped.

"Excuse me."

"Was. Ellen. Lost her to cancer six years ago."

They exchanged personal insights that probably neither had shared with someone of the opposite sex in a long time. Maybe it was the alcohol. Or maybe it was something else. Ryan was forthcoming—unless it touched on his PI work. It wasn't lying, but it wasn't the full truth, either.

The restaurant closed at eleven. Leaning on Ryan, Nancy made it as far as the passenger seat of her lunar-blue Mercedes GLC-300 SUV before falling asleep. He didn't know where she lived. So he drove to Pirate's Hideaway, carried the semiconscious Nancy upstairs, and tucked her into bed.

"Sweet dreams." Ryan turned off the light and resumed his guard post on the great room couch, prepared for another round of texts or whatever might come his way.

——— 🐙 ———

Monday morning's spectacular sunrise operated as a silent alarm. Ryan awoke with a start and checked his phone. Odd. There had been no text messages overnight.

Eventually, Nancy emerged from the master bedroom. How could she look so stunning, so together, after what must have been a fitful night sleeping it off?

"Good morning," Ryan said. "Feeling better?"

"Sure." She sounded less than sure. "Do I smell coffee?"

Ryan poured her a cup. "Did you find the toothbrush I left you?"

"I did. Thanks." Nancy added creamer and took a sip. "Oh, that's good." She looked at Ryan. "Listen, about last night—"

"No need." Ryan sipped his coffee. "Certain anniversaries are . . . well, difficult."

"You know, last night's kind of fuzzy. Was I any trouble?"

"Not at all. Didn't think I should search your purse for your address. Took some effort to get you upstairs, but you were sawing logs the instant your head hit the pillow."

"Thanks for being a gentleman." Nancy blushed. "I don't usually—"

"Don't give it another thought. Glad I was there to help."

Nancy nodded. "I'd like to make it up to you."

"Okay." Had he really heard what he thought he did? "Let me take you out tonight."

"How about I drop by and make dinner? Just the two of us."

"Sure." Ryan's heart seemed to skip a beat—*just the two of us.* "I'll look forward to it."

"Around seven? We can enjoy the sunset."

———

Except for anticipating Nancy's visit, Monday was largely mundane—inspecting the house, responding to texts, and scouring the internet. No breaks for a swim in the backyard pool or a dip in the surf. Whatever free time he might have, he'd reserve for dinner.

No news from his state police source about tracing the phones. Exploring the maze of websites containing tax, real estate, and business records, though, had narrowed the field to three companies who were the primary players in all the party-castle transactions over the last ten years. One Richmond law firm had represented most purchasers throughout. Next step? Connect the dots to Pirate's Hideaway. But that could wait. Six o'clock. Time to get ready.

Nancy seemed harried, like it had been a long day. They dined in the screened porch adjacent to the kitchen. After a couple of glasses of wine, eating the seafood salad Nancy prepared, and increasingly intimate conversation, she seemed more relaxed. Remarkable orange, blue, and yellow hues of the sunset over Back Bay capped their evening together.

Nancy sipped her Chardonnay. "I didn't have much time after work." She placed her glass on the table. "Do you mind if I borrow your master bathroom to freshen up?"

"Feel free. Plenty of towels in the closet."

"Great." Nancy smiled. But it was more than a smile. "And I'll need help with my zipper."

To Ryan, their lovemaking, in the shower and again afterward, seemed inevitable, given his immediate attraction to her and her apparently reciprocal feelings. As sunrise peaked over the horizon, he worried. Inevitable or not, so few hours had passed since he picked up the key to Pirate's Hideaway. He rearranged the sheet, covering Nancy's naked shoulders. Maybe she was the someone special he had been waiting for after Ellen. Or just a memorable one-night stand.

Ryan slipped out of bed and put on his pajama bottoms. *Let her sleep as long as she wants. Surprise her with hot coffee and pastry.* He tiptoed out of the bedroom, eased the door shut, and headed for the kitchen.

"Dammit!" Ryan hopped on his left foot and sat on the back edge of the sofa. Nancy's purse lay on the floor, near the barstools, where she'd left it last night. Lipstick, a small metal box of mints, and several items Ryan couldn't identify skittered across the floor.

His right big toe throbbed. No sounds from the bedroom. Good, he hadn't disturbed Nancy. He got on his hands and knees. He could return everything to her handbag, and she wouldn't be the wiser. No need to tell his new lover what a klutz she had slept with.

He dragged Nancy's purse along on his quest. Damned heavy. Real estate agents must need a lot of stuff. He crawled toward a rectangular shape masked by the shadows of the kitchen table.

Ryan shifted to a sitting position. He exhaled, tightness spreading through his chest. A phone. But not Nancy's iPhone. A flip phone, like the dozens of prepaids he had encountered over the years. Prepaids—burners—were often used to avoid calls being traced. Ryan peered into Nancy's purse. Rancid, bile-filled acid reflux crept from his stomach toward his throat. Two more prepaids. *Why does she need one burner, much less three?* Ryan gritted his teeth to suppress his urge to vomit. There had to be a logical explanation.

The sound of running water signaled that Nancy was probably about to emerge from the bedroom. Not enough time to write down the phone numbers. He had to stay calm, return the purse to its original resting place—with the phones inside—and act like everything was normal.

"Good morning, beautiful," Ryan said as Nancy approached the kitchen. She was beautiful. Traitorous, maybe. But beautiful.

"Making us some coffee." He bit his lip to avoid saying something he might regret.

"Thanks." Nancy kissed Ryan's cheek. "And thanks for last night. I really needed it."

"I think we both did." Ryan returned the kiss. "Maybe we can—"

"Definitely."

Her eyes seemed unfocused. Like she was preoccupied. Or staring at something in the distance no one else could see.

"Listen, I hate to, but I have to run. I've got a client meeting." She smiled. But it was less than a smile. "And I need to get ready." As she turned to leave, she said, "Call me."

He had violated a fundamental tenet of undercover work—no personal relationships. *Don't get involved.* But he had no reason to think that Nancy would become a suspect. All she had done was hand him a house key and a welcome packet last Saturday. Now, along with everything else, he had to deal with a conflict of interest. It might cost him his client. Or his PI license. Maybe both.

The texts started again. Standard scare tactics. Nothing new. For the remainder of Tuesday—well into the evening—Ryan multitasked between responding to texts, checking on the physical security of Pirate's Hideaway, and internet research. Yesterday, he connected three companies and one law firm. Today, he drilled into other parties involved—the real estate agents. His face warmed as he learned more. *Damn!* Nancy was the acquiring agent in almost all of the deals in the last five years.

He stared at the computer, mesmerized. A text arrived. *Hi, Lover.*

He practically fell off his chair and crawled to an adjacent corner, numb.

Another text, *See you at midnight.*

Finally, *Sleep well.*

He had flown dozens of combat sorties. Dropped bombs. Been responsible for death and destruction. Regardless, Nancy's betrayal paralyzed him. His Navy training screamed "FIGHT." But he couldn't. He curled up in a ball, defeated. Despite his anger, he drifted off to sleep.

— 👧 —

Ryan's alarm chimed. Almost midnight. No choice. Run now and he'd never quit running.

He relied on ambient light from outside as he donned his tactical gear. Let them think he was asleep. He secured the Glock in his thigh holster.

He checked his phone for the latest email. *Great!* His state police source had traced the burners through credit card records. He read the results and put his head in his hands. His jaw quivered. It's always someone you think you can trust.

Noise. Footsteps on the wooden walkway leading to the side entrance on the first floor. Can't let emotion interfere, not now. Time to buck up and get it done. He crept down the inside stairway to the recreation room, located a dark corner, and waited.

A solitary figure, dressed in black, opened the door. No tools. A key—like Nancy had given him last Saturday. A flashlight beam sliced through the darkness. The figure stopped in the middle of the room. A plastic bag crinkled. Something plopped onto the floor. The figure turned toward the door.

Ryan aimed his flashlight at the intruder. "Hold it right there."

The figure swiveled and lunged.

As Ryan dodged, he dropped his flashlight, pulled out his ASP, and engaged the release. After a series of ominous clicks, the baton expanded to its full twenty-one-inch length. Ryan swung the one-pound rod of concentrated steel, striking the intruder's thigh just behind the knee. The figure screamed and crumpled to the floor.

Ryan secured his adversary's hands and ankles with zip ties. He turned on the lights, then removed the intruder's ski mask.

"What the hell?" Jake blinked, obviously in pain. "You think I'm still paying you, after this?"

"You're the one behind everything. Wasn't positive until state police traced the burner phones to your credit card. Pretty amateurish, wouldn't you say?"

"You got nothing. Just an owner checking his property."

"And delivering a dead opossum?"

"Go to hell."

"Fine. But tell me why you hired me."

"Wanted to make sure I wasn't a suspect when we bought this house and Dolphin's Cove." Jack grimaced. "Spied on you from The Sanctuary. Thought I could scare you off, too."

"Not hardly."

"But then you fell for my ex—Nancy."

"Nancy?" His head throbbed. "How's she involved?"

"She's not. My name doesn't appear on any paperwork. So she has no clue it was me."

"But she was the acquiring agent—and the burners."

"Prepaids are part of the business. We deal with a lot of high-viz and foreign investors who want to remain untraceable. And Nancy as the acquiring agent? Perfect. Figured I could vector lucrative commissions her way without anyone being the wiser. She'd get rich. I'd get her alimony reduced."

Ryan called the cops. Within minutes, Jake was in a police cruiser headed for jail. Soon, crimson and gold rays would grace Wednesday's morning sky. His sizeable retainer from Jake was safe in the bank. Pirate's Hideaway was his through midmorning Saturday. Now he'd have time for a swim. And a walk on the beach. Maybe a margarita or two. And Nancy.

THE LAST LAUGH

BY MAGGIE KING

He who laughs last, laughs longest.

"YOU HAVE ARRIVED AT your destination."

Emily Bates turned off her GPS, muting the disembodied voice of her guide, and parked her Honda Civic in front of Julie Ruthers's apartment complex on the outskirts of Charlottesville. She walked through a courtyard under a canopy of leafless trees, branches making lacy black patterns against a cloudless sky. A sharp January wind quickened her pace, and she pulled her jacket tightly around her. As she scanned the apartments for the number fifteen, the scent of garlic, onions, and cinnamon wafting from the bag of Bodo's Bagels she carried reminded her how hungry she was.

Emily and Julie met in a karate class. Both had trained as gymnasts at young ages, so karate came easily to them. They often met for coffee at Greenberry's Coffee Company, where they discovered they knew many of the same people. More years had passed than either cared to admit since they'd earned degrees from the University of Virginia.

A few days before, Julie had invited Emily to her place for breakfast. "I'll make my famous egg casserole. How 'bout this Saturday at ten?"

"It's a date," Emily said. "I'll bring bagels."

Emily found number fifteen and pressed the doorbell. When Julie didn't appear, she beat a *rat-a-tat-tat* with a tiny brass knocker. Still no answer. Had Julie canceled? Emily pulled her phone from her purse. No text, email, or voicemail.

She tried the doorknob, not expecting it to turn in her hand, surprised when it did. Cautiously, she stepped inside. A warm and savory aroma suggested Julie's promised egg casserole.

"Julie," Emily called.

Silence. Such silence.

Furniture crammed the small living room, and stacks of books were piled on the floor in front of the now-empty built-in bookcase. Paintings filled nearly every inch of wall space. Emily recognized Julie's work from her Facebook postings. Julie favored the Impressionist style, with a hint of Jackson Pollock. Emily was no art expert, but years before she'd had a memorable fling with an art history professor. He taught her about art, and they taught each other skills in the bedroom. Last Emily heard, he was serving time for art fraud.

In the kitchen, cabinet doors gaped open, contents removed. Dishes, pots, and pans covered the counter, floor, and a small round table. A decluttering project could explain the disorder. Emily chuckled. She had her own decluttering projects to tackle, but never got around to them.

A light over the range top revealed the egg casserole with a sizeable slice missing. Emily stepped into the kitchen, pulled off a leather glove, and felt the pan. *Warm.* A yellow mug with *Julie* artfully painted on its side, an empty half-gallon milk container, and a coffee maker with its glowing red light competed with the cabinet contents for space on the counter.

Did Julie forget about her breakfast date with Emily? The egg casserole indicated otherwise. Had she run out to the store to get more milk, neglecting to lock the door?

"Julie," Emily called again. "I'm here for your famous egg casserole."

Julie continued to be a no-show.

Emily tossed her purse and bag of bagels on a chair in the dining area, adding her jacket, scarf, and gloves to the pile. Nothing to do but wait.

A metal lamp in a birdcage style hung over the dining table. Emily caught sight of herself in a mirror on the wall. Her straight dark hair with a bold white streak, full red lips, and red turtleneck reflected back to her.

An odd assortment of items littered the table: a can of soda, a box of rubber gloves, a closed laptop, a couple of books, a silver letter opener, a roll of duct tape, a stack of bills, and a thick Bible.

Clutter everywhere. Where did Julie plan to serve breakfast?

Several Post-it Notes and a sheet of paper marked pages in the Bible. Emily peeked at the single-spaced sheet with the heading *Amends List*. Was Julie in a twelve-step program? Such programs emphasized making amends as a major step in substance abuse recovery. Giving into temptation, Emily pulled the sheet from the Bible, noting the page it marked. The list was lengthy. Had Julie harmed that many people? A few names toward the list's end struck a familiar chord, but Emily couldn't place them. Sonya Westerson's name appeared handwritten at the bottom of the page, like an afterthought. Julie often mentioned Sonya, a woman she met at UVA where they struck up a lifelong friendship. What amends did Julie owe Sonya?

Emily replaced the amends list in the Bible.

Where was Julie?

Unable to contain her restlessness, Emily started down a short hall that led to the bedrooms. She passed a bathroom tiled in a retro Pepto Bismol pink. Vomit flooded the bathroom floor. Emily cringed. Had something in the egg casserole disagreed with Julie, sending her to the emergency room?

A room full of canvasses propped against walls and on easels suggested Julie's studio. Emily walked across the hall and stood in the doorway of another room with walls painted a vivid shade of lavender. Drawers had been pulled open, contents dumped on the floor. The open doors of the closet revealed an empty clothes rod; a mountain of clothing and shoes blanketed the floor.

Julie's into decluttering in a big way, Emily thought.

She turned to leave, then stopped, eyes wide at what she saw reflected in the dresser mirror: a headboard covered in a purple floral chintz, and a mass of platinum blond hair.

When Emily first came in the room, the door had blocked her view of the bed. Now she looked behind the door and gasped. Julie Ruthers lay on her back. Through the strands of hair that fell across her face, Emily detected a couple of bruises and what looked like burns.

She checked Julie's pulse. *None.*

Oh, Julie. What happened to you?

Emily stood, stunned. Normally, she was easygoing and not much fazed her. But normally she didn't stumble upon dead bodies. However, she quickly assumed the take-charge attitude responsible for her success as a wealth advisor. She dashed back to the dining room and grabbed her phone.

The front door opened, startling Emily and interrupting her call to 9-1-1. She spun around and found a woman who looked equally startled.

"Who are you?" the woman asked.

"Emily Bates. Who are you?"

"Sonya Westerson."

"Oh!" How was Emily going to tell Sonya about Julie, her decades-long friend?

"What are you doing here?" Sonya demanded. "How did you get in?"

"The door was unlocked."

"Unlocked?" Sonya glared at the door, like she expected it to offer an explanation, before locking and bolting it.

Emily struggled for words, but finally managed, "Sonya, something happened to Julie."

"Oh?" Sonya carried a half-gallon of milk to the kitchen. A few minutes later, she returned with a mug of coffee and tossed her puffer jacket toward the living room. It landed on a stack of books. A red and black lumberjack shirt billowed around her slim figure. Close-cropped auburn hair hugged her head like a helmet. Her brows drew together, and she repeated her question. "What are you doing here?"

Emily sighed. "Julie invited me for breakfast. Now about Julie—"

"I killed her," Sonya said, with little concern.

"*You?*"

"What, you don't think I could kill someone? I'm so sick of people thinking I'm incompetent."

So the woman hoped to elevate her self-esteem through killing?

"Yeah, I'm sure you could kill someone," Emily said. "But

why Julie? She was your friend."

"Can I get you some breakfast?" Sonya gestured toward the kitchen. "Julie fixed a lovely casserole."

"No." Even if it didn't contain the poison that killed Julie, Emily wanted no part of the casserole. She was no medical examiner, but her best guess was that Julie had been poisoned.

"Coffee? Coke?" Sonya eyed the Bodo's bag on the chair. "Something to go with those bagels?"

"No, *thank you*. Why did you kill Julie?"

When Sonya still didn't answer, Emily huffed a sigh. Spreading out her arms to encompass the whole of the apartment, she asked, "So was Julie decluttering? Or were you searching for something? The bedroom looks like a tornado hit."

Sonya's eyes narrowed. "How long have you known Julie? I never heard her mention you."

"We met about a month ago. In karate class."

"Then I guess you don't know how messy she is."

Emily couldn't counter that claim, so she switched tacks. "Sonya, why are you still here? Most people who kill don't stick around the crime scene or return to it. But you went to the store for milk and came back."

Sonya shrugged. "I needed milk for my coffee. Julie ran out."

Emily knew she should bolt and call the police. But anger over Sonya's cavalier admission that she'd killed Julie, in addition to a curious nature, drove her decision to stay and get answers.

Besides, she had nothing to fear from Sonya Westerson, at least not physically. A video of Emily demonstrating her karate skills was posted on YouTube. But what if Sonya carried a weapon? That oversized shirt she wore could hide a gun. But if she had a gun, wouldn't she have used it to kill Julie?

Emily repeated her question. "Why did you kill Julie?"

When Sonya flashed an arch smile, Emily shook her head in frustration.

If Sonya had never committed murder before, she might be in shock and need time to collect herself. Emily would give her time—but not much.

Emily sat at the table and picked up a copy of *Contract Bridge for Beginners*. "I almost forgot that Julie is, rather *was*, in a bridge group with Margo Trevor, one of my clients." Emily winced at the past tense.

"Clients?" Sonya prompted.

"I'm a wealth advisor."

"Oh, my! Wealth advisor. Aren't you something." Sonya pushed a pile of books off a chair and sat. She set her mug on the table.

"Margo is Julie's painting instructor, the one who's teaching her to create all this atrocious crap." She waved a hand at the paintings on the walls, some with simple narrow frames, others with wide, ornate ones. "Margo invited her to join the bridge group."

"I take it you're not in the group?"

"Hell, no. Who wants to hang around with a bunch of rich bitches?"

"Margo's the nicest person in the world. Sure, she's rich, but she's not a bitch."

"Well, *excuse* me." Sonya held up her hands in mock surrender.

The disorder throughout the apartment triggered an idea in Emily's brain: Was Sonya robbing Julie? She had dodged Emily's question about searching for something. Trying for a cagey approach, Emily said, "Margo told me she and her mother were burgled a few weeks ago. Just after New Year's. That makes about four burglaries in wealthy Charlottesville neighborhoods in the past couple of years. In each case, they robbed while the homeowners were eating dinner."

"*They?*" Sonya examined her well-chewed nails, curling her fingers toward her, then turning her hand, fingers up.

"One of Margo's neighbors saw two people running through the yard. She thought it was a couple of neighborhood kids cutting through."

"*Hmmph.* Did they get caught?"

"No, not yet. Funny, the thieves seem focused on jewels, and nothing else."

Sonya yawned loudly. "Sorry. I didn't get much sleep. Coffee?" She got up and carried her mug to the kitchen.

"No, nothing." Emily went on with the subject of the burglaries. "Margo and I think it sounds like the Dinner Set Gang."

"Dinner Set Gang?"

"Did you ever see that *60 Minutes* segment about those guys who robbed homes while the owners were downstairs eating dinner? Although I doubt they'd be operating in this area. They're either still in prison, or dead. But someone could be doing the same thing."

"Smart of them. No one has alarms on at dinner."

"That's true. And the burglaries occurred in November and December when people typically dine after dark."

Sonya plunked her mug on the table, spilling some of the coffee. "I bet it was Margo's butler or cook."

"Margo fiercely defends her staff," Emily said.

Sonya had nothing to add. Her small, dark eyes studied Emily. The absurdity of chatting about art and stolen jewels with a woman who'd killed her friend—a friend who lay dead in a nearby room—wasn't lost on Emily.

Time's up, Emily thought. *You've had enough time to pull yourself together.* "Why did you kill Julie?"

When the arch smile reappeared, Emily yelled, "Sonya, a woman is dead, and you killed her. Now tell me why and tell me now!"

"I won't be bullied!"

"Fine. I'll call the police. They can bully you." Emily picked up her phone.

"Okay, *okay*. I'll tell you about Julie. We met in college."

When she stopped and Emily gave her a look, her words came out in a rush. "I did her homework for her, her papers. She wouldn't have graduated if it hadn't been for me. As thanks, she bequeathed her cast-off boyfriend to me. Peter. We married. He wasn't so bad back then. Still had all his hair and a flat stomach. On our tenth anniversary, he told me he married me out of pity, figuring no one else would marry me."

"Ouch! That's terrible."

"Julie seduced my son when he was twenty-one. She liked them young. I came home one day and caught them in his bed. They laughed at me, and continued to get together, like I didn't matter. Peter approved, thought I was a prude. Said, 'She can teach him plenty.'

"Now my son is thirty-three. He and Julie resumed their

tawdry affair over the summer. His wife's divorcing him. They have a three-year-old."

Emily didn't know how many other seduction-worthy relatives Sonya had, but perhaps the woman didn't want to chance them falling under Julie's spell. "Wow. I . . . I'm sorry," she said. "Why were you friends with her?"

"She was my only friend." Sonya sipped her coffee.

Some friend. But Emily kept that opinion to herself.

"Two days ago I turned fifty-eight." Sonya leaned forward, perhaps to emphasize the seriousness of what she had to say. "Peter didn't even acknowledge my birthday. Just came home, plopped down in the recliner and demanded a beer. That was it. I'd had enough. I got his beer and poured it over his head."

Emily gritted her teeth. "How does that explain—"

"I'm tired of being bullied, laughed at." Sonya picked at a ragged cuticle, taking out her frustration on her nails.

A lifetime of bullying would drive some to murder. "But why kill Julie *now*?"

"She took me out to lunch for my birthday."

"And?" Emily prompted when Sonya didn't elaborate. "That's hardly a motive for murder."

Sonya smiled, but said nothing.

Emily opened her Facebook app. She recalled one of Julie's Facebook posts—a post that contradicted something Sonya had said.

"What are you doing? Calling the police?"

Emily slanted a look at Sonya. "I should, but not just yet. I'm checking something on Facebook."

Sonya went off on a rant about Facebook, which she'd apparently abandoned, citing privacy concerns, divisive political posts, and a host of other reasons. Emily let her go on, offering an occasional *"uh-huh"* as she scrolled through Julie's posts.

"Julie likes to post pictures of the bridge group," Emily said. "Here's one from November." She showed Sonya the picture but held onto the phone.

Julie posed with a group of fourteen women, including Margo Trevor. All but one woman was tagged—Sonya Westerson.

"You said you weren't in this group."

"I went a couple of times. Bridge isn't my thing."

Something hovered around the periphery of Emily's consciousness—a hunch, perhaps? *Something about that amends list . . .*

The doorbell put the hunch and Sonya's bellyaching about Facebook on hold. The visitor pressed hard on the bell. Sonya and Emily looked at each other, frozen in place, like in a tableau. Then the pounding started, accompanied by shouts of "Sonya! Sonya, open the goddamned door! I know you're in there."

Sonya groaned. "That's Peter. What a jackass. Probably wants his SUV back." She stood and moved toward the door. "Go away, Peter," she bellowed.

Peter continued to pound, treating us to his colorful vocabulary.

"I've gotta get rid of him." Sonya opened the door, ushering in a blast of cold air. Emily caught a glimpse of a man with a shaved head and a massive belly hanging over tattered jeans. Sonya stepped outside, leaving the door open. She and her husband shrieked at each other.

Emily pushed the door closed, muffling their volume. She pulled Julie's amends list from the Bible and checked the names she had thought familiar against the tagged ones on Facebook. Each one matched.

A group of wealthy women, she thought. *A good source of burglary victims.*

Emily pulled on her leather gloves and moved into the living room. She stood before a painting with a two-inch deep frame. Drops of paint in every color of the spectrum dotted the canvas. When she pulled gently on the right side of the frame, she heard rustling. She lifted the picture from the wall and turned it around.

The back of the canvas was chock full of jewels. Diamonds, rubies, emeralds, and amethysts, stuffed in clear plastic sandwich bags and taped in place, glittered and winked at Emily. She found three more paintings with the same two-inch frame, both backed with bags of jewels. Phone in hand, she documented her discoveries in pictures.

Sonya stormed back in, slamming the door. After going through the locking process, she dragged a chair from the dining area and wedged the back under the doorknob. Peter continued his tirade outside.

"Is this what you were looking for, Sonya?" Emily swept a hand at the displays, posing like a game show host. "Guess you hadn't had a chance to check behind these frames. Quite a stash!"

Sonya's face clouded, her anger at Peter replaced by her anger at Emily's discovery.

"I'm guessing you and Julie were the newly resurrected Dinner Set Gang."

Sonya folded her arms, her face a study in defiance.

"Now tell me why you *really* killed her."

"Another thing she bullied me into. I didn't rob those people. *She* did! I was just the lookout."

"Go on," Emily prompted through gritted teeth.

Sonya took a deep breath. "The other day at my birthday lunch, she . . . she sprang her plan on me."

"What plan?"

"To turn herself in, and . . . and name me as her accomplice. Oh, she assured me that she was *so* sorry she got me involved. Happy Birthday to me!"

"Wow! What did you say to all of that?"

"I pleaded with her to reconsider, but she wouldn't budge." Tears trickled down Sonya's cheeks. "Can you see me in prison?"

"Truthfully, no. But that's where you're headed. And murder carries a longer sentence than burglary."

Sonya pulled a tissue from a box on the dining table. While she mopped her face and blew her nose, Emily asked, "How did she come up with this Dinner Set Gang idea? And why?"

"She needed cash. She was in a lot of debt. Her ex cleaned out the bank accounts, maxed out the credit cards, and split. Her teaching job doesn't pay enough. She remembered that *60 Minutes* show with the dinner gang. Everything fell into place. She got Margo to invite us to the bridge group with the rich bitches. I needed money as well, so bullying me this time wasn't hard. I could be the lookout. She said it would be fun, an adventure. We cased the places for a while, and she found excuses to wander around the houses while everyone was playing bridge. It was all amazingly easy."

Aha! My Facebook hunch was right.

Sonya continued. "All those women had good climbing trees next to second-story windows and decks. Julie had no problem getting inside their houses."

"Those gymnastic skills," Emily said. "She used her special talents for her life of crime."

"She said we should wait a while to fence the jewelry." Sonya waved a hand at the treasure before her. "She never would tell me where she hid the loot."

After a pause, she continued. "Then she goes to this church that's big on making amends. Amends? I should be first in line for amends. I came here last night to try again to get her to reconsider turning us in. I also wanted my share of the loot. I need money if I'm going to leave the jackass." She hooked a thumb over her shoulder at the door. The jackass continued to pound and yell.

"So, what happened when you got here last night?"

"She still wouldn't budge. Said she had to turn us both in and give full restitution to the rich bitches."

Until this moment I hadn't considered the *how* of Sonya's crime. "How did you do it?"

"I pretty much figured Julie wouldn't give me my share. So I had a plan B. I found a recipe for liquid nicotine and stole Peter's cigarettes. I shredded them, soaked the tobacco, reduced the yucky mess to a potent liquid, and brought it here with me last night. When I didn't get anywhere with her, I added it to her lavender body lotion. And then I left."

"And then you left," Emily repeated. Her words hung in the air for a long moment before she asked, "So tell me about today. When did you come back?"

Sonya looked at the ceiling for a moment before saying, "Oh, seven-thirty or so."

"And Julie was dead?"

"She was."

"And that's when you started hunting for the jewels?"

Sonya nodded.

"And you helped yourself to breakfast."

"Sure. Julie's egg casserole is really good. Sure you don't want some?"

Emily ignored the gesture of hospitality. "Where did you find the instructions for the nicotine?" she asked.

"Google."

Good old Google. Accessory to murder.

Emily loomed before Sonya. She felt like a character in a black comedy. More black than comedy.

Sonya stepped back. "You're going to call the police, aren't you?"

"Yes."

She considered Emily's words, then nodded. "Okay. Do it."

Emily started to tap out 9-1-1.

Sonya grabbed the silver letter opener.

Emily caught Sonya's arm a nanosecond before losing a piece of her nose. The weapon and Emily's phone dropped to the floor with a clang and a thud. Sonya screamed. Emily managed a swift kick to Sonya's midsection, landing the woman on the floor. Emily quickly turned her over, planted a suede boot on her back, and reached for the roll of duct tape on the table. After binding Sonya's hands and ankles together, Emily reached for her phone.

Sonya continued to shriek, letting loose a litany of obscenities. "Peter, get me a lawyer," she raged.

Emily retreated to Julie's art studio to mute Sonya and Peter's volume while she called the Charlottesville Police Department. She averted her eyes from the bedroom and bathroom. Call made, she returned to the living room to wait for the police to arrest Sonya and tackle a highly contaminated crime scene. With a self-satisfied smile she said, "Justice will prevail."

"So, Emily, how are you going to prove you didn't kill Julie?" Sonya pulled at the duct tape binding her wrists and ankles. "How are you going to prove you weren't Julie's partner in crime? The wealth advisor and the jewel thief—match made in heaven. I'm sure the police will be *quite* interested in my statement. Your word against mine!"

Emily's smug smile vanished. She knew Sonya's harsh, raucous cackle would ring in her ears for some time to come.

Sonya had the last laugh.

CHALK IT UP TO MURDER

BY TERESA INGE

JOJO BENNINGTON GLANCED AT the patrons sitting on the bar stools as she entered the Raven, a boozy landmark restaurant in Virginia Beach. She strolled past a gallery of photos that included boxers, military heroes, and other prominent guests.

Known for the best crab cakes on the East Coast, customers could always count on getting a good meal and a good cocktail at a good price, and visitors always remarked about the specials on the hand-lettered chalkboard near the bar.

"It's about time," Lou Ayers yelled from behind the bar as Jojo bustled in. Lou had owned the bar since 1969 and took great pride in his specials.

"Sorry I'm late," Jojo walked toward the bar. "I had another gig that ran over."

"Yeah, well the only gig I'm concerned about is that you update my boards. Got it?"

She sat her portable chair and tackle box on the floor next to the board.

"Can you do larger print this time," yelled a regular on one of the stools.

"What do you have in mind," she opened her most treasured possession, a vintage green tackle box and grabbed her chalk and accessories. An odd place to house the tools of her trade, but it somehow kept her close to her deceased father, since he had given it to her as a child.

"Just make them bigger. It's hard to read the small print."

"Might be time to get new glasses," she laughed. *Or time to erase the entire board and start fresh,* she thought, *since Lou is picky about his boards.*

"Here's the specials." Lou handed Jojo a sheet of paper.

"That's a lot of specials." Her eyes widened.

"Well, it's June and tourists like options," Lou said.

"I don't think I can get all of this on the board."

"Try." He turned away.

Jojo unfolded her chair and sat in front of the board. The top section of the slate was pre-painted with a burger special, steak dinner, and other local favorites. She always struggled to work around what Lou wanted on the board. She read the dailies from the sheet and began putting chalk to board.

"You have real talent." A man with rugged good looks and sandy hair loomed behind her with a bar towel across his shoulder. As she stood back to ensure the letters were large, even, and legible, she caught a whiff of his lingering aftershave.

"I'm Dalton Elliott, the new bartender." He extended his hand.

Jojo rubbed her hand across her jeans and shook hands. "Sorry, chalk can be messy."

"How'd you learn to do that? Write on a chalkboard, I mean."

"I loved to draw with chalk as a kid. And I would get annoyed if the hopscotch squares were not drawn in perfect order when I played the game. So, it kinda of grew from there." Jojo shrugged.

"I don't pay you to stand around and talk to the chalkboard artist," Lou yelled at Dalton. He turned toward Jojo. "I see you got all the specials in after all." He walked behind the bar and pulled out cash from the register. "Here you go, sweetheart." He hesitated when handing her the money. "Make sure you're on time next time."

"Okay, Lou."

"By the way, the girl that used to be your assistant, what's her name?" Lou tapped two fingers against the bar.

"Tess?"

"Yeah, her. She came in earlier and said she could do digital boards."

"Oh, really?" Jojo hoped her face didn't show her true reaction to the mention of Tess Sinclair, her previous assistant.

"I told her to get lost. I might be a stickler for being on time and doing the job right, but I'm loyal. Plus, my customers like the chalkboards."

Lou rummaged through the business cards in the basket by the register. "Here." He handed Tess's card to Jojo.

She glanced at the services offered on the card and stuck it in her pocket. As she folded her chair, two loud voices from the far end of the bar caused everyone's head to turn.

"Say it again," the man who had yelled at Jojo earlier to make the letters larger stood from his stool, yelling at the man next to him.

"Take it somewhere else." Lou motioned his arm toward the door and a large man in a black shirt and jeans grabbed the men and escorted them out of the bar.

Jojo grabbed her chair and box.

"Seems they didn't like the chalkboard," Dalton said.

"What do you mean?"

"They were arguing that you spelled *libations* wrong."

"What?" Jojo turned toward the board.

After the fiasco at the Raven, Jojo corrected the board and headed to her next job several blocks down the Boardwalk. She wondered how she had misspelled libations, but tried to take it all in stride, especially with being late and Lou yelling at her. And the Tess situation bothered her more than she cared to admit. She entered the 19th Street Ice Cream Shop to add the specials for the week.

"How's it going, Jojo?" Tina, the manager, stuck her head out from inside a cooler.

Jojo looked at the digital board on the wall.

"You like it?" Tina closed the door and walked toward the counter holding an ice cream container.

"Where did you get it?"

"Oh, that sweet girl, Tess that works for you." Tina placed the ice cream in the dipping station.

Jojo's eyebrows knitted together. "She doesn't work for me anymore."

"Oh really? I thought she was part of your service. She recommended that I buy the board. Can I get you something, dear?"

"No. I was going to update the weekly specials but since that's taken care of, I'll just head out."

A crowd of kids burst through the front door and Tina began scooping ice cream. Jojo headed home to dress for an evening wedding gig on the beach.

— 🎎 —

After showering and dressing in a flowery sundress, Jojo grabbed Tess's card she had placed on her dresser. Award-winning Designs. Ha! Jojo knew the true story and that Tess could only bluff her way for so long. She was not surprised that Tess had started her own business but stealing her customers was a whole different ballgame. She set the card on the dresser and would deal with Tess later. She did one last look in the full-length mirror and looked forward to creating unique designs and colors for the beach wedding.

Jojo shouldered her bag filled with extra chalk and boards. She had already created the large standing boards for the bride and groom and miniature boards to be placed at the guest tables with each guest's name.

"Where have you been?" Liza Rosen, Virginia Beach's premier wedding planner, grabbed Jojo's arm.

"You said four o'clock arrival." Jojo looked at the time on her phone.

"Yeah, yeah . . . all that's changed now. Listen, I need you to modify a couple of the chalkboard name plates. We've had guests who were invited at the last minute, and the bride is insisting we add their names. Brother. Why do people always think I can change everything at the last minute?" Liza rubbed her head.

"I'll take care of it."

"That's not all. There are changes in seating assignments."

"Like big changes or small changes?" Jojo asked since she would have to modify the symbols to match the table. Each table had individual chalkboards with a symbol such as a seashell, turtle, or lighthouse.

"Just put them behind the main bar for now. I'll be right there." Liza spoke into her phone and then turned toward Jojo. "Check your phone. I texted you the table changes. Do you have extra boards?"

"Yes."

"Good. Get to work. Go!" Liza waved her arm toward the tables and rushed in the opposite direction to solve whatever was placed behind the bar.

Jojo looked at the list which was more than she had anticipated. She walked toward the first table on the list and began updating the boards.

"So, you're the chalkboard artist?" A fifty-something woman, dressed in a tight blue dress, appeared with a cocktail in hand. From her slurred speech, it must have been five o'clock somewhere much earlier in the day.

Jojo looked up from the table. "Uh . . . yes."

"The chalkboards are such a novel idea for my daughter to spend money on. But what do I care? It's only my money."

"You're Gina's mother?"

"The one and only. Patricia Winslow, front and center." She took a long swig of her cocktail. I have to admit, when Gina first told me about the boards, I was skeptical, but your work is very good. She leaned over Jojo's shoulder to get a better look.

Jojo smelled alcohol on her breath. "It's okay. I love doing the boards for weddings."

"Can you create this for me?" Patricia tapped on her phone and waved it around. Jojo got a glimpse of a black-and-white lighthouse photo.

"Sure. I can create the image. Mind if I take a picture of it?"

Patricia held up the photo as Jojo snapped it with her phone. "I'll be at the front table creating extra boards for guests later. I'll do it then."

Liza approached the table. "Patricia, you're being summoned by the queen bee. Something about a bow for the mother of the bride."

"A bow? Do I look like I would wear a bow? Oh, never mind. Where is my sweet daughter anyway?" she sneered.

"The bridal suite in the hotel," Liza said.

Jojo glanced at the last table on the list. She suppressed a gasp at the new addition to the table of eight, Tess Sinclair. Tess and Gina were first cousins, but Tess was not in the bridal party nor invited to the wedding. Jojo knew they had not spoken in two years. Until now. Jojo wondered what brought about the change.

"Almost done?" Liza tapped her watch.

"Yes, all done."

"Everything is coming together. The bride will enter the beach at twilight to catch the sunset as it sets behind the hotel. Then after the ceremony, guests will return to their tables for the reception."

As Jojo placed her chalk in the toolbox, Tess quietly approached. Tess's scowl removed all chances of this being a happy visit.

Jojo gripped the table.

"I'm supposed to finish the boards, but I'm running late," Tess smirked.

"What do you mean?"

"When Aunt Patricia said that Gina had hired a chalkboard artist for her wedding, I offered my expertise to help."

Jojo frowned since Tess had little experience doing mini boards. "Actually, I finished the job that I was hired to do." Jojo bit her tongue since now was not the time to chat with Tess about the digital boards with her clients.

"Gina said I could help since she didn't think you could handle all the boards alone. So here I am. Better late than never."

Liza clapped her hands toward the bartenders, wait staff, and ushers. "I need everyone in place. Guests will start arriving in fifteen minutes. Move it people."

Jojo took her place at the veranda near the large standing chalkboard that welcomed guests to the ceremony. Liza and her team had transformed the venue into a beautiful beach wedding with all the trimmings.

Jojo noticed Dalton Elliott, the new bartender from the Raven, tending bar on the veranda. She made her way toward him.

"What can I get my favorite chalkboard artist?" Dalton grinned.

"I'll take a bottled water."

Dalton grabbed a bottle and twisted the top.

"I didn't know you were working at the wedding?" Jojo sipped her water.

"Yeah, I'm part of a bartender's rotation for Liza's events. It's a good way to earn extra cash." Dalton placed wine glasses on the bar. "Is this your first time working with Liza?"

"Yes. I hope I did a good job with the chalkboards."

"I noticed the mini chalkboards on the tables. Nice keepsake."

As guests arrived, the bar lines grew long, keeping Dalton and the bartenders busy.

Jojo sat at the front table creating random chalkboard designs for guests. Patricia stopped by to pick up her board. "Love it. Lighthouses are my favorite." Moments later, Liza made an announcement for everyone to make their way to the beach.

— 🎎 —

A white makeshift altar adorned the veranda with rows of white chairs on each side. The groom and wedding party stood at the altar. As the music began, Gina's father escorted her down the aisle. Melancholy thoughts consumed Jojo as she envisioned her own future wedding. She missed her father, who wouldn't be able to escort her down the aisle.

During the ceremony, the bride read a poem, and the groom shared a story of how they met. After saying their vows, guests cheered as Jojo's eyes darted toward Patricia lying on the ground. Someone murmured that she's probably drunk. Liza and Tess fanned her with their hands. Gina mortified at her mother passed out.

After a few minutes, Liza yelled from the front row, "She's okay. The humidity got to her." They helped Patricia to her seat as the bride and groom walked down the aisle.

Jojo hurried toward the small crowd. "Is she okay? Was it just the humidity?"

"Yeah, that and all the vodka she drank." Liza smirked and instructed guests to make their way to the cocktail reception before dinner.

Jojo walked up the aisle to check the stand-up chalkboard for smudges since it was inevitable that someone would bump into the board or place their hands against it.

"I would have done that board differently." Tess stood near the board with a glass of wine.

"Excuse me?" Jojo huffed.

"It needs different images."

"That's not what the bride wanted. Besides, it's none of your business," Jojo admonished.

"Actually, it is since I was hired at the last minute to correct your work." Tess turned and walked away.

Liza approached Jojo. "You okay?"

"I don't understand why Tess keeps telling me she was hired to do this job. You hired me to do the chalkboards."

"Patricia told Tess she could help and of course Tess ran with it. But no, I am not paying Tess to do the job that I hired you to do."

After the photographer finished with the wedding party, guests headed to their tables for dinner. Jojo sat at the table across from Tess since she was invited to eat. Steak, lobster, shrimp, and seafood salad made a delicious feast.

A groomsman tapped his glass with a fork. He led the first of many toasts. From the reserved table, Patricia raised her glass to toast, but spilled wine on the groom's mother. The woman turned in her seat, throwing red wine back at Patricia. She sat the glass on the table, then punched Patricia's face. Patricia balled up her fist and popped the woman right in the kisser.

Gina stood at the head table, motioning to get the situation under control.

Jojo leapt to her feet, and Tess followed close behind.

"Are you okay?" Jojo grabbed Patricia's arm.

"I didn't mean to spill wine on her dress," Patricia slurred.

"Come with me. I'll clean you up," Jojo said.

A hand touched Patricia's shoulder from behind. "I'll take care of her. Afterall, she is *my* aunt." Tess walked Patricia to the bridal suite.

Jojo inhaled deeply.

Liza approached. "Don't let Tess's rude behavior bother you."

Before Jojo could speak, Gina appeared in her wedding dress. "Thanks for getting my mom out of here. She and my husband's mother don't get along."

As the deejay announced the bride and groom's wedding dance thirty minutes later, Gina rushed to the dance floor with her hand raised. "I'm here. Just had to go freshen up."

Jojo and Liza stood nearby.

"Well, here's to no more drama," Liza laughed.

"Good thing. And speaking of drama, I'm going to check on Patricia. Be back soon."

"I'm sure she's passed out," Liza said.

Wedding guests stood in line at the open bar as Jojo walked to the bridal suite. *No bartender. That was odd during the middle of a reception.* As she stepped into the elevator and pressed the button, Dalton exited, not noticing Jojo as he pushed a cart of ice containers.

"Knock, knock. It's Jojo." The door was ajar. She pushed it open. "Anyone here?"

Jojo found Patricia on the floor with a large gash on her forehead. Trembling, she knelt and checked her pulse. To her right, lay the lighthouse board. Broken. Had Patricia fallen on the board? On a hunch, Jojo took a picture of the board.

— 👧 —

"Thirty minutes later, Jojo sat in a conference room in the hotel talking to detective Josh Harding from the Virginia Beach police department. Liza sat across from her. Jojo had texted her earlier for support.

"Let's go over this once more." The detective pulled his notebook from his pocket. "You entered Patricia's room to check on her?"

Jojo nodded.

"That's when you found her body?"

"Yes."

The detective scratched his head. "What I don't understand is how she got to her room being intoxicated and all?"

"She didn't. Her niece, Tess, escorted her back."

Another officer poked his head in the room. He motioned for the detective to follow him.

"Jojo, you okay?" Liza whispered.

"Yes. Just the shock of finding her like that."

"Did you see Tess in the room?"

"No. I never saw her passing in the hall or anything."

The detective entered the room. "There's a development."

Jojo raised her eyebrows.

"Tess Sinclair and Gina Winslow gave statements that you and Patricia had a disagreement earlier. Did you have a grudge against Patricia?"

Jojo's legs trembled. "No. Patricia said it was a waste of money to hire a chalkboard artist. But in the end, she was fine with it."

"And you didn't notice anyone or anything suspicious in or outside the room?"

Jojo thought about the lighthouse board. She also remembered Dalton coming off the elevator. "No."

The detective closed his notebook. "I need you to stay in the area until further notice."

A short while later, Jojo headed to the beach to pack up her chalkboards and tackle box. She had not been cleared to leave and rubbed her forehead as Detective Harding approached.

He stood at the front table. "How's it going?"

Jojo frowned.

"Looks like you're packed up." He pointed toward the supplies.

"I want to go home."

"Since we're investigating a murder, I need you to stay a while."

"Murder? You think someone killed Patricia?"

He nodded.

"Am I a suspect?" Jojo tried hard to stifle a sob.

His voice softened. "I need to cover all bases and need you close by for questions."

"Can I visit Liza?"

"Yes. Just don't leave the hotel or beach area. I'll be back later."

Jojo texted Liza who was on her way back to the table.

"Does the detective have any suspects?" Liza asked.

"Besides me?"

"Look. I know you didn't kill Patricia."

Jojo gave her a quizzical look.

"For one thing, there's no motive."

"I wish the detective thought so." Jojo paused. "But what I don't understand is what happened after Tess escorted Patricia to her room?"

"I heard that Tess told the detective she put Patricia to bed, slipped off her shoes, and left. Are you sure you didn't see anything else?"

"Come to think of it, I saw Dalton exiting the side elevator as I got on the main one."

"What was he doing?"

"Getting ice." Jojo tapped her lip. "You know. He seemed distracted."

"What does that have to do with anything?"

"I don't know. But there's something else." Jojo held up the lighthouse photo on her phone.

Liza moved closer.

"The lighthouse board was lying next to Patricia when I found her. I'm thinking she was killed with it during the struggle. The gash on her forehead appears to match that."

"Please be careful, this could be dangerous," Liza said.

Jojo worried about what a murder investigation would do to her business. She asked Liza, "Have you seen Gina, Tess, and Dalton?"

"No. Is there a connection?" Liza asked.

"I don't know, but I have to clear my name and solve Patricia's murder. Can you bring them back here to the table?"

Liza smiled. "I've got you covered."

Jojo pulled a chalkboard from her bag. She sat her tackle box and chalk on the table and recreated the lighthouse. The same image that Patricia was killed with.

From the corner of her eye, Jojo spotted Gina approaching.

"Liza said you wanted to see me?" Gina said.

Jojo displayed the board on the table.

Gina's eyes darted toward the board. "What's this about?"

"Oh, it's a lighthouse I created. Do you recognize it?"

"No."

Jojo reached into her pocket and pulled out her phone. She accessed the lighthouse photo and set the phone on the table.

"Where did you get that?" Gina asked.

"Next to Patricia's body, right where you dropped it after killing her."

Gina's eyes teared up as she picked up the phone. "This was her favorite lighthouse." She glared at Jojo. "You think you're so clever. You can't prove anything."

"On the contrary. The police will find your fingerprints on the board. Plus, the hotel surveillance cameras will show you leaving the bridal suite before I found Patricia."

"Not true. Tess put her to bed."

"Yes, but she didn't kill her. You killed her when you freshened up in the bridal suite before the bride and groom dance."

Gina exhaled. "When I got to the room, she was asleep. So, I went into the bathroom. Next thing I knew, she stood at the door screaming at me for not having her back at the confrontation. She wouldn't stop. I don't know what got into me, maybe years of her drinking. But I pushed her. She fell back. When I checked on her, she spit on me. That's when I saw the lighthouse board and hit her."

Jojo stood to make a quick getaway.

Gina's eyes widened. She slammed the phone against Jojo's head, knocking her off her feet. Dazed, Jojo pulled herself up by the table. Gina grabbed Jojo's throat. She squeezed hard with both hands. Jojo reached for something on the table. Anything to save her life. Her hand snaked toward the tackle box. She grabbed the handle and slammed the box against Gina's face.

Liza, Dalton, and Tess appeared at the table.

"What the hell?" Dalton said.

"Gina admitted to killing Patricia," Jojo coughed and rubbed her throat.

Detective Harding approached the table. "Surveillance cameras show Gina was the last to leave the suite before you arrived."

He grabbed Gina's arm to arrest her for Patricia's murder.

———— 🜲 ————

Two weeks later, Jojo entered the Raven.

"How are you doing, kiddo? I mean from the murder and all," Lou said. After Gina's arrest, Tess took over Patricia's affairs and quit the digital board business since clients complained the boards didn't work properly, so they returned to Jojo.

"Just trying to get back to normalcy."

"This should help." He handed her the specials.

Jojo unfolded her chair and pulled the chalk and supplies out of the tackle box. As she added the specials, she glanced at the dent on the box from hitting Gina. It had saved her life and served as a reminder that her father had protected her.

Dalton approached. "Did you see the new libation that I created on the sheet?"

Jojo looked at the sheet. Tropical Green Tackle.

"For the tackle box." He smiled. "Maybe we can enjoy one together sometime."

"Maybe." Jojo added the drink to the board, ensuring to spell it correctly.

UNFINISHED BUSINESS

By Smita Harish Jain

"LOOK FOR A MAN in tight-fitting pantaloons and a frock coat," the invitation said, "and don't forget to wear comfortable shoes."

The Fredericksburg Specters and Spirits Tour, a three-hour exploration of the city's most haunted sites, was billed as the highlight of the weeklong Halloween celebration put on by the Fredericksburg Tours and More Office. The event—dubbed by the locals as "Woo-Woo Week"—was the brainchild of the city's newly elected mayor, Timothy Lewis. Posters all over Downtown and on the city's social media sites announced the tour with the tagline, *The specters come in droves, and the spirits come in glasses.*

"It'll be a gold mine! Think of the tourist revenue it will generate!" Tim said, when pitching his idea to the city council. He spoke in his usual excess of exclamation points. At twenty-six, he was the city's youngest mayor.

"So, you want to introduce our ghosts to their families?" Don Simons, the longest-serving member of the council asked, skeptical.

Tim had grown up in Fredericksburg and knew the city took pride in its spectral residents. Inviting their living relatives to meet these war heroes and prominent citizens from the past would be a tourism coup, he reasoned.

"Hey, maybe the ghosts will give us a real show if they know their family members have come to see them," Sally chimed. The mayor's secretary could be counted on to have his back, and he rewarded her with a quick wink. "They might even do more than their usual door slamming and moving things around."

"People will be talking about it for years! It's a great marketing opportunity for the city!" Tim said.

"We even found a descendant of one of our ghosts to lead the tour," Sally added.

"I don't know about this. Do we really want to stir up the spirits of dead people on a night that's already filled with ghouls and demons of the human variety?" a second council member cautioned.

"And let's not forget about Josephine," a third member said.

The tour was scheduled to coincide with the next possible sighting of the Lady in Blue, a governess named Josephine who came once every ten years to the historic Surrey Estate, which had been a Confederate headquarters during the Civil War. She was murdered after giving birth to a son believed to be fathered by the Surrey patriarch himself, James.

"If she shows up, there's no telling what might happen," Don said. "The last time she came, the city was overrun by those ghost-chasers from Culpeper."

"That's just it! Josephine, I mean the Lady in Blue, was killed on Halloween before it was even called that. The synchronicity of the two events taking place during Woo-Woo Week will be too much for any paranormal enthusiast to pass up! They'll come by the busload to catch a glimpse of the 'famous, wronged woman who has been haunting the James Surrey Estate since 1780.'" Tim quoted from past announcements about the visiting ghost.

"There'll be no keeping the kooks away," Don warned a second time.

Mary Fitzsimmons, the vice mayor, had been listening to the exchanges and added, "The tourism income *would* offset the costs of cleaning the city."

As much as the stodgy members of the council wanted to disagree, they knew the young mayor had a winning idea. The buzz in the city had been building for months, and the local merchants wanted the dollars the event would bring to their shops.

"Let's do it," Mary said, not sounding thrilled with the idea of bringing together the relatives of dead people.

"Awesome! I'll go along, too, since I'm eligible!" Tim said.

———— 🎎 ————

"Welcome, everyone. My name is Richard, and I'm going to be your guide tonight," a large, muscular man said. He wore a white linen shirt and buckled shoes to complete his period costume and looked every bit the Revolutionary-era man-about-town. "So, where is everyone from?"

All ten descendants answered at the same time, then laughed at the incomprehensible jumble.

"Why don't you go first, Mr. Mayor," the tour guide suggested.

"Absolutely, Richard. I'm Timothy Lewis, and I'm representing the family of Colonel Fielding Lewis, Revolutionary War munitions supplier and brother-in-law of George Washington. Just call me Mayor Tim!"

"Mike Stanson. Family of Theodore Ambrose, Second Lieutenant, Battle of Fredericksburg, Civil War." The man standing next to the mayor sported a high and tight Marine haircut and a no-nonsense demeanor.

"I can't wait till we get to the Confederate Cemetery. That's where my great-great-great-grandpa is buried. I wanna take some selfies," a gum-snapping teenage girl informed the group.

One by one, each descendant told their story, brandishing a sheaf of papers that documented their claim to a ghost, their right to be part of this historic tour. Each one had been checked by Richard personally.

By the time the introductions were done, the group learned they had four military descendants, three descendants of the original immigrants to Colonial Virginia, two business-owner descendants, and one member of a wealthy, old Fredericksburg family on whose land the city was established in 1728.

"What about you?" Sylvia, an older woman who had come alone, asked Richard, batting her eyelashes at him.

"About a year ago, I discovered that my ancestors were from Fredericksburg, so I moved here when I retired, to find out more about them."

"Ooh, are you a genealogy buff, too? I once—" Sylvia tried to engage him further, but Richard cut her off.

"We're going to visit several historical murder sites, as some would have you believe, where every one of your ancestors' apparitions have been spotted multiple times," Richard said. "We're sure to see many spirits tonight."

Some of the spirits would come in the form of signature drinks named for the more famous ghosts, another perk provided by the Tours and More Office. By the time the dead bodies were found, most of the people on the tour would be three sheets to the wind and of little use to the police. The killer had counted on that.

"Virginia Hall, the second oldest dormitory at the University of Mary Washington, has been the site of two ghosts." Richard made his voice sound ominous. "The first is a young girl who hung herself for reasons unknown and now haunts the building."

"Cool!" Gum Snapper said, aiming her camera in the direction Richard was pointing.

"The really interesting story, though, is about the man that everyone saw but no one reported. You see, this is an all-female dorm, so the girls just assumed he was sneaking out of some coed's room and didn't want to get her in trouble. It was only after a resident woke up in the middle of the night and saw the phantom strangling her roommate that others confirmed seeing him, too. The roommate said she didn't feel a thing, but when they looked, she had red bruises on her neck that weren't there when she had gone to bed," Richard said.

"Oh my!" Sylvia cried, feeling her own neck.

"It happened right there. If you look closely, you might see his face." Richard pointed to a window on the front of the building. Since school was still in session, they weren't allowed inside.

"I read that a Catholic priest was brought in to exorcise the ghosts," Mike said, flipping through a notebook filled with handwritten notes.

Richard glared at him, not too happy to have his information challenged. Mike might have been right, though, since neither ghost showed up to greet them.

"Darn! I wanted a picture with the girl ghost," Gum Snapper said.

From there, they walked up College Avenue and took a left onto William Street. The tour had started after nightfall, so the only light on their path came from the headlights of passing cars, cell phone camera flashes, and the few small homes that lined the street.

The construction in and around the university, especially at Sunken Road, had finally stopped. The city's residents and, some joked, the ghosts of the fallen from the Battle of Fredericksburg—known to still occupy the area—had complained about it enough that the council gave additional funds to ensure a speedy end. City dwellers said they'd rather listen to the gunfire of the dead soldiers' military drills than the incessant noise of the jackhammers.

After two more stops, Richard steered the group to a small cafe on Littlepage Street. "Let's take the chill off," he said. "Nicodemus Nectars for everyone." He ordered for the group from the preset menu created by the Tours and More Office, making sure to get Gum Snapper one without alcohol.

While everyone waited for their drinks, the mayor did his "Chamber of Commerce duties," as he liked to say, making a good impression on tourists. If he did his job well, the Chamber would have lots of smiling photos and effusive quotes to describe visitors' experiences in the city.

He started with Marcie, a young woman who was sitting alone, her backpack occupying the chair next to her.

"I'm Mayor Tim," he announced, as if she could have missed his introduction at the start of the tour.

"Marcie," she said, jerking her head in a what's-up gesture without making eye contact. She was wearing baggy pants, a baggy jacket, and a wool beanie. Her hands were buried inside her pockets.

Tim leaned over to move her backpack from the chair so he could sit.

"No!" She grabbed the bag and cradled it in her lap.

Startled, Tim took a step backwards, then decided to play the mayor card, "Just seeing how our valued guests are doing," and lowered himself into the chair.

"So, what happened to your ancestor?" he asked.

The question had become the tour participants' greeting for each other. Tim thought it sounded like a pickup line.

"Hugh Mercer. Confederate general. Civil War. No one's sure where he's buried. There's a monument to him in Fredericksburg, though, 'cuz he was born here." She spoke in spurts, giving just enough information to answer the question.

Tim cocked his head to one side and thought about Marcie's words. Every kid in Fredericksburg has played hide-and-seek or tag at the Hugh Mercer statue, and every kid knows he was a Revolutionary War hero. It was his grandson, Hugh Weedon Mercer, who fought in the Civil War. Hugh Mercer died thirty years before his namesake was even born.

Before Tim could correct her, Marcie got up and left. Mike, who had watched the entire exchange, joined the mayor.

"She's got her history wrong, doesn't she?" He glanced at his notebook, then back at Tim.

"It's an easy mistake, I guess," Tim sounded doubtful.

Mike wrote something in his notebook, and Tim noticed that the page was filled with the names of tour participants, some with lines drawn through them. When Mike saw him looking, he flipped the notebook shut and thrust it into his coat pocket.

The two men made small talk until Richard called for the tour to resume.

The group walked along Washington Street to their next stop, the Confederate Cemetery, and Sylvia quickened her pace to walk next to Richard. He wasted no time moving away from her and closer to Marcie, who was now flanked by Richard and Mike. Both had been staying as close to her as possible all tour. Tim was no prude, but weren't they way too old for her?

"Don't be surprised if the spirits of the fallen dead fill you as soon as you go inside," Richard said, when they reached the cemetery.

"And the spirits named for the fallen dead," Sylvia slurred, which made the group chortle. Clearly, she had consumed more than the Tour Office-sanctioned one drink per stop, per descendant freebie.

As soon as Richard opened the gate to the Confederate Cemetery, Gum Snapper ran inside and started taking selfies next to the gravestones. The flashes from her camera were the only light in the hallowed space.

She pursed her lips and cast a seductive look at the lens. "Just hanging out in a cemetery on Halloween night. No biggie."

Clearly, she hadn't come here to honor history or the sacrifice of her fallen ancestor. Tim started to lament what he had wrought upon his city.

"Over three thousand soldiers from four key battles are buried here. If you're really quiet, you can hear their whispers. Many of them complain about the raw deal they got, being put on the front lines by their commanding officers and getting robbed of their futures and what was rightfully theirs."

What? Tim thought. Richard seemed to be making up things as he went.

By the time they got to Historic Kenmore, Tim knew something was off about this tour. Mike was taking notes on the most random things; Sylvia wouldn't stop stalking Richard; Marcie's backpack seemed to grow bigger after every stop; and their tour guide didn't know what he was talking about. Tim had brought these people together, and he needed to figure out what was going on.

"A copy of the plans for the critical Battles of Princeton and Trenton, in which General George Washington led the Continental Army against British troops, are rumored to be hidden inside Fielding Lewis's study—given to him by his friend, the general himself, for safekeeping," Richard told the group.

"How much are those worth?" Gum Snapper asked, perking up.

"A small fortune. Treasure hunters often come on historic tours to get their hands on such items, but to date, no one has been able to find these battle plans," answered Mike while checking his notebook.

"Whose ghost lives here?" Sylvia asked, moving closer to Richard.

"Colonel Fielding Lewis himself has been seen poring over paperwork in his study. He died before paying off all his debts, worried that he would leave his beloved wife, Betty Washington, destitute," Richard said.

"Why didn't he just sell off the battle plans?" Gum Snapper asked.

Before someone could explain to her the importance of the battles as turning points in the Revolutionary War, Marcie entered the master bedroom where everyone was gathered. When she saw Tim staring at her, she moved her backpack to under her big coat and slipped herself back into the group.

"Fielding Lewis used his own personal fortune to build guns for the Revolutionary War, expecting to be reimbursed when the war was over. That money never came, and now his ghost spends his time at his old home, fretting over his unpaid bills," Richard said between clenched teeth. "Every one of these ghosts has unfinished business. The same can be said of humans," he said in full dramatic *voce alta*.

Richard's becoming more unhinged with every stop, Tim thought.

They took their second break, this time for Frazer Fireballs at a small bar right next door to the Rising Sun Tavern, known to be haunted by its former owner, John Frazer. Richard and Marcie sat together, and Sylvia watched them while she nursed more than her share of the whiskey-filled drinks. The mayor and Mike Stanson sat by themselves in a far corner of the room.

"She's been stealing historical artifacts and selling them to collectors on the black market for years," Mike said, after informing Mayor Tim of his true identity—Michael J. Stanson, agent, FBI Art Crime Team. "I've never been able to catch her, because she's always passed off the stolen items to an accomplice before I could get to her."

"Do you think she has an accomplice this time?" Tim excitedly whispered.

"Probably. It's her MO. I'm waiting till I know who, so I can nab both of them."

"How does she know what to steal? Is there a list of all this stuff somewhere?" Tim asked.

"Usually, people request the items they want, but really, every one of these old places is filled with valuable pieces. Unless they're in museums, there's very little security around them. Treasure hunters just need access to the places where the items are, and historical tours make it easy," Mike said.

"So, I handed her my city's most valuable artifacts on a silver platter," Tim said. Realizing what he had allowed to happen diminished Tim's usual verve.

——— 🎎 ———

The famed James Surrey Estate on Plantation Way consisted of a three-story manor with brick facades, white trim boards, and Tuscan-style columns. Also on the massive grounds were a smokehouse, an icehouse, a dovecote, and rows of huts where field laborers, stable hands, and other workers once lived. Josephine had most often been seen walking near the stables, so descendants scrambled there to set up their cameras. A single photograph of the Lady in Blue could earn them several hundred dollars on the right websites. Some of them brought electronic voice phenomena recorders, just to give them every chance for getting something saleable.

Edward Surrey, the sole heir to the Surrey fortune and the current occupant of the manor, addressed the group. He leaned against a cane in one hand and read from an index card in the other.

"Josephine was strangled in the hut used by the smokehouse workers, one of whom was her lover, after giving birth to their bastard son." His voice was monotone, even bored.

The hut where Josephine was killed was behind the manor and still intact. While patches of the brick exterior had worn over the years, the basic structure of the hovel was supported by a concrete masonry foundation and provided cover to anyone who went inside.

"What happened to the child?" Sylvia asked, holding on to a fence post for support. She reeked of alcohol, and people gave her a wide berth.

"He was sent to the local church orphanage, and that's the last anyone knows of him." Surrey shrugged.

"Wouldn't his descendants also be heirs and entitled to some of this?" Gum Snapper said and indicated the large expanse all around them. She definitely had a one-track mind.

"It's only a rumor that James Surrey was the father of the child. No one has ever been able to prove it."

"Margaret Surrey, James's wife, had the boy sent to the orphanage because she didn't want a reminder of her husband's mistake in her home. The orphanage papers will show who the child's parents were," Richard said.

A slow smirk spread across Edward's face. "What orphanage papers?" he asked.

He finished up the history of the Surrey Estate and all the sightings of Josephine, then returned to his manor.

Richard shouted behind him, "Josephine will have her revenge!"

Richard had become too involved in his ghosts and had finally lost it, Tim decided.

As it got closer to midnight, the time the Lady in Blue usually took her walk around the estate, the voices and muttering softened to whispers. Some in the group held their breath, while others swiveled their heads from side to side looking for her. After several minutes of quiet waiting, they jumped when a shriek pierced the darkness all around them.

"What the hell was that?" Mike was the first to speak.

"It came from over there," Tim said, pointing in the direction of the workers' huts.

The two men ran towards the back of the manor, and the rest of the group followed. Inside the first hut, they found Sylvia standing over the body of Edward Surrey, lying in the exact spot Josephine was found over two hundred years ago. A rope was tied around his neck.

A collective gasp filled the cool night air. Gum Snapper pointed at Sylvia and said, "What did you do?"

Sylvia couldn't speak. She could barely stand. She stared at the body, shaking her head in bursts, looking both confused and curious.

"I thought I saw Richard come this way. I was hoping to—" she said, stopping when she saw Richard running towards them from the direction of the main house.

"What was that scream? Is anyone hurt?" he said.

Sylvia squinted her eyes and looked from Richard to the main house, then back to Richard. She shook her head. "There *was* someone here," she finally stammered.

The group looked in every direction, then someone finally whispered, "Josephine."

"I knew she'd come back," Richard said.

"This is unbelievable!" someone else exclaimed.

"Looks like she took care of her unfinished business."

The group went on making claims and assumptions, each more far-fetched than the last. Mike had heard enough.

"This wasn't a ghost. This was murder," he said and motioned everyone to move away from Edward's body.

While Mike called the police, Tim searched the area.

"Where is Marcie?" he asked.

———— 🁡 ————

Several days later, the local members of the tour group sat at what would have been their final drink spot and discussed the events at Surrey. Without Richard there to order for them, people asked for the establishment's specialty, Blue Lady Aquatinis.

"So, Richard and Marcie were in on it together the whole time?" Sylvia asked, still trying to put all the pieces together.

"When Marcie told Richard what she had found in her research for the Specters and Spirits Tour—that his great-great-great-grandmother was the famous Lady in Blue—it was easy for her to get his cooperation. In exchange for stealing the orphanage papers for Richard, she would get a cut of his upcoming inheritance, and she could take whatever she wanted from the other tour sites," Mike explained.

"While everyone was waiting for Josephine, Richard went to the main house to confront Edward about the papers he had destroyed, demanding he tell the truth about what was in them, take a DNA test, do something. When Edward refused, Richard lost it completely and strangled him. He dragged his body out to the hut, so people would think it was Josephine settling an old score," Tim said.

"That's nuts. Who was going to believe a ghost killed a human?" Gum Snapper said, the first thing Tim agreed with her on since they had met.

"It was just a distraction, to give Richard enough time to get away," Mike said.

"But why kill Marcie?"

"Without the orphanage papers, Marcie was the only link

between him and the Surreys, and the only person who knew he had a motive to kill Edward. The police found her body in Edward's study, where Marcie had been trying to break into the safe."

"What Richard didn't know was that Sylvia had followed him."

"So, I did see him!" Sylvia said.

"You sure did," Mike said, "but—"

"But no one believed me because I was sloshed," she finished and dropped her head.

"It was your suspicion about Richard that helped me put the pieces together," Mike said. "Nothing in her backpack tied her to Richard, so I had no way of finding her accomplice. When I had my office look into Richard's background, they found his connection to the Surreys, just like Marcie had, and the pieces fell into place quickly. If it weren't for you, Richard might have had time to get away." Mike stretched out his hand and placed it on Sylvia's.

For the first time since the tour started, Sylvia smiled. *Maybe she would have some unfinished business of her own,* Tim thought.

THE LADY GINGER

BY SHERYL JORDAN

"THIS IS A BEAUTIFUL house, the Lady Ginger. Char said the builder designed the house in honor of his great-grandmother, Ginger Parker. This model is bigger than the original design because the Hunters wanted specific changes. I'm glad she showed us this one first. It hadn't even been on the market long and we got it for a steal," Eboni marveled as she and Ember walked to the front door.

"Let's take a quick look around." Ember ran from room to room, admiring their luxurious home.

"Okay." Eboni smiled at her sister's excitement as she walked to the kitchen. She saw someone in the backyard.

"Excuse me, what are you doing on my property?" Eboni asked a man she had never seen before. She walked through French doors from the house to a grilling area and bar dominating the patio space near the huge pool with Lake Smith's forty-two acre natural reserve in the middle of Virginia Beach as its backdrop.

"I'm Matt Blakeslee with Blakeslee Pool Services," the man replied.

"My realtor told me the previous owners paid the pool service contract for the year. I'm Eboni Snoe. We closed on the property today," Eboni said, slyly checking out Matt's athletic build in his formfitting red shirt and black shorts. She walked closer to Matt, extending her hand.

"Nice to meet you, Ms. Snoe." Matt's green eyes sparkled as he shook her hand, admiring the yellow sundress clinging to her slender figure. He stared as the hot sun kissed her cocoa-brown skin and highlights in her dark hair.

"Have you worked for them long?" Eboni asked.

"Uh, for about ten years." Matt blushed, clearly trying not to stare at Eboni. "They had the house built about eleven years ago. While attending college, I worked for another pool company that the Hunters had their service through. I was assigned to their service. When I started my own pool service company, they hired me. I've been working for them ever since."

"So, what are you doing here today?" Eboni asked.

"I'm testing the pH levels. I shocked the pool yesterday, so I had to come back to ensure the chlorine is at the proper level," Matt said.

"How often does this need to be done?" Eboni smiled at the thought of Matt's repeat visits.

"Every Thursday," he replied.

"Eboni! Where are you?" Ember yelled, running into the backyard. "Who's this?" Ember cooed as she looked the tall man up and down.

"This is Matt from the pool service. Matt, this is my sister Ember." Eboni rolled her eyes.

"It's a pleasure to meet you," Matt said.

"The pleasure is all mine." Ember looked straight into Matt's mesmerizing eyes. She tapped her watch. "We need to meet Jaxon soon."

"Oh yeah. Can you lock all the doors while I finish talking with Matt?" Eboni asked.

"Sure, but hurry up." Ember disappeared inside the house.

"Do you have a business card in case I need to contact you about the pool?" Eboni asked.

Matt pulled a card from his pocket. "Here ya go. Feel free to call me anytime."

"Thank you." Eboni smiled and palmed the card. A panicked scream from inside the house interrupted their conversation.

"What the heck!" Eboni ran toward the French doors with Matt close on her heels. Ember, pale and panting, came running from the office in the front of the house.

"What happened?" Eboni asked.

"I think someone was in here. When I locked the side door, I thought I heard footsteps by the garage door. I didn't see anyone there, but when I turned to go to the foyer, I thought I saw someone near the laundry room." Ember's voice quivered.

Matt ran out of the garage door to the front yard. Eboni and Ember waited for what seemed like an eternity. They turned their heads in unison when they heard footsteps.

"I didn't see anyone," Matt said, catching his breath.

"I'm calling the police." Eboni grabbed her phone.

"And tell them what? I *thought* I heard and saw someone," Ember said.

Eboni flashed a sheepish grin. "I guess you're right. Let's lock up and get going." Eboni turned towards the garage door. "What is this?" She picked up a velvet bag in the doorway to the mudroom.

"That wasn't there earlier when I was looking around when we first got here." Ember reached for the bag, reading the logo "Hunter's Diamonds."

"Someone was really in here," Eboni stared at her sister.

"Yeah, maybe. Let's just go meet Jaxon. Thank you for checking around Matt." Ember locked the front door.

Eboni and Ember rushed to the apartment to help Jaxon and a few friends move their belongings to the new house. They told everyone what had happened. All agreed no one should be alone in or outside the house while they unloaded the truck.

"I'm having a locksmith meet us at the house tomorrow morning."

After loading the last of the items on the truck, they drove to the new house. They unloaded and ordered pizza and wings to eat before they began unpacking. Eboni gave them a tour of the house while they waited for the food to arrive. Shortly after the tour, the doorbell rang.

"Hi, here's four pies and twenty-four buffalo wings. I need you to sign here." The delivery driver handed the food and receipt to Jaxon.

"Thanks," he said.

"So, the Hunters finally moved out, huh?" The driver peered around Jaxon's tall frame in the huge foyer. "I thought they would have moved after two of their crazy triplets went berserk on them."

"Wait, I want my sisters to hear this," Jaxon said. "Eboni, Ember, come here. I think you should hear this."

"What's going on?" Eboni asked.

"I'm sorry, what's your name?" Jaxon asked the pizza girl.

"Kelly, my family lives a few blocks over," she said.

"Kelly knows something about the family who previously owned your house," Jaxon said.

"They had triplets. Two boys and a girl. Teddy, Terry, Tammy. My older brothers went to school with them and always talked about how weird they were. They all looked almost identical. Same height and weight, honey-blond hair with hazel eyes. They didn't have many friends but seemed perfectly happy being with themselves. Everyone called them the three Ts. If you saw one, you saw all of them. They were inseparable."

"What happened to them?" Jaxon asked.

"Rumor has it that Teddy and Tammy beat their parents really bad because they didn't get them the cars they wanted for their sixteenth birthday. They went to juvie for several years and then to prison. Another rumor is they did it because their parents canceled the five-million-dollar trust funds they were supposed to receive in monthly allowances when they turned twenty-one. Their family owned a diamond business. When the Ts found out their trusts were canceled, that was it," Kelly said, sliding her finger across her neck.

"What happened to Terry?" Eboni asked.

"He lived with his parents until he finished high school. He was even weirder without his brother and sister around," Kelly added.

"Have you seen them lately?" Jaxon handed her the signed receipt.

"No, I don't think so. The other night on my way home from work, I saw a girl and guy sitting in a car a couple houses down the street. It could have been them, but I don't know what they look like now," she replied.

"Interesting. It was nice talking with you, Kelly," Jaxon said.

"For sure. I got more pies to deliver." She smiled as she walked away.

Jaxon and his sisters repeated their conversation to their friends while they ate the pizza and wings.

"Wow, what if Teddy and Tammy got out of prison and came here to finish off their parents?" Eboni asked.

"Girl, that would be so crazy. If someone was in the house, they had to see your car in the driveway with personalized plates that say Eboni." Ember laughed.

"She has a point. What if something is hidden somewhere in the house, and they came to get it back?" Jaxon asked.

"That could be," one friend said. The others nodded in agreement.

"Well, I hope they don't ever come back for any reason," Eboni said.

"Yes, indeed. Let's get these boxes unpacked, so we can relax the rest of the night. You two have had quite the day," Jaxon said.

— 🖤 —

Early the next morning, the three of them drove back to the house. A basket filled with flowers, wine, a cheese and cracker tray, candles, and a card sat on the front porch. Before going in, they checked all entries to the house and to the pool house to ensure all were locked. As they passed the crawl space door, Jaxon stopped suddenly.

"Why the hell is that open? It wasn't open when we left," Jaxon said.

"Are you sure it was closed?" Ember asked.

"I thought so. Maybe I'm just imagining the worst with all the talk about the Ts," Jaxon said as they walked to the front door.

"Aww, this basket is beautiful!" Ember picked it up and opened the card.

"Who's it from?" Eboni leaned over her sister's shoulder to see the card.

"It's from Char. It says, 'Congratulations on your new home. Just a little housewarming and thank you for choosing me to help you on a big decision. Enjoy, Char!'"

Eboni pulled out her phone and clicked Char's contact. After

Char's perky voicemail, she said, "Hi Char, this is Eboni Snoe. Thank you so much for the lovely basket. You're the best. Talk to ya soon."

Jaxon unlocked the door and hesitated. "What's that smell?"

"All I smell are flowers and candles." Ember set the basket on the table in the foyer.

"Okay, let's get the rest of these boxes unpacked and get some groceries. I don't want to starve to death while I'm staying here," Jaxon mumbled, taking a box to the family room. "I don't smell froufrou flowers." Jaxon moved furniture and looked in the dark corners.

"Jaxon, what are you doing?" Ember stared at her brother.

"You don't smell something rotten?" he asked.

"Not really." Ember rolled her eyes. "But you always notice smells before everyone else."

"You ain't lying about that. Remember when there was a dead possum in Mom and Dad's garage? All of you thought I was crazy," Jaxon said.

"I'll put a candle in here," Ember said, lighting a candle.

They finished unpacking the downstairs and took a break for sandwiches and chips.

"I love this house. It's the perfect home to provide a temporary haven for victims of violence. At first, I thought you were crazy, looking at a house with eight bedrooms, eight bathrooms, three half-baths, and close to six thousand square feet. I love it, though, and am so thankful Grandma gave us this money after Grandpa died," Ember said.

"Yes, it's a blessing. I may sell my house and buy in this neighborhood," Jaxon said, smiling.

"That would—"

"What was that?" Eboni paused and looked at her siblings.

"How would we know? We're in here with you." Ember stared at her sister.

"Don't be such a smart-ass. I kept hearing things while we were unpacking last night," Eboni said.

"I didn't hear anything, and why didn't you say anything?" Ember glared at her sister.

"I heard creaking noises off and on, but I thought it was the unpacking. I heard something again today, but thought it was the house settling," Jaxon said.

"That doesn't explain why I feel like we're being watched, even now," Ember said. "Creepy." She cleared the trash, and the trio returned to unpacking.

Dusk fell as the orange sun began to set.

"Come on," said Jaxon. "We need to get groceries before it gets too late."

The three piled in Ember's car, which she threw into gear before they clicked their seatbelts. Then, as suddenly as she started, Ember slammed on the brakes.

"What the heck?" Jaxon muttered, swearing under his breath.

"Did you see that?" Ember sputtered.

"What?" Eboni asked.

"Two figures. All in black like twin ninjas or something. They disappeared around the house."

"You're imagining things again," Jaxon said. "Do you want me to drive?"

"No. I know what I saw," Ember whispered.

— 🎎 —

"Okay, let's get in there and get the stuff," a woman said. They walked to the backyard and up the stairs past the grilling area to the French doors. The other person, a man, pulled a lockpick from his pants pocket and began working on the lock.

"What's taking so long?" the woman asked.

"I almost got it," the man said.

The lock clicked unlocked, and they quietly walked in. They climbed the back staircase to the second floor. The man led the way to a great room at the end of the hallway.

"Hmm, it's almost the same as when I was last here," he said, sitting on a recliner.

"Just get the stuff so we can leave before they come back," the woman demanded.

"You always were the bossy one." He stood and looked around the room.

He walked to the built-in bookcase and felt for a secret panel. *Click.* The small door slid open.

"Damn it, there's nothing in here. Everything's gone!" He punched the wall.

"Did you hear that? I heard someone gasp. It sounded like it came from the wall," the woman said.

"The wall's whining because I punched it." The man laughed.

"I'm serious. Let's finish searching the rest of the house and get out of here."

Turning to leave the room, the man stopped, causing the woman to bump into him.

"What are you doing?" she asked.

"Shh, I heard laughing," the man whispered, raising a finger to his lips. "I feel someone watching us."

"Yeah, like someone is in the walls."

"Let's get out of here. We'll have to find a way to come back," the woman said. They went downstairs to find their brother Terry pointing a shotgun at them.

"Tape her up." Terry tossed a roll of duct tape to his brother.

"What the hell are you doing here?" Tammy asked as Teddy bound her hands and feet with the tape.

"I live here. I never left. Mom and Dad thought I moved out after high school, but I have been living in these walls. This is my house!" Terry declared, smiling at their surprise.

"Stop it, Terry!" Terry hit Teddy in the back of the head with the butt of the shotgun, knocking him unconscious.

"There. Now to get you to my room." Terry secured his brother's hands and feet with tape then carried his brother to the garage and put him through a secret door leading to the passageway. Terry then dragged Teddy into a small room. He returned to get his sister.

Tammy had managed to crawl to the French doors.

"Where do you think you're going?" Terry carried her towards the garage.

"Why are you doing this to us?" Tammy asked.

"Because you guys ruined everything by beating Mom and Dad and treating them so badly. They never trusted *me* after that. They couldn't wait for me to finish high school to put me out of the house. They took everything you did out on me. They hate me . . . and I hate you!"

"They took our trusts—"

"Shut up!" he yelled, putting tape over her mouth. He dragged her to the room he put his brother in. He taped Teddy's mouth, not sure what he was going to do with his siblings.

Terry went into the backyard, shutting the doors behind him. The fresh air would help him think." *I didn't expect them to show up after all these years*", Terry said to himself. Not paying attention, he walked out the back gate as a car backed into the driveway.

"Oh, my God. Look!" Ember screamed, slamming her foot on the gas pedal instead of the brakes.

"Stop the car." Jaxon flung open the door and jumped out.

"Where did he go?" Eboni asked.

"I don't know, but I clipped his leg with the car," Ember said, putting the car in park.

Jaxon chased the intruder past the pool and into the woods on the side of their property. Ember called the police, while Eboni chased after Jaxon.

"Jaxon, come back," Eboni yelled. She was gaining on Jaxon but lost him when he entered the woods.

She stopped running, listening for sounds just as someone grabbed her arm. Eboni screamed and swung a punch that connected squarely with someone's face.

"Ow, damn, sis!" Jaxon groaned in pain.

"Jaxon, you scared the crap out of me!" Eboni whispered harshly.

"I didn't want you to go in the woods. He got away." Jaxon wiped his mouth.

"I'm sorry. My reflexes kicked in."

"Where is Ember?" Jaxon asked.

"In the driveway, calling the police," Eboni said.

Sirens echoed in the distance.

"Let's hurry." Jaxon grabbed her by the arm and pulled her toward Ember's car, where she waited with the doors locked.

Two cruisers pulled into the driveway, their red and blue lights bouncing off the front of the house.

"Tell us exactly what happened," a police officer said, tapping on the driver's window. Ember rolled down the window and repeated the night's events.

"Has anyone been inside the house since you came back from the store?" the officer asked.

"No, we stayed outside," Jaxon said.

"Good. Do you mind if we bring in a K-9 unit to search for intruders?"

"Not at all," Eboni said, looking at Ember, who nodded in agreement.

The K-9 unit arrived, and the officer opened the door with the key Eboni handed him. The dog went wild, barking and jumping around while Eboni followed.

"He only responds this way when he thinks there's a body nearby." The officer watched the dog closely. Eboni lingered behind. The canine and his officer searched the first floor and then headed up the front staircase. The dog immediately ran to the walk-in closet in the first bedroom. No one there, but the dog whined, then ran to the next room. He repeated this until all rooms on the second and third floors were thoroughly searched.

The team had returned to the main floor when the canine ran to the French doors and began barking. They went outside, and the canine sniffed his way to the crawlspace door, where he barked and scratched at the door. His officer pulled open the door, and the odor of a decaying body overwhelmed them.

The K-9 officer reported their findings to the lead officer, who called in to the station. The officers first to arrive finished securing the house when homicide detectives arrived. They spoke about their findings until the medical examiner arrived.

"Well, I'll be damned! I remember this house. The address seemed familiar. Remember the Hunter case we worked five years ago? This is the house," the officer said to his partner as they walked towards the Snoes.

"Hi, I'm Detective Harris. This is Detective Franklin. We didn't find anyone in the house, however, we did find a body in your crawl space," Detective Harris said.

"What?" Eboni covered her mouth with both hands.

"I told them I smelled something," Jaxon said.

"Who is it?" Eboni asked.

"We won't know until the medical examiner finishes up here," Detective Franklin said.

"Oh, dear God. I can't believe this is happening," Eboni said.

The crime scene investigators took photos of the entire house and bagged a purse and cell phone found next to the body. The forensic team bagged the woman's hands and removed the body from the crawl space.

"The woman has been identified as Char Johnston. Do you know her?" Detective Harris asked.

"Yes, she's our realtor," Eboni said.

"Why would someone kill Char and put her body in our crawl space?" Ember grabbed the nearest chair and steadied herself.

"That's what we need to find out," Detective Harris said. "When was the last time you saw or heard from Ms. Johnston?"

"At the closing yesterday morning," Eboni said.

"She left a housewarming basket on the front porch. It was here when we arrived this morning," Jaxon said. "She must have dropped it off when we weren't here. We left about midnight last night and didn't return until about eight this morning."

An officer approached the detectives, signaling them to step away from the group. They spoke in hushed tones.

"The forensic team heard a male voice yelling at someone, and then stomping. He said he was going to kill his siblings. They heard whimpering and other muffled voices. He has at least one hostage," an officer reported.

Detective Harris grimaced as he approached the Snoes. "Have you heard noises or voices in your house?"

"Yes, more than once. And I had the creepy feeling we were being watched."

"I need you all to go with this officer," Detective Harris said. "We need to get your statements."

The SWAT Team arrived and Detective Harris filled them in on where they suspected the hostages were being held. SWAT quickly assessed the situation. They went to the third level of the house and drilled a tiny hole through the ceiling below them and inserted a tactical surveillance camera to get a visual of what was going on in the secret room. They saw a male and a female tied up. Another man was pacing back and forth, holding a shotgun, ranting about how they ruined his life. The SWAT Team positioned themselves around the house and found the passageway door in the garage. The team commander gave the signal for the rest of the team to bust in the room when the man set the gun down and began pacing without it.

"SWAT! SWAT! Get down now! Get down right now!" SWAT members yelled, busting the door down. The man was confused and rambled on. They took all three into custody to sort out what occurred and why the three of them were in the house.

Detective Franklin explained to the Snoes that there were people in the house, in a hidden passageway. They were believed to be Teddy, Terry, and Tammy Hunter. He recounted the night Teddy and Tammy were arrested on their sixteenth birthday and eventually sent to prison until their twenty first birthday, which would be next month.

"They were released early for good behavior. Terry has been living in the secret passageway all along, it seems. We suspect Char saw him coming out of the house and confronted him when she dropped off the basket, so he killed her, then hid her body in the crawl space," Detective Franklin said.

"Do you have somewhere to stay while we finish our investigation and close the case?" Detective Harris asked, handing Eboni his card with the case number on it.

"Yes, they can stay with me for however long they need to." Jaxon hugged his sisters.

"Also, we may need to contact you for additional questions."

"Yes, of course," Eboni said.

"I bet Grandma never had this in mind when she gave us our inheritance!" Ember said, trying to break up the dark mood as they got in their cars.

A DINNER TO DIE FOR

BY VIVIAN LAWRY

STELLA POKED HER HEAD into my room at the Blue Moon. "You're wanted in the parlor."

I glanced up from painting my toenails. "Who wants me?"

Stella shrugged. "He didn't say, but it felt like he knows you." I arched a brow. She shrugged again. "Just the way he said, 'Kindly tell Miz Clara she has a guest.' He's a peculiar little man, about so tall." She held her hand shoulder high. "And he's white as rice, even his hair and eyebrows. His red eyes are fringed by pure white lashes." Stella shuddered. "I don't mean bloodshot eyes. His look like live coals."

I laughed at her spot-on description of Colonel Levereaux. "He's been my most valuable customer since the early days of this bloody war between the North and the South. Give him a sweet tea and tell him I'll be down directly." I spent five minutes twisting blond curls into a loose knot on my head. I donned my prettiest chemise, pinched my cheeks and bit my lips for good measure.

He stood and bowed when I entered the parlor. "Lovely as always, my dear."

"I'm pleased as anything to see you." I curtseyed. "To what do I owe the pleasure?" He usually sent his carriage to take me to his farm out in Hanover County.

"I was coming into Ashland anyway, so I thought I'd deliver my invitation personally." He gestured toward a loveseat, and we sat, thighs touching. He leaned close and lowered his voice. "I'm having a party, and I'd like the pleasure of your company."

I cocked my head. "A party? Should I invite some of the other girls?"

"Oh, no, no. That wouldn't do a'tall." He stroked his skimpy beard and peered toward each corner of the room. I couldn't imagine why, seeing as how his eyesight was extremely poor, and the room was empty. His voice sank to a whisper. "My guests are all Butterflies—just a few of our close mutual acquaintances. I'm sure you can handle all our needs quite nicely."

"I see. And thank you for your confidence."

"Need I say you'll be richly compensated?"

I tilted my head and fluttered my eyelashes. "I'm always happy to oblige *you*."

When I met the Colonel in 1861, I ended up staying at his farm for a week. By the time I returned to the Blue Moon, he had introduced me to the Butterfly League, a group of gentlemen who treated me well and paid generously for my favors—and silence—concerning their unusual ways of taking sexual pleasures. (I require all clients to wear French letters—always—for everyone's health and well-being, and I neither inflict nor tolerate pain. But I'm very accommodating about anything else.) With the Butterflies, I make more money with less work than any time since I entered the life at age sixteen. Whatever the Colonel wanted, I'd do my best to provide.

I leaned closer, pressing my breast against his arm. "Tell me more."

"The party will begin with dinner on Friday. Who knows when it will end?" He chuckled and patted my knee. "I'll send my carriage for you before noon. Prepare for several days, just in case."

I nodded. "I'll arrange it with Miz Pettigrew. As long as she gets her cut, she doesn't care where I work." I thought, *And I'll pay her extra to keep my room at the Blue Moon empty.*

———— 🦋 ————

Although Miz Pettigrew swore she'd keep my room locked, when I left for the farm, I'd packed all my French letters, all the petticoats with coins sewn into the hems, my prettiest unmentionables, and my favorite lavender toilet water.

Colonel Levereaux handed me down from the carriage. "Come set a spell on the verandah. You are first to arrive." He placed my hand on his arm. He wore his at-home clothes: white suit, white straw hat, three-inch heels, and a bright green feather boa. His white mane hung loose, brushing his shoulders. As we walked toward the house, a flight of pigeons dyed pastel colors scattered before us and flew up like winged confetti. I never tire of the Colonel's birds, but I was surprised he still had them. There wasn't a pigeon left in Richmond, all having been shot for the table.

We sat on white-painted wicker chairs, nibbling peanuts and sipping mint juleps the Colonel's man brought. "So what is the occasion for this party?"

The Colonel puffed out his bony chest. "My cousin—also a Levereaux—owns Live Oaks Plantation on the river. He allows blockade runners to dock there on their way up to Richmond and provides whatever aid is needed. In return, he sometimes receives goods as well as gratitude."

"Will your cousin be at the party?"

"Oh, no, no. He isn't one of us. But we've been especially close since serving together in the Mexican War. I saved his life—twice—and he often remembers me in my hour of need. He sent a wagonload of goods from the most recent blockade runner—mostly foodstuffs!"

"A *wagonload* of food?" My eyes felt ready to pop right out of my head. Bread riots rocked Richmond only last week. And most people entertaining these days hosted starvation parties, where only water is served and all the talk centers around food and favorite recipes. "What are you going to do with it all?"

The Colonel sipped his julep and sighed. "First, I'm going to enjoy this party. I've invited only Butterflies whose preferred pleasures involve food and drink. For a time, we will put aside all thoughts of war—of those so recently lost at Gettysburg. Once we've indulged ourselves, I'll decide. The Army needs all the food it can get. But many families are doing without as well, what with all the men and boys off fighting those infernal Yankees instead of tending their farms." He cut a sideways look at me. "The amount of food, and its source, must remain secret. The goods would be seized—and my cousin imperiled. A private citizen taking goods from a blockade runner is illegal."

"Do you need assurances of my silence, sir?"

"Not at all, my dear. Not at all."

— 🐞 —

As the afternoon wore on, half a dozen Butterflies arrived, all of them known to me. As evening approached, the Colonel announced that it was time to dress for dinner.

"Clara, there's a nice bath waiting in your usual room. You have your choice of lavender or rose water. Sally will help with your hair. You need not dress."

Nevertheless, I descended to the parlor wearing a silk wrapper. The Colonel was alone except for his servants. His pet goose waited by a long, cloth-covered table, a napkin tucked under one wing. "Come, Clara. Leave your wrapper here and make yourself comfortable on the table."

Hmmm. This wasn't the Colonel's usual pleasure. I climbed onto the purple cloth and found it padded. There was a pillow for my head and another to rest behind my knees. I'd no sooner settled than the other guests trickled in, eyeing me and smiling broadly. When all were assembled the Colonel whipped a purple napkin off a nearby tray.

"Gentlemen, I have *salt.*" The assembly murmured and chuckled. "*And* I have pre-war tequila and fresh limes." He smiled proudly. "It's time for our before-dinner libation."

The Colonel came to my side. "I acquired a taste for tequila during my service in Mexico." He dribbled salt down my breastbone, put a wedge of lime between my lips, and then poured tequila into my navel and both upturned palms. I smiled. *It's a good thing my bellybutton is a little cup instead of a knob.*

One of the Butterflies said, "Oh, Colonel! You arranged this for me?"

"I arranged it for all of us. Let me show you how it's done."

First he sucked up the tequila, then licked the salt, then took the lime from my lips, bit into it, and finally swallowed. One by one the Butterflies stepped forward. The Colonel kept my body supplied. I must say the licking and sucking were titillating. Of course, my pleasure or lack thereof was irrelevant. I was working.

"Now then, let us move on to hors d'oeuvres."

I thought my part was finished, but instead the Colonel sponged my body, lips, and hands, and then decorated me with slices of hardboiled egg and cucumber, olives, tiny ham biscuits, cubes of beef jerky, and dabs of peanut butter. The Butterflies surrounded me, partaking of the food and chatting about the war. "I mean no treason, but we will lose this War of Independence on our bellies. We cannot feed our Army or our citizens."

Nothing in his tone hinted at the irony of such a comment under the current circumstances.

Charles rose from my belly murmuring, "These tidbits are even better than liquor," just as Robert leaned in. Charles' head collided with Robert's face.

Robert pinched the bridge of his nose. "You oaf! I'm damned lucky it isn't broken!"

"You should've waited your turn," Charles growled.

"Are you, sir, suggesting that I am greedy?" Robert's face glowed red. "Or just ill- mannered?"

The Colonel stepped forward. "Now, gentlemen, there's plenty for everyone. And this is a party, not a barracks brawl."

Both men fell silent, the nibbling continued, and I tried to remember what I'd heard about a long-standing feud between Charles and Robert. Somebody shot somebody's cousin over cards? Something to do with a woman? Or a disputed land boundary?

When we adjourned to the dining room, the Colonel sat at the head of the table, and I sat opposite him, the Butterflies lined up between us. Although the Colonel ate only dumplings, as was his wont, the rest of us feasted: Florida Johnycake and Confederate biscuits, Captain Sanderson's boiled pork and bean soup, Miss Lesley's stewed mutton chops, roast rabbit with Boston mustard, fried catfish with Confederate ketchup, Mrs. Haskell's 1861 mashed potatoes, braised turnip greens, and fried corn.

The Butterfly on my right insisted on feeding me, watching closely as I licked my lips, chewed, and swallowed. The Butterfly on my left wanted to be fed, preferably by hand, and licked my fingers after each morsel. The Colonel had planned the seating masterfully. Cages of colorful songbirds serenaded us. Charles and Robert pointedly avoided speaking to each other.

As the table service was removed, the Colonel said, "Now for dessert! Gentlemen, enjoy your brandy. I'll call you when all is ready." He took my hand. "Come with me, my dear." He led me to the small dining room.

Once again, I found myself on a padded table, comfortable with pillows, while various parts of my body were daubed in whipped cream, jam, custard, more peanut butter, and cherry pie filling.

When the men joined us, their *ooohs* and *aaahs* filled the room. The Colonel said, "Now, same rules—no hands . . . lips and tongues only."

One Butterfly devoted himself almost exclusively to the blackberry jam on my toes. I closed my eyes, listening to the slurping and sighing, trying not to giggle when someone's beard tickled. Although parts of the experience were sensual, by then I was tired of lying still. Finally, the Colonel said, "Now, the grand finale!"

His man Jonah brought forth an enormous molasses apple pie with ice cream crust. "Mrs. Cornelius's recipe," the Colonel boasted. At a nod from the Colonel, Jonah picked me up and plopped me down in the middle of the pie. I gasped at the cold. The Butterflies gaped and cheered. The Colonel's man set me on my feet again.

The Colonel grinned. "Because it's Robert's birthday, and he is particularly fond of apple pie with ice cream, perhaps he would like to have his dessert in private." The Butterflies guffawed.

Robert extended his hand to me, smiling. "If this should be my last day on earth, I'd die a happy man!"

Robert took great pleasure in licking and sucking the pie from my lady parts. He then pushed my thighs tight together and dribbled brandy from the decanter on the bedside table down my belly and into the cup made by my thighs. While lapping it up he murmured something about the perfect pairing of brandy and seagrass.

When I'd satisfied all Robert's needs, I returned to my room and another soothing scented bath. At last, I was no longer sticky. Sinking into bed, I'd barely closed my eyes when the Colonel stepped out of my wardrobe, feathers in one hand and a pot of chocolate in the other. He was naked, painfully thin—a smiling polished skeleton. "My pleasure at last," he said.

I smiled and rose, reaching for the goose feathers and chocolate. "I wondered that you served no chocolate for dessert." The Colonel's special pleasure was for me to paint his body with chocolate. I sang to him until the chocolate hardened, too. When the time was right, he moved cautiously, causing the chocolate to crack and fall. We fed the chips to each other and then spooned together for the night.

Breakfast was another cheerful feast, everyone enjoying real wheat pancakes, not the usual fare of corn cakes. The Colonel crowed, "Yes, the cargo included flour! And coffee!" With nothing but ground acorns and chicory at the Blue Moon, this was the first actual coffee I'd had in months. Heavy cream and sugar were passed, heaping teaspoonfuls plopping into cups.

One of the Butterflies looked around. "Where's Robert? If he doesn't come down soon, he will miss this latest bounty."

"Maybe he had a late night," another Butterfly said, waggling his eyebrows at me.

Charles scowled. The Colonel motioned and his man left.

Moments later the man returned, his face as pale as a black face could be. "Massah, Mr. Robert be in 'is bed. He's dead!"

Everyone looked at me. "He was perfectly well when I left him!"

All rushed to Robert's room and beheld the ghastly sight of his twisted features and the vomitus on his bedding. A doctor Butterfly stepped forward and examined the body. "It appears he has been poisoned."

The room resounded with gasps and exclamations. The Butterfly next to me muttered, "It looks like he didn't die happy after all."

"But how could he be poisoned?" the Colonel asked. "Everything was eaten by several people, and all of us are fine!"

"Not everything." I shuddered and gestured toward the nearly empty brandy decanter. "Last night that was full."

The Colonel said, "That doesn't signify. I had decanters of brandy placed in all the bedchambers, and all were filled from the same cask." The Colonel sniffed the decanter, dipped his pinky into the liquid, and touched it to his tongue. "It seems fine to me."

Someone said, "We must call the sheriff."

I couldn't let that happen. "Consider, gentlemen. The sheriff would ask why we all are gathered. He would want to know what food was consumed—and one thing would lead to another. All of us would be exposed." I sighed. "He would land on us like a duck on June bugs."

The men looked at each other. The Colonel said, "We must deal with this ourselves. We must find out what happened." He inhaled deeply and turned to his man. "Jonah, take his body to the icehouse —as far from the ice as is practical."

I wanted to shout, "And then what?" but remained silent.

We examined the room. The armoire held his clothes, neatly hung and folded. His writing implements rested on the desk, apparently unused. The bedding and the body had been removed, but the stench of vomit and body fluids released by death remained. No one was inclined to linger.

The remaining five Butterflies, the Colonel, and I made a glum gathering in the parlor. The Colonel shook his head and said, "Poor Robert. Cut down in his prime."

One Butterfly said, "As far as I know, his plantation is more successful than most through these dark days. Yesterday he mentioned that he expects to have cotton off to Europe this season."

Another Butterfly said, "Um, yes. He confided to me that he has a contact to get around the blockade. And although his kitchen gardens have been raided by both armies, he has other gardens hidden in the woods."

"Sounds as though his life was pretty good," Charles said, a sneer in his voice.

"Not in all respects," said a fourth Butterfly. "I know two of his sons died at Gettysburg—one on our side, the other in the Union Army."

"Oh, dear Lord. As recently as that," I said. "He didn't say a word about it, but then he talked a lot less than was his wont."

The Colonel scratched his sparse beard. "I'm surprised he came."

The Butterfly who knew about his sons said, "Maybe he was

trying to put all his losses behind him. His wife died of a heart attack early in the war, when word came that their eldest had died of dysentery."

My heart ached. "Did he have no other family? Is there no one we should notify?"

"Only one daughter, I believe," said the Colonel. "She lives in West Virginia."

Several of us sighed. *Probably estranged*, I thought, *if she stayed in West Virginia after they separated from the Commonwealth and went with the Union.*

The Colonel straightened his slight frame. "Without the law, it's up to us to figure this out. First, what do we know about Robert? Outside the League, I mean. Does he have any enemies?"

Charles frowned. "Doesn't everyone?"

"None that I know of," said another, "except you. What's this ongoing bad blood between your families?"

"What the hell are you goin' on about?" Charles scowled. "That's ancient history. Robert's daddy ran off with the woman promised to my granddaddy. Surely you don't think I murdered Robert!"

One Butterfly said, "You know as well as I do that family feuds get passed down from one generation to the next practically forever! You're the only one here with anything akin to a motive."

Another Butterfly said, "And while the five of us were on the veranda with our cigars and brandy—after Robert, Clara, and the Colonel had gone off—didn't you say you wanted a little walk to settle your stomach? Who's to say you didn't go into Robert's room and slip him a little something?"

All the color drained from Charles' face. "Slip him a little something? Are you suggesting I carry poison around as a matter of course? Hells bells, I didn't even know he'd be here!"

The Colonel said, "Gentlemen, remember yourselves!" But all the other Butterflies glared at Charles.

After a supper of cold meats, breads, cheese, and fruit, we were ready to retire to our respective rooms. One of the Butterflies cocked his head toward Charles. "What about him? Is he gonna be free to roam around and kill us in our beds?" Other Butterflies muttered indecipherable comments.

The Colonel heaved a sigh. "Let's not be precipitous!" He held up his hand. "I know there appear to be no alternatives, but let us proceed in a rational way. In the morning, we'll convene our own court. All will be free to ask questions or present evidence."

"But what about tonight? I say, lock him up!"

The Colonel looked at my stricken face and Charles's resigned one. "Charles shall have the comforts of his room. I'll hold his weapons, and I'll post men at his door and windows." He stared from one Butterfly to the next. "I trust that will suffice?"

With that, we all retired.

— 🎎 —

I waited for a knock on my door, but none came—thank goodness. Robert's death seemed to have subdued everyone. I kept thinking about Charles. With me he'd always been gentle, just quietly nibbling bits of bread and jam off my body while growing greatly aroused. He asked about me, my life, my problems, which very few clients ever did. And he seemed eager to return to his family as soon as this wretched War of Northern Aggression ended. I couldn't believe he did it. But with no alternative, would the assembled men decide to lynch him?

My thoughts roiled. *What have we missed?* As the clock struck midnight, I crept into Robert's room, candlestick in hand. The windows were open and the smells from the morning were dissipating. Cicadas serenaded the night. Everything looked as before—clothes, decanter, writing desk.

Looking more closely, I spied a tumbler under the bed. I retrieved it and sniffed the dregs. I sniffed again. It smelled off, like bitter almonds. I compared the smell of the glass with the decanter. *Definitely different!* This was where the poison had been. I'd tell the others in the morning.

I opened the armoire and searched the pockets of Robert's clothes. Nothing. *I wonder whether the clothes he was wearing were searched?* Then I remembered that he'd been found in his nightshirt.

His traveling writing desk still sat on the table. We hadn't opened it, so I did. Paper, quill pens, pencils, nibs—and a journal.

I clutched it to my breast and returned to my room.

I started at the latest entry and read back through earlier entries. Robert was not loquacious. The latest entry said, "Levereaux invited me to party. Will go. At least I won't be alone." Then he listed items pertaining to his plantation production. Back in mid-July, I found the entry for the day he learned of his second and third sons' deaths. "All is lost. My dear, beloved sons are lost. I cannot mourn Samuel without also mourning Matthew, however misguided his loyalties to the Union."

Paging backwards, I read the facts of his life and loneliness; his depression following his sons' deaths at Gettysburg; his love for the daughter who would no longer speak to him. Farther back he railed against the war that had halved his family, two sons with the Confederacy, one son and one daughter with the Union. Eventually, about a year back, I came across this entry: "I struggle to go on without Martha, but I must for the sake of our remaining children. I have cyanide. If ever I have nothing more to live for, I shall take it."

SHE SIMPLY VANISHED

By Maria Hudgins

THE VIEW WAS SPECTACULAR, and I was alone with no one to share it. I stood atop the ramparts on Fort Monroe, specifically beside the flagpole called the Flagstaff Bastion. A half-mile out in the water, toward Norfolk, lay the ancient Fort Wool at the entrance to the harbor, its huge flag flapping like the one beside me. As I imagined the history, the ships entering Hampton Roads Harbor over four centuries from the first settlers to the first Africans, to the Union blockade in the Civil War, I drew up my collar against an east wind. I don't know what made me glance down to the seawall and spy the lone pedestrian on the sidewalk.

I pointed my iPhone at Fort Wool and took a picture. Such a perfect day and perfect view. I took a couple more, tucked my phone back in my jacket pocket, and paused to enjoy the moment. The man stood still on the pedestrian walk down below but facing west, in the direction of the Chamberlin. As he stood there, a woman in a filmy green dress approached him and stopped. They were talking, so I assumed they knew each other, but maybe not. I turned my gaze to the west, wondering if I could see the bandstand that stood just this side of the Chamberlin, wondering if she had come from there. I knew they often held events like concerts and weddings there, so it might explain why this woman was wearing a fancier dress than one would normally see on the walk. Trees blocked my view of the bandstand area. I turned back to the scene in front of me.

The woman was gone.

Impossible. She was there, talking to the man, no more than thirty seconds ago. She couldn't possibly have disappeared that fast, because I could clearly see a good quarter of a mile in every direction. If she had been running in either direction along the walk or across the lawn toward the road I could have seen her. Between the walk and the waters of the harbor was a four-foot wall. Surely she hadn't scaled the wall and jumped into the water, so where could she have gone? Straight up?

I puzzled about this, sure that I had misinterpreted or missed something. The man she had been talking to was now walking eastward down the pedestrian walk. He was wearing dark jeans and a light blue shirt, sleeves rolled up just below the elbows. He walked like an athlete, his shoulders much wider than his hips. No hat. Dark hair. With his back to me, he would soon be out of my view. A child on a bicycle pedaled past him, traveling west.

I couldn't forget about this. The woman had vanished. But on the other hand, I couldn't go to the police with absolutely no evidence. *There must be a simple explanation,* I thought. *My phone. Is she in one of the pictures I took?* I pulled out my phone and checked. There was the one of Fort Wool across the water, and another of the same scene, but taken a minute or two later. In this second one, the man was there, walking west, but the woman was not. I used two fingers to expand the shot and saw that his shirtsleeves were rolled up as I had already noticed, but now I saw that he was wearing aviator-type sunglasses. He also appeared to be wearing a necktie, but I couldn't be sure, given the small size of the image.

Such a little thing. I should forget about it, but I couldn't. Like a name you can't remember, it haunts your mind until you come up with an answer. Or at least a possible answer. I had to investigate. I turned and descended the slope off the ramparts and down to my car parked at the entrance to the Casemate Museum.

I drove around to Fenwick Road and met a crowd leaving the bandstand.

Cars were backed up waiting to turn onto this same road. There had obviously been a wedding. White streamers and flowers festooned every column and the entire rail of the bandstand. Given the traffic snarl, I knew I couldn't find a place to park from the Chamberlin to the next parking spot, so I took my first chance to turn left and continue around this tiny island called Old Point Comfort. It used to be property of the US Army but was now transitioning into an upscale community with lovely old homes, playgrounds, and campgrounds.

As I drove along Fenwick Road paralleling the seawall, I kept my eyes peeled for the man in the blue shirt. He could have been walking to his car, which could be parked in any of several small lots, or he could be heading for the Paradise Ocean Club about a mile from the bandstand. I turned into the parking area of the club. Still early in the day, the lot was mostly empty, but I looked around, peered through the entrance to the outdoor area of the restaurant, and watched workers picking up trash at the pool and volleyball court. The man wasn't here.

Back in my car, I thought about it and decided I would rather make a fool of myself than have a woman's disappearance on my conscience. I knew there was a police station around here somewhere and it should be easy enough to find, given the fact that Fort Monroe had only three roads. I found the Hampton Police Department's small substation not far from the Paradise Ocean Club. Inside, I introduced myself to the first person I met. He, in turn, introduced me to Corporal Jay Winters.

Still standing near the front door, I explained my presence in terms that I hoped would not sound as silly as I felt.

Corporal Winters shifted his weight from one foot to the other, hitching up his hefty belt as if the burden of listening to me was one more hardship a policeman had to endure with grace.

"I'm not sure what you are asking me to do," he said.

"I saw this woman, and she disappeared. There's no way she could have vanished like that. What if she's in trouble?"

"What sort of trouble would that be?" He tilted his head and shrugged.

"I'm sure I don't know but—" I knew it would turn out like this. "Look," I said, holding out my phone and tapping the photo folder. "This is where she stood. Right there! Talking to that man."

Corporal Winters took the phone and studied the picture. I hoped he was noting the great distance between the woman and any place she could have gone. He expanded the shot just as I had done. "Who is the man?"

"I don't know."

"Did it seem like she knew him?"

"I don't know, but I rather think she did. You might say hi to a stranger, but you wouldn't stand there and talk to him."

"One of them could have been asking the other for directions."

He had a point, but it didn't help explain how she vanished like that. "I watched them for maybe thirty seconds and then something caught my attention—or maybe it was nothing—and I turned to my right, looking down toward the Chamberlin." I wondered if I had really heard or seen something that distracted me. "When I turned back to them, the man was still there, but she was gone."

"You aren't giving us much to go on here, Mrs.—"

"Dennis. I know this sounds like nothing, but I do hope you will keep an eye out for a woman in a green, sort of chiffony-looking dress. I do wish I had noticed what color hair, how tall—I'd make a terrible detective, wouldn't I?"

With the slimmest possible hope that Corporal Winters and the Hampton Police would keep an eye out, I left the station and hurried to get off the island before the predicted storm hit. I tried to forget the whole thing, but couldn't. Several days passed. I scanned the *Daily Press* for any news of a disappearance. The Sunday paper did have coverage of a wedding at the bandstand on that same day. It had to be the reason for the traffic snarl I had run into. The Hawes-Rose nuptials had been the occasion for the fluffy decorations, the crowd, and the snarl. William Hawes and Laura Rose had been united in holy matrimony and the bride's attendants, it said, wore apricot. This eliminated one idea. The woman in the green dress had not been a bridesmaid. But really, I had no reason to believe she had been a part of the wedding at all.

—— 🐾 ——

On Friday morning, fishermen discovered a body washed up on the rocks at Fort Wool. I started to call the police, but then decided I'd get diverted into the usual runaround as they switched me from one wrong extension to another. I would get nothing by phone. Instead, I would drive out to Fort Monroe again and stand there like Poe's raven, threatening to haunt them forever until I found out everything I could about this body. Some things require eye contact.

Corporal Winters remembered me. "There's a patrol boat out there now," he said. "They haven't told us anything yet. They have to document everything first, and then they'll take her to the coroner, who will do the autopsy."

"You said *her*. So, it's a woman?"

"I meant to say, *it*. " He winced at his mistake.

"Did they tell you what color dress she's wearing?"

"No. They haven't told me anything, and I shouldn't have said *she*. But the body has been in the water for some time, and it may have lost any clothing it may originally have had. But you could help us here. The woman you think you saw on the walkway, what color hair did she have?"

My body tensed when he said, *think you saw*. "I can't remember her hair. I only remember her dress was green."

Pure agony! I had to wait and wait, scouring the paper every day, looking for every bit of local news I could find online. Had they identified the body? Could it be the woman in the green dress? Were they looking for the man in the blue shirt? Were they questioning members of the wedding party? Did other clues lead them to the retirement community at the Chamberlin? To the large marina just around the side of the island? There were so many possibilities.

I can't help my tendency to obsess over anything unexplained, no matter how tiny. So, I felt a need to do a little sleuthing. Parking my car in between the Chamberlin and the bandstand, I trekked to the spot on the walk where the woman had stood. The seawall, I now saw, was about three and a half feet high. Leaning over it, I discovered the shore was lined with huge boulders guarding the land against erosion. The boulders extended out some fifteen feet from the wall and told me the woman would not have hit the water if she had jumped over. She would have hit the rocks.

The entrance to the Casemate Museum was close by, so I visited, hoping to find someone who had been there that day and seen something, as they might well have done, since I had been standing atop the part of the fort that housed the museum. Since decommissioning, the museum was free and open to the public, but few if any employees were ever on site. I looked around for someone to talk to, but found only animated figures and interactive exhibits. Outside, I ran into a matronly woman in a yellow traffic vest who listened to my story.

"I remember that wedding. Yes. You're talking about the day before the storm, right?"

"What I need to know is, did you see a woman" I didn't know what to ask, so I lamely, added, "in a green dress, walking along the seawall and stopping to talk to a man . . . and, like, running away or . . . something?" I got the look I deserved. I straightened up and, in my best adult voice added, "Maybe climbing on that wall? Was there any confusion or shouting or anything?"

"Was someone attacked? Is that what you're getting at?"

"I don't know. I was watching from—" I pointed to the top of the ramparts. "And this woman just disappeared before my eyes. I looked away for a second and—"

She looked at me with sympathy and suggested I check with the police.

"I already have."

Mentally licking my wounded ego, I marched along to the Chamberlin and into their beautiful lobby with windows overlooking the harbor. Consciously avoiding eye contact with employees, I searched for an elderly person who looked unoccupied. I found a woman and a man sitting in the small Poe reading room. I took a seat myself and, edging more carefully into the subject this time, asked, not about a woman who disappeared, but about the wedding at the bandstand a week or so ago. The one with the bridesmaids in lovely apricot dresses.

"I remember it. I watched it from the Solarium, up—" the woman pointed to the ceiling. "I do so love to see things that go on over there. I love the bands, too. The little ones dancing."

I interrupted her to ask about a woman in a green dress who might or might not have been at the wedding.

Again, I got that look of pity, this time from a woman old enough to be a bit peculiar but actually in better control of her faculties than I appeared to be.

The police had a Jane Doe on their hands.

I had to talk to Corporal Winters again. Despite his demeanor—he reminded me of the dark glasses, pot belly, toothpick-chewing stereotype—I felt that he might be a good cop. Some cops cultivate that image deliberately. I found him at the big police headquarters in downtown Hampton, bent over a box of take-out Chinese noodles. He drew in a deep breath and motioned me to sit in the chair beside his desk.

"I've been wracking my brain to figure out what it was about that man—the one in the blue shirt—something very familiar about him—I wish I could put my finger on it." I knew I must sound like an idiot, but I wasn't lying. There had been something about him.

"You still got that picture you took?" Winters asked.

I pulled out my phone and showed him.

"Send it to me." He told me his email address.

I sent him the one I took when the man was facing west, before the woman in the green dress arrived, then clicked forward to view the next few photos. I had also taken a shot of the man's back when he was walking eastward down the walk. This one was taken from much too great a distance to tell much about him. He had been near the spot where a pier jutted out into the water.

Winters held his own phone, studying the photo I had sent. The chopsticks he had been using when I interrupted him still dangled from his right hand, dripping a small puddle onto his desktop.

"You know there was a wedding down at the bandstand at almost the exact same time?"

"I told you that," I said.

"But do you know who? The bride was a Rose. Last name Rose. One of the richest families in Tidewater. Groom was a Hawes. Don't know them." He went silent a minute and then heaved a huge sigh.

I knew all this. I had the newspaper coverage clipped out and stashed at home. William "Billy" Hawes had certainly married up. I had known him in high school. Good football player, but not much of a student. Went to Virginia Tech on scholarship but flunked out before he finished. I'd had a bit of a crush on Billy. I still remembered admiring his backside as he walked down the hall at school.

I shook myself back to the present. "The body. Have they identified the body they found at Fort Wool?"

Winters told me they had not, but that it was a woman with reddish hair. Her clothes were mostly gone, but they found remnants of green chiffon tangled in flotsam near the body.

"I told you this woman was wearing a green dress," I said, my tone betraying my irritation. They should have told me this already. My hint should have told them where the woman came from and when. I had handed him a great lead.

Corporal Winters said nothing. He stared at his phone and let his chopsticks fall to the desktop. Then he looked at me directly for the first time.

"There's other stuff, but I can't talk about it."

"About the wedding?"

"I can't say."

"Do you know who this man is?"

Silence. I realized I could go no further. Knowing that Winters really couldn't tell me more, knowing that if I probed too much I'd get myself thrown out of the building, I swallowed hard and thanked him for his time.

Instead of driving home, I motored out to Fort Monroe again and parked close to the bandstand. From here it was a short walk to the seawall. I trudged down the walk, past the spot where the man and woman had been standing, and reassured myself that there was no way she could have left by the grass, by the walk, or by any other route. I peered over the wall and watched as gentle waves lapped the boulders. *No sign of a disturbance here.*

I walked on to the east as the man in the blue shirt had done—something about that man—where had I lost sight of him? A short distance ahead was a break in the seawall and the start of a pier. At the end was an L-extension, where a small dinghy tied to its piling bobbed with the passing ripples. It hit me all at once. What if the man in the blue shirt had a boat waiting here? What if the woman in the green dress had met him, following a plan, jumped over the sea wall onto the boulders, and simply waited for him there until he brought his boat around from the pier?

But why?

I didn't know, but at least I now had a plausible explanation for *how*.

The *why* had to wait two more weeks. With my epiphany at the pier, I also had another vision—the man in the blue shirt walking away and Billy Hawes walking down the hall at school— same walk, same build. But not the same man, because Billy was at that moment getting married back at the bandstand. Billy had a brother, hadn't he? Slightly older, but also a football star a few years before I got to high school?

I would have loved to be a fly on the wall when they questioned James Hawes in an interview room at the police station. It took him a while, but Corporal Winters had been relentless. It seemed the elder Hawes brother, James, had been contacted by Penny Hawes, Billy's first wife. Well, not actually his first wife—more like his current wife. They had never finalized their divorce, despite Billy's best efforts to do so. He had given up. He had met the beautiful and wealthy Laura Rose, asked her to marry him, and did so without worrying too much about the fact that he was still technically married. No one knew Penny's whereabouts. She seemed to have disappeared. Who would ever know?

Then Penny popped up. She wanted to make Billy's wedding the worst day of his life. She renewed her old friendship with his brother James who convinced her he hated Billy as much as she did. He made up lots of past grievances that never happened. When he learned of her plan to ruin the wedding, he saw a chance to save the wedding and take care of Penny once and for all. James was looking forward to becoming a part of the Rose family and, incidentally, the Rose fortune. No one had seen Penny for years. If she were to fall into Hampton Roads Harbor, suitably weighted with a cinder block or two, no one would miss her, would they?

James told the police he would have preferred to take care of Penny before the actual day of the wedding, but this was the only opportunity she gave him. Penny couldn't take the chance that, after her performance at the wedding, she might run away and find no means of escape. She told James, her coconspirator, "Meet me on the seawall, just before she walks down the aisle. Wedding starts at two. Have the boat ready."

James's confession had to be pulled out piece by piece. He had to make certain Penny Hawes—still using her married name—came to him before she barged in on the wedding ceremony and ruined it.

How had he managed to move her from the walkway to his boat? I asked Corporal Winters about this. There were dozens of people around—not close, but certainly within shouting distance. Winters pointed out the extreme difference in their sizes. Penny, five-foot-one and ninety-five pounds, versus James, six-three and two-hundred-twenty pounds of pure muscle. A quick grab, a twist of the neck, and toss her over the wall. I shivered at the realization that one human could kill another that quickly and easily.

James insisted he hadn't intended to kill her. He only wanted to kidnap her briefly until the wedding was over, but that made no sense to Corporal Winters because it wouldn't solve the real problem—that the wedding taking place that day would be null and void due to the groom's being already married. But if the first wife was dead or permanently missing, the marriage would be legal. This became a favorite topic for discussion and arguments in the Hampton Police Department for years.

REVELATION

By Rosemary Shomaker

"FIVE FUNERALS THIS YEAR," Vickey Martin said as she sped along the James Madison Highway. "Please not another."

Vickey had left Baltimore for Culpeper immediately after her mother called. She shivered. Would she soon attend her grandfather's funeral? She parked at the hospital, set her sights on the front doors, and forged ahead to deal with matters at hand.

As Vickey neared Room 2207, her shoulders slumped. The anxiety of seeing the family patriarch in decline weakened her, and she regretted not stopping in the hospital cafeteria for a cup of fortifying coffee.

The institutionally wide door was half-open, and Vickey heard Uncle Mike within. He was her great-uncle, but his brother status to Grandpa Lew prevailed.

"Those were the good old days. You and Blessed Bess were good to take me in," Mike said.

Vickey bristled at her grandmother's "blessed be the meek" nickname. Remembering her mother's one-visitor-at-a-time admonition, she stayed in the hall.

"Couldn't ignore my best buddy, Mike. You know, I'll always look out for you."

"You had no choice. Emmie and Elise were sickly, and Mama had to spend all her time with them. I was a surprise baby, and she foisted my care on you."

"I wasn't in school yet. I was proud to help." Lew continued, "Once you returned from the Army, seemed fitting you'd live with me, Bess, and our girls."

Vickey heard the grind of a motor and pictured Grandpa Lew adjusting the hospital bed to sit straighter.

"I put in long hours for the sheriff's office and then for the town's police department. When I became police chief, the hours became longer. I wasn't home much, so I was glad you were there for my kids.

"Building that playhouse for the girls was pure gold. You, Alice, Lucy, and Liz would be in those far maple trees for hours, making shutters for the playhouse, painting it inside and out. You especially helped us deal with Liz's teenage dramas." Lew's voice dropped. "Her wild accusations were insulting."

The Room 2207 conversation hummed in the background as Vickey focused on twice-divorced Aunt Liz. She'd escaped Culpeper and held prominent government positions in Washington, DC. By age four, Liz refused the nickname Beth Ann and demanded to be called Liz. How the urbane name entered her consciousness was a mystery.

The familiar male voices rose and fell. Vickey leaned against the doorjamb of the empty patient room next to Grandpa Lew's. She wrinkled her nose. The antiseptic odor of the hospital was at odds with the crushed leaves, apples, and woodsmoke aromas conjured by the clear skies and autumn foliage she saw through the room's window.

The sharp hospital scents induced Vickey's recall of her disagreeable aunt. Liz's stormy adolescence coincided with Mike Grayson's joining the household and with Gran Bess' adoption of Duke, her first dog. When a young Liz screamed that Uncle Mike molested her, she'd rocked the family and hurt Grandpa Lew. He punished Liz for accusing Mike and chalked it up to Liz's attention-seeking personality. Bess stayed mute and concentrated on training Duke. Before Liz finished high school and left for college, a fire of mysterious origin destroyed the playhouse Uncle Mike had built.

Dogs. That redirected Vickey's grim mindset. She'd see the family dog, King, at her childhood home. The family list of German shepherds began with Gran Bess' Duke, followed by Knight, and then Baron. Her mother acquired Rex before she married. Vickey grew up with Rex and then Viscount. Now King ruled the Barberry Street rambler of her childhood.

A nurse marched past Vickey pushing a waist-high cart of small items Vickey couldn't identify. Vickey said a few words to explain her loitering, but the nurse took no notice of her.

Uncle Mike's voice focused Vickey's wandering thoughts back to the present.

"Good thing Alice brought you in. It's your heart again, right?"

A weakening voice replied, "My retirement and medications kept the old ticker working these past years, but now the old pump can't keep up. New pills they gave me a few months ago helped, but now walking around the house exhausts me."

"You'd be in hot water with Blessed Bess if she still walked the earth. What with you skipping meals and ordering pizza."

"True. Bess took great care of me. Now her likeness does."

Vickey moved closer to the door. They meant her mother, and she wanted to hear more.

"Alice has the same comforting, nondramatic way Bess had. She doesn't make demands, and she gets work done."

The Grayson relations maintained that Vickey took after Gran Bess and Alice, except for the part of her that echoed Liz. Did she exhibit the docility of her grandmother and mother and the contrariness of her aunt? Neither was a compliment.

Vickey heard the hum of the hospital bed changing position. Maybe Grandpa Lew was reclining the bed, giving Uncle Mike the hint to leave.

Alice Martin appeared at the end of the corridor.

Vickey advanced to meet her. "Hi, Mom. I was about to shoo Uncle Mike away. He's been with Grandpa since I arrived."

"Grandpa needs to rest before dinner. Let's go in and send Mike packing. We can stay for a bit and then go to Grandpa's house to let King out before deciding the plan for the night," Alice directed.

"King's at Grandpa Lew's?" Vickey asked.

"I've been sleeping there in my old room—the one I shared with Lucy—and King's been with me. We began sleeping there when Grandpa grew weak." Alice pushed the door fully open and entered Room 2207 with Vickey in tow.

As if startled by the interruption, Mike blurted, "Liz is in town, and she's taking me to dinner tonight! How about that?"

Everyone stared at Mike.

"I've got an important errand to run before I see Liz," Mike continued. At the door, he turned back. "Alice, regular time on Sunday? Tie up that beast of yours, and I'll be there."

"No," Alice said to the empty doorway. "Papa may still be here, and I'm not planning on cooking for you." The echo of Mike's footsteps signaled he was yards away and mindless of her comment. She scowled. When she glanced at Vickey, they both rolled their eyes.

Lew said, "Alice, how long has Vickey been your partner in eye-rolling? You and Lucy would both raise your eyes just like that!"

"Very funny, Papa. Get some rest and eat a good dinner. I'll call you later," Alice said.

She and Vickey kissed Grandpa Lew's forehead and left the room.

In the elevator Vickey learned Liz had arrived Tuesday, was staying at Alice's, and planned to take Uncle Mike dining in Sperryville.

"Maybe she wants to mend fences with Mike before it's too late," Alice said.

Her mother's comment stumped Vickey—too late for whom or for what?—but she didn't ask.

— 🎎 —

As Vickey followed Alice to Grandpa Lew's on Madison Road and along South Blue Ridge Avenue, her thoughts roamed. Grandpa Lew was a welcomed Sunday night dinner guest at their house after Gran Bess died, whereas Uncle Mike's attendance didn't win him any fans.

Vickey's father hadn't liked Uncle Mike. The animosity worsened when her father heard from a coworker of complaints against Mike of inappropriate conduct towards female teachers. Mike's teaching assignments moved from school to school until he was posted to division headquarters.

Her father had said, "Mike Grayson was promoted past his proficiency to get him out of the classroom and to where they could keep an eye on him."

A relieved Alice had added, "The teachers may be safer now. And the children."

Uncle Mike rose through school division ranks and kept coming to Sunday dinner. Vickey's father wasn't the only one who disliked Uncle Mike. Vickey's job was to shutter their dog in her room when Mike arrived.

Now Sunday dinners were held at Grandpa Lew's. King would not let Uncle Mike into the Barberry Street house.

Alice turned off Old Rixeyville Road and drove the dirt lane to Grandpa Lew's front door. Vickey stopped farther back, mesmerized by the golden fall regalia of the tall maples near the house. The aromas of woodsmoke, apples, and crushed leaves she pined for in the hospital corridor poured in her car's open windows.

Vickey caught up to her mother as Alice opened the back door. Out King bounded. He greeted them with prancing and licks and then ran to the property's other stand of maples on the edge of the woods separating the Grayson and Pritchard properties.

"Where'd you like to sleep on this visit?" Alice asked.

"I'd just as soon go home and sleep in my old room," Vickey said. "I can keep Liz company."

They rolled their eyes to the sky, knowing the difficulty of keeping such company.

— 🎎 —

The next morning, yelling jarred Vickey from sleep. She sprinted to the living room from her bedroom to find Culpeper Police Officer Herbert Sealy inside the open front door. Liz paced from door to couch, arms aflutter. They talked over one another with increasing volume.

"Dang it, Mrs. Fulcher! Anchor yourself! Since I'm the only officer not related to you, Chief Grayson sent me."

In the mayhem Vickey latched on Officer Sealy's words. Uncle Pete was Police Chief now, but were they related to most of the town's police officers? Between Grandpa Lew's seven siblings and Gran Bess's eight, maybe so.

Vickey skirted the pair to close the door. She took Liz's hand and stood next to her. "What is this, Officer Sealy?" she asked.

She hardly heard the reply since Officer Sealy's words reignited Liz's yelling. Vickey registered something about trouble at Uncle Mike's townhouse. She dropped Liz's hand to call her mother.

She caught Alice on her way to the hospital. Before Vickey could mention Aunt Liz's situation, Alice told her Grandpa Lew had been sedated last night because he was agitated. Seems they over-suppressed him; he was unconscious but in no danger.

Vickey told her mother the police were asking Liz about some problem involving Uncle Mike. An unflustered Alice said she'd call their attorney and come to the police department.

Vickey disconnected the phone and turned back to the commotion.

Liz continued yammering and flitting around the living room. A frustrated Officer Sealy boomed, "That's it! You'll listen to this! Mrs. Elizabeth Ann Grayson Pierce Fulcher, we need to talk to you about last night. You can detail for us Michael Grayson's actions before his assault."

"What assault? Is he okay?" Vickey asked, alarmed.

"It was high time for that old bastard to suffer!" Liz sneered.

Vickey hugged her aunt, more to still her than from compassion. The hug gave Vickey the opportunity to say into her ear, "Aunt Liz, don't say anything. Mom's calling Mr. Cooper. Go with Officer Sealy now, and I'll follow in my car."

"Bert told me Mike was attacked, Vickey," Liz said as they sat across a table from Officer Sealy in a sparsely furnished office. "I will answer his questions. I have nothing to hide. We are all friends here." Liz smiled at Officer Sealy.

Vickey leaned toward Liz and whispered, "Aunt Liz, something's happened they aren't telling us. Please wait for Mr. Cooper."

"Mike did nothing against his will, dear. I can't get in trouble by telling the truth."

A composed Officer Sealy asked Liz about Thursday night, encouraging her chattiness.

"I treated Uncle Mike to dinner at the Three Blacksmiths in Sperryville," Liz replied.

Once they'd finished dining around half past ten, Liz drove Mike home, arriving at his townhouse by eleven o'clock. She had stayed in front of his home until he turned on the inside lights. She then went to Alice's house in Belle Parc, arriving at quarter past eleven, and went directly to bed.

"The old fool decided himself to eat all seven courses and have wine with dinner."

Vickey left the office. In the lobby she called her mother again. As the call connected, she pleaded, "Mom, get Mr. Cooper here, quick!"

"Stay calm, Vickey," Alice said.

"Aunt Liz enjoys having an audience and won't stop talking! Attention-seeking Aunt Liz, right?" Vickey rolled her eyes to the ceiling, expecting that her mother did the same on the other end of the phone.

"Sam Cooper insists on shaving, honey. I'm leaving his house now, and he'll follow."

Vickey returned to the office. Officer Sealy continued to interrogate Liz about the route from Sperryville to Culpeper, the time her car pulled up to Mike's home, and if she walked him to the door.

Liz stood defiantly and said, "Darn it, I left him at his townhouse. I hope he got sick as a dog from all that rich food!" She added more quietly, "You said he was attacked. Did he go to the convenience store for antacids? Was he mugged on the way?"

A grave Officer Sealy said, "No, Mrs. Fulcher. He never left his townhouse. He's dead. The food didn't kill him. It was the repeated stabbings."

Liz sank onto a chair. Quietly she said, "With his diabetes and clogging arteries, I prayed the heavy food would kill him, but I didn't stab him. He was alive at eleven o'clock when he entered his home."

When Alice and Mr. Cooper strode into the sheriff's office, Vickey exhaled in relief.

Alice hugged a crying Liz, faced Officer Sealy, and demanded the facts.

Officer Sealy said a neighbor saw Mike Grayson's front door open early this morning. When she knocked and no one came to the door, the neighbor called the police.

"We had trouble at that address before, so we were wary,"

Officer Sealy said. "Last month Mr. Grayson attended a funeral for a former teacher, and the teacher's husband threw him out. The husband later came to Mr. Grayson's home and beat on his door, challenging him to a fight. He alleged Mr. Grayson's harassment of his wife ruined her life.

"This morning we found Mr. Grayson deceased in his living room. We'll be talking to the man from the recent incident."

Officer Sealy advised Mr. Cooper that Liz was not under arrest. Mr. Cooper drew Liz into an empty office to confer. Liz was released, and Sam Cooper left.

"Vickey, if you will drive us home, I'll leave my car here," Alice said.

"Sure, Mom."

Alice and Liz talked quietly in the backseat as Vickey drove.

When they arrived at the Barberry Street rambler, Alice said, "Liz and I are going to have some lunch. Vickey, would you go to Grandpa Lew's and let King out into the yard? Bring him back with you, please." They were asking for privacy, and she gladly left. She had an errand of her own to run.

— 🎎 —

Vickey drove to Fairview Cemetery. She walked amid eternal resting spots, shaken and upset, heedless of any pursuer. She passed clusters of graves and hesitated at the refrigerator-sized Grayson headstone. Under the half identified for Elizabeth Ann Haskins Grayson rested Gran Bess. The other half waited for Grandpa Lew.

Now there would be another gravestone—for Uncle Mike.

When Vickey came to Wade Martin's headstone, she pressed her hand to the 2-0-1-8 date of death and felt the autumn sun's warmth on the surface.

Vickey said, "Hello, Dad. If you have influence up there, please get a reprieve for Grandpa Lew. I can't bear to have you both gone."

A chill crept up her spine as she thought of Uncle Mike. "You may have already seen Uncle Mike in heaven," she started. "Unless he went to the other place," she finished, horrified.

She stared at the headstone, willing her father to comfort her.

A man spoke, but it was not her father's voice.

"I saw your car turn into the cemetery. I'm sorry I didn't talk to you separately in the office, but your mother was a force to deal with."

After staring at Officer Sealy, Vickey turned her eyes to the headstone. "News of Uncle Mike's death is a shock. Since my father's death, Mom is no longer passive. She has grown bold."

Officer Sealy nodded.

"First to arrive with a casserole, as usual. But instead of stepping into the background, she now steps up to schedule visitors and manage the bereaved households."

"I've noticed that," Officer Sealy agreed.

Vickey looked west to the Blue Ridge Mountains. "I thought it was a good thing, like Mom coming into her own." She shrugged. "Keeps her busy, I guess."

Officer Sealy appeared uncomfortable. "I'm sorry for your family's troubles," he said, and he walked solemnly to his car and drove away.

Vickey touched the Wade Martin inscription in farewell. She swayed as she turned and grabbed a nearby marker for support. "Sorry, Aunt Lucy," she said to the narrow gray headstone that steadied her. Lucy Grayson had pounded out her existence on Continental Automotive Systems' assembly line, only to spend her retirement volunteering daily at the Culpeper Humane Society. "I'm so sorry, Aunt Lucy," she said again, thinking of Lucy's downcast gray eyes and small, unexpressive mouth—eyes that shone and lips that curved in a smile only when around dogs.

Thickening clouds hid the sun, and Vickey felt the gravestones gathering portentously toward her. That sensation propelled her from the cemetery to her car, and she left to deal with the living.

— 🐾 —

Vickey collected King from Grandpa Lew's and drove to Barberry Street.

Once home, King went right to Alice. Her hunched shoulders and creased brow relaxed as she caressed King's fur.

"Liz is lying down. Come to the patio with me, and I'll brush King," Alice said.

Outside, Vickey's tension erupted. "What is this about? Someone killed Uncle Mike? What's Liz got to do with it? What do we tell Grandpa?"

Alice sat and began brushing King. "I've called cousin Myra. She's lead nurse for Papa's floor. She's posting a 'no visitors' sign on his room and ordering staff to say nothing about Mike."

Vickey perched on the edge of a lawn chair. "Were burglars in his townhouse? Did Liz see anything suspicious? Why did she rant about Uncle Mike's dinner choices?" She met her mother's eyes. "Why does Liz hate Uncle Mike? He's intelligent, if a bit conceited. Is it because Grandpa favored him over her? Did she make up that molestation stuff to needle Grandpa Lew?"

"She didn't."

"Didn't what?"

"Didn't make up the molestation incidents. It's the truth. Mike sexually molested her."

"What? How do you know?"

"Because he did it to me, too."

Vickey's throat constricted. She slid back in the chair, nauseated.

"What's more, that playhouse was an evil place, disregarded by those fifty-foot-tall maple trees." Alice stood and tossed aside the dog brush.

"Those indifferent trees didn't protect us. Gran Bess didn't take action. Grandpa Lew didn't believe us. Liz didn't set fire to the playhouse. I did."

Vickey's stunned brain drew new connections. Liz's rage. Alice's docility. Aunt Lucy's limited life. Was it possible that a girl who torched a playhouse could later stab a man to death?

Vickey already knew.

— 🐾 —

Vickey set aside her dread. Alice, Liz, and Mr. Cooper returned to the police department Friday afternoon for more questioning. Vickey took King to Grandpa Lew's house and then spent the rest of the day at the hospital, deflecting attention and ensuring no mention of Mike's death would permeate Grandpa Lew's subconscious. The doctor monitored his blood pressure and heart rate and described his altered state as benign rest after his Thursday night agitation.

Before dinner, Alice relieved Vickey from her post at Grandpa's bedside. Vickey went home to Barberry Street, where she and Liz catatonically readied the house for the next day's arrival of Vickey's brothers, summoned by Alice because of Grandpa Lew's condition and to help deal with law enforcement.

Liz excused herself to lie down.

Vickey heated a can of soup. On her fifth spoonful, Alice called, "Vickey, bring Liz to the hospital right away!"

"Oh, no! Mom, is Grandpa Lew—"

"No, it's good news. Grandpa Lew is awake and wants to see us." Alice's curt voice had a softness now.

At the hospital, Vickey led a war-torn Liz into Room 2207. Liz brightened at the sight of her father and said, "Papa! Good to see your eyes open."

"Yes, Liz, and these eyes are blessed to see you! My poor tiny girls. Come here. I've been waiting for you."

Vickey hung back while Liz and Alice moved into their father's seated embrace. She doubted Grandpa Lew noticed her in the room's dim corner.

"Girls, I'm sorry for how I failed you. Mike returned yesterday afternoon with Reverend Daniels and told me everything. He's got a lot to answer for, but he wanted my forgiveness. I guess he thought I was dyin' on him," Lew said.

He looked into the faces of his two surviving daughters. "You told me, Liz. Alice, yours and Lucy's actions said as much, too. I chose not to believe it. I am so sorry."

Strangled wheezing escaped Liz's mouth as she stared at her father. Tears tracked down Alice's face, but grim determination sealed her lips.

"He's asked for my help when he talks to you both," Lew continued. "Liz, he hoped dinner with you would bolster his courage. How did it go?"

Before Liz and Alice said anything to their father, Vickey quietly left the room and exited the hospital. Her nerves quivered and her stomach lurched, but she knew to drive the Old Rixeyville Road to Grandpa Lew's.

—— 🐦 ——

Vickey forgot the beauty of the golden maples as she parked at the house. She stumbled to the back door and let King out. He nuzzled her, and as his deep brown eyes met hers, she wiped away the droplets falling from her cheek onto his nose. She experienced the heartbreaking déjà vu of two generations of Grayson women wiping tears they'd shed from the consoling countenances of German shepherds. Vickey unleashed her tears and wept, her body shuddering with sobs.

King pressed his body to hers as she knelt with her arms around him. After a minute she stood, and King leaped away and ran to the old playhouse site. He dragged something from the dirt—the leather sheath of her father's skinning knife. Inches away lay the knife with what Vickey knew were Alice Martin's fingerprints and Mike Grayson's blood.

"King, leave it," she commanded. He dropped the leather case, sniffed the soiled knife, and backed away, a low thrum in his throat. *Officer Sealy won't find a weapon in any teacher's home, and he'll never find it here.*

Vickie willed her tears to stop as she headed for the back door. King followed. Once inside, Vickey opened the pine cabinet and unsheathed one of her grandfather's hunting knives. She tossed the leather to King, left the knife in the cabinet, and grabbed a swatch from the rag bin.

Vickey left King happily chewing inside the house and made her way to the blighted area by the maples. She gathered the abandoned sheath and knife with the cloth, scuffed the sterile dirt with her shoes to smooth it, and then walked past the Grayson property line into Pritchard's woods.

Vickey rolled a log to a sweet gum tree and stood on it to reach a hollow where a thick branch had long ago separated from the trunk. She dropped the knife, along with its case and the rag, in the beckoning hole of the tree. She rolled the log away from the tree and scattered leaves to hide the drag marks.

Her heart raced as she left Pritchard's woods and re-entered her grandfather's yard. Satisfied with her disposal of the knife, Vickey prayed the playhouse avenger discarded last night's bloody clothing as efficiently.

THE HALLOWEEN OPEN

By Max Jason Peterson

THE DENBIGH FENCING CLUB had never been so proud. Fencers from around the region crowded into the American Legion building in Newport News for the Halloween Open. The line for on-site registration snaked into the fencing lanes. Once the tournament opened, fencers between bouts waited outside in the mild Virginia fall under the bright blue October sky.

The annual event was hosted by a different club in the Eastern Virginia division each year. Denbigh had put its distinctive stamp on the tournament by calling for painted fencing masks. Not everyone allowed them, but some clubs had looser rules. The *fleur-de-lys*, flaming skulls, and owls staring back from the black mesh masks gave extra menace to flashing steel.

But what made this Saturday particularly memorable was the club's two top fencers heading into direct elimination for men's foil. Keith Semper and Jerry Greenfield were ranked fifth and seventh out of thirty-eight seats. The club's enthusiasm had attracted the attention of local college scouts. Someone might earn a rare and coveted fencing scholarship.

Tall even when he slouched, his tight black curls cupping his head like a helmet, Keith sat in the front row of the small viewing rink, watching the fencers finish their pools. Beside him sat Marie Dover, petite even for seventeen, with rows of ornamented braids on either side of her heart-shaped, fawn face.

On his lap, Keith held the fencing mask that Marie brought that morning. He grinned at the snarling wolf's head painted on the mask's black wire mesh. Saliva dripped from its fangs.

"It's fabulous, Marie. You really are the best!"

"I stayed up late every night this week to finish it. I'm blowing off my homework for you, Keith."

"Nah, you don't want to do that. You need those grades to get into art school. You're going to be great."

"Really?" Marie glowed.

"You're going to make it," he said, his brown eyes serious.

"With or without you, right?" she said lightly.

"I need to talk to you about that." A worry line creased his forehead. "But the direct eliminations are starting. I need to watch these guys."

Coach Linda Rodriguez gave pointers to Helen Rheingold, a blonde whose pink cheeks glowed as she awaited her next bout in the pool. Coach kept an eye on all her fencers, as much as she could with ten on the strip today. A small, intense woman, Linda had been an Olympic alternate before her knee injury. Her eyes rested on Keith, holding his mask on his lap, his free arm around Marie's shoulders, a strange, soft bewilderment on his face.

Under the windows, Jerry Greenfield worked on the club's backup blades. These loaners always had a kink to work out, a nick to sand smooth, an electrical line to dig out and repair. Red-haired, his pasty face marred by acne, Jerry helped Coach with everything he could to pay for club dues and, more rarely, new equipment. He spent a lot of time helping other fencers, even at the cost of his own practice time.

Keith turned and flashed Jerry a troubled look over Marie's head. Jerry set the weapon in its bag.

"Nice helm," Jerry said. "Marie paint that for you?"

"Yeah. Pretty fierce, isn't he?"

"That snarl is so you, man," Jerry joked.

Muffled against Keith's chest, Marie said, "He wants to go to Harvard."

"Really? That's great!"

Marie's eyes were red and puffy. It might have been the fumes Jerry smelled from the painted mask. "It's too far," she moaned.

"It's only four years, right?" Jerry said. Keith said nothing.

"If anyone in Virginia offers him a scholarship, I want him to take it. I don't care what school I go to. I can make art anywhere." Turning to Keith, she pleaded, "We could live in married student housing."

"We'll see, Marie," Keith said. He handed the mask to Jerry and stood, pulling Marie's arms from his neck. He walked to where the seating was posted on the wall, studying it as if he hadn't already memorized his bout order and opponents' names.

Jerry turned the mask so the wolf's eyes blazed up at him. The strong smell made him uneasy. "Marie, you had a window open, right? I mean, this isn't exactly good for you, what with your, um, condition."

"Yeah, Jer, like that's what I'm even worrying about right now."

"Well, maybe you should be. It doesn't look like Keith's going to," he blurted.

She sighed and looked down. "Don't blame Keith. It's complicated."

Jerry put a hand on her shoulder. "Never mind. You know I'll always stand by you, right? No matter what."

She nodded. But when she looked up, her eyes went to Keith, tall in his fencer's whites, frowning, arms crossed on his chest as he watched Helen struggle through her bout. When she won, he walked over to meet her, standing on the sidelines while she secured her weapon, adjusted her straps, and stretched. Soon they were laughing together. She handed him a water from her pack.

With the swift, five-touch bouts, the women's second pool finished quickly, though using just one strip. Coach and the referees prepped three lanes for men's foil direct eliminations, while saber continued in the far corner. Fencers slipped carefully between the lanes, heading for the restrooms or the equipment bags heaped among the folding chairs at the back. With the first two seats excused from the opening round of competition, Keith sipped a homemade smoothie from his travel mug. Then he donned his wolf mask and took the second lane.

Coach watched her stars. Jerry did fine, holding his own with the spirit and heart he put into everything. But Keith didn't seem up to his usual form. He defeated his opponent in the direct round, but when he came off the strip and pulled off his mask, his face ran with sweat and his brown skin had a bluish tinge. His exhaustion might be due to his ongoing, intense discussion with Marie. But then Keith held her hand to his heart, and Marie looked calmer. Since Marie was running his water, and only one person was authorized to interact with the fencer on breaks, Coach decided not to interfere. He didn't need extra pressure disrupting his focus.

Anyway, there wasn't much time left. He and Jerry beat the odds. The others stood aside to watch as Linda's two top fencers went after one another for the only *A* ranking that would be awarded that day.

At the break after the first three minutes, Keith pulled off his mask even before retreating to his end of the lane. He gasped like an overextended swimmer breaking the surface. Turning away, Keith hunched over his inhaler, hiding it in cupped palms. The opponents were supposed to retreat to their corners, not fraternize, but Jerry asked, "You okay, man? Do you need a time out?"

Keith shook his head vigorously, his face creased with pain. Jerry glanced quickly toward Coach, who watched but didn't step in.

"Look, I've got a spare mask in my bag. Maybe you ought to trade. That thing hasn't had enough time to air out."

Keith wheezed. "Marie stayed up all night painting it."

"Forget about that, man. She'll understand."

But Keith shook his head again, their break half gone. Jerry shrugged and returned to his end of the strip, draining his water bottle but watching Keith.

———— 🐱 ————

During the next period, Keith seemed to be conserving his energy. By the second rest period, Keith still led, 10-9 out of the fifteen touches needed for victory.

In the final period, Keith came back with a vengeance. Jerry rallied in response to his friend's aggression—one's energy feeding the other, each striving to top him, like always. They stood at game point together, saluting each other as the referee said, "Good luck."

The end came, swift and simple—one lunge.

Jerry's foil landed over Keith's heart.

Keith fell.

The referee called the touch and the end of the match. Keith didn't stir.

Jerry unhitched the cable and knelt by Keith's side. He worked the wolf mask off. Coach and Marie ran up. The referee instructed everyone else to keep back.

"He's not breathing," Jerry said.

Marie sobbed, clutching Keith's ungloved left hand. Coach checked his pulse and started CPR. The paramedics arrived with oxygen and took Keith to the hospital.

— 🧸 —

Coach Linda Rodriguez kept her head. While the emergency team worked, she examined Keith's equipment. There was no break in lame, padded jacket, or underarm plastron. Like all electric foils, the tip of Jerry's weapon had no sharp point, only a button to trigger the scorebox. Jerry's tap above the heart hadn't even scratched Keith's plastic chest protector.

At the hospital, Keith's mother, Susan, and stepdad, Louis, clung to one another until a nurse said, "Family only." The swinging door provided Linda's last glimpse of the young man she'd trained for eleven years.

Keith died that night without a single mark more serious than a bruise.

Afterward, Linda didn't go to her own place in the Waypoint at Uptown townhouses on Lucas Creek Road. She headed straight next door.

Detective Isadore Schwartz answered her knock, still wearing the suit and topcoat that served as his plainclothes uniform, his russet curls framing his kind olive face.

"Linda? I saw the news."

She told him what she knew. Dor placed some quick calls. She spent the night curled into him, hanging on as if he were the only thing that made sense. She'd gone through enough in her thirty-five years, but the loss of one of her kids was a tragedy she couldn't fathom. Still haunting her soul, she could feel the press of her husband's hand on hers before ICE took him away. His desperate parents, fleeing El Salvador with their infant, paid dearly for his forged US birth certificate. Toño, top of his class, won a coveted government position as a civil engineer. The background check brought ICE. He'd been just as surprised as she was. In the detention camp, which denied both visitors and timely medical care, Toño died from a ruptured appendix.

Dor kept her up to speed with the routine investigation.

"Right now, the cause of death is a fatal asthma attack. The mask had contact with a mild detergent, an ammonia-based cleaner, and various paints and fixatives, but it's not clear if the odor caused the attack. Asthma can be induced by exercise. Without a reasonable suspicion of foul play, the city won't spring for an autopsy. But Keith's parents could."

Linda hated suspecting her fencers. But Jerry had been Keith's chief rival, and Helen had a crush on Keith and might have been jealous of Marie. With Dor, she talked to them, trading fond memories of Keith. They cried together. Linda put her arms around the kids she'd trained.

Linda and Dor walked to second court, the townhomes alternating between brick and siding. They stopped at a wide end unit near the little pool.

Susan Fournier took Linda's tawny hands in her warm, sepia fingers. "My boy was a fighter, and he died doing what he loved. Thank you so much for helping him all these years. You brought real joy and purpose to his life after his father died."

Louis Fournier sat in an armchair, nodding his smooth umber head in agreement.

"Keith and his stepfather were buddies," Susan said. "Louis always hoped Keith would run the hardware store after him. He loved Keith like a son."

"I wanted to adopt that boy. But I understood when he said no. He loved me, he called me Pop, but he didn't want to replace the dad he lost."

"Were you disappointed when Keith planned to go away to college?" Dor asked.

"Who'd be disappointed that his kid's going to college?" Louis huffed. "And who's to say he wouldn't get a business degree and come back to run the place?"

"He had a good shot at a fencing scholarship. He wanted to try for the Olympics. But he worried about your approval," Linda said.

"He didn't need a scholarship. We'd have paid for college," Susan said. Louis looked pained.

Dor said, "What about Marie? Did Keith mention wanting to start a family?"

Susan shook her head.

"At your hardware store, did Keith have any problem with fumes from paint or wood-finishing products?"

"Keith didn't react well to polyurethane," Susan said. "What's this about? The way the mask smells? Did you ask Marie what she used to seal her painting?"

"We'll speak to Marie," Dor said. "Would you consider requesting an autopsy?"

Susan looked queasy, pressing her hand to her heart. "Oh, I don't think I could do that. Cut my boy open? I don't think so."

"But Ms. Fournier," Linda pleaded. "Keith was so young . . . in such good health. If he was stolen from us, we need to know why."

Louis put his head in his hands and moaned. Susan patted his back, then sat on the chair's arm and rubbed his shoulders. He leaned into her, slipping an arm around her waist.

"If you don't mind, Ms. Fournier, what caused your first husband's death?" Dor asked.

"They called it heart failure. But they always say that, don't they? He was only forty-four. But we didn't have the money to find out the truth. And what did it matter? He was already dead." She covered her face with her hands. Louis drew her into his bulk, rocking her and murmuring, "They're together now."

Linda felt humbled in the face of their love, their grief. "I'm so very sorry. I loved Keith," she whispered. She hugged Keith's mother quickly, then bent down and patted his stepfather's back. Louis reached up and hugged her awkwardly.

—— 🎎 ——

Linda and Dor crossed into third court and approached a double stoop, where two doors shared brick steps. They knocked at the door with a haunted house artistically scratched into the black paint. Marie's mother, Satoko Dover, called up the stairs for Marie.

The girl came down, her eyes tired and sad. The same purple blouse and hot pink skirt she'd worn yesterday were wrinkled.

Marie flopped into the black leather armchair by the front windows, under which a small table showed family portraits: a young girl laughing between black-haired Satoko's golden smile and a tall, lean army lieutenant whose brown hand rested protectively on her shoulder.

With an apology, Satoko left the room to complete needed tasks before work.

"You did an amazing job on Keith's mask," Linda said. "I've never seen that level of realism on black mesh."

"I treated it first, so the metal would hold the paint."

Dor asked Marie about the sealant, paint, and primer. "Those masks get ripe, especially the bibs. Did you need to wipe it down with chemicals?" Linda asked.

"Keith keeps all his stuff super clean. He'd never give me his mask smelling like that."

"It did have a strong odor."

"Because the sealant just went on! I wanted time to air it out, but Keith said he needed it for the Halloween Open."

Dor held up his hands. "We're not accusing you."

"Just because I'm an artist doesn't mean I have my head in the clouds," she said, eyes blazing. "Keith has some rivals in your club, and they have access to his equipment. Ned's always complaining about how he can't get higher than third seat because of Keith and Jerry. He needs a scholarship, but no one's going to look at him till Keith leaves for college, and then it'll be too late." Tears spilled down her cheeks. She lifted her chin as if they weren't there.

"You're right, Marie. Please help us," Linda said. "We don't actually know *what* happened to Keith—or why. Were you with Keith the whole time?"

"Yeah. A bunch of us went to Keith's house that morning. We were excited to show off the masks. I brought the wolf, and Jerry and Helen showed up. Keith's mom really admired my painting. After she left for work, Keith's pop dropped us off at the tournament." She drew a shaky breath. "Ms. Fournier wouldn't let me go with them to the hospital. I ended up walking home."

"I'm sorry," Linda said. "I should have asked you to ride with me."

Marie shrugged. "You had other things on your mind."

"What did he eat or drink? I saw Helen give him some water."

"Helen's got a crush on him, but they're buddies," Marie said. "And Keith didn't want to get weighed down with food or take his mind off his game. He only had that smoothie he brought from home. His mom makes them special. I think he's lactose intolerant. He never touches anything with cow's milk. It's been like that since he was little." She put a hand over her mouth. On her finger, something sparkled as brightly as her tears.

Linda said quietly, "Is that ring from Keith? I didn't know he could afford diamonds."

Marie flushed. "He gave it to me right before that last match. It's his mom's first engagement ring. He said his father would want me to have it."

"So you and Keith were getting married?"

Marie freed the leg she'd been sitting on. "I would have done anything for Keith. He wanted to go to school, so I'd probably have worked to support us. Between that and our baby, my art would be on hold, except for finger painting. I loved Keith, but it made me angry. Now that he's gone, I don't know what to do. The baby is part of Keith. Maybe it's my duty to sacrifice everything for him. But what about me?"

Marie looked trapped. Before Linda could say anything, Satoko rounded the corner from the dining room.

"A girl is supposed to have a chance in America! She loves art like Keith loved fencing. Just because she's a girl, she shouldn't have to give up her dreams. She wins contests. She should be the one with a scholarship!"

Linda rose, holding up apologetic hands. "You're absolutely right. As his coach, naturally I rooted for Keith. But as a woman, I should never have taken Marie's dreams lightly."

Marie stood up straight, as if strengthened by her mother's defense. Though sad, her dark brown eyes stayed steady as she said, "The world has gone crazy. Someone like Keith can't just die like that."

For her day job, Linda worked in the hospital records department. She spent Monday's lunch in the medical library, following up a hunch. What if Keith didn't just have lactose intolerance, but a milk allergy? Asthma, respiratory allergies, and food allergies often went together. Teens were at greatest risk for death from food-triggered anaphylactic shock. In some cases, the onset occurred thirty minutes to an hour or longer after ingestion. Many children with a milk allergy outgrow it, but some do not. The initial symptoms could be mistaken for milk intolerance.

Linda called Dor. "What if there was dairy yogurt in that smoothie? Some soy yogurts taste as rich and creamy as the real thing. He trusted his mom's smoothies, and his mind was on the bouts, and Marie."

Dor promised to follow up with the attending physician.

"It can be difficult to impossible to distinguish between asthma and anaphylaxis, even when the patient recovers," Linda warned "But his dad's death might be another clue. He was young for a heart attack. Anaphylaxis can stop the heart, and it runs in families."

"Between all that and Keith's age, I can get an autopsy. He died quickly enough they may be able to analyze his stomach contents." He shared his own findings. "Did you know Keith worked twenty hours a week at the hardware store without being paid? He's on the books as a volunteer."

"I thought the business was doing fine."

"It stays afloat partly due to family contributions. That probably *is* doing well for a local business competing with Lowe's and Home Depot. It helped support the family. But to pay for college, they'd have to sell the business. Keith had a lot riding on those scholarships."

"So did his stepdad."

"Even more than you'd think. Keith's grandfather on his dad's side founded the store, and he willed it to Keith," Dor said. "A minor can't legally own property, so his mother is estate custodian. She appointed Louis to manage the store on Keith's behalf. Keith would have turned eighteen on March 21, plenty of time to sell it for college. Then there's the death and disability insurance on Keith."

"I helped set that up. My own coach drummed into me how important it was, with scholarships and sponsorships all resting on your health."

"The policy's a large one, and his mother is the sole beneficiary. But Keith willed the store to Marie."

— 🐱 —

On Halloween, puffy pumpkins dangled from the vines of their mother's arms. Tiny Catwomen and Batmen rode trikes and wagons. Pumpkins burned on townhouse stoops where adults sat with spooky soundtracks and cauldrons of treats.

Susan wore a purple cape over a black T-shirt with the bat symbol. She looked tired beyond belief. "Keith *adored* Halloween. We would have handed out candy together. I'm doing this for him."

She settled them in the living room. "Are you going to release my boy's body, Detective Schwartz? I need to get him decently buried."

"I'm doing what I can, Ms. Fournier," Dor said.

"Did you know Keith gave Marie your first engagement ring?" Linda asked.

"His father's ring?" A smile battled the heavy lines of grief. "Well, isn't that something." Her eyes clouded. "I told him Marie was just distracting him from his studies."

Louis broke in. "Marie was pregnant."

"And you didn't tell me?"

"I wanted to be a father to him. He asked for advice, then pleaded with me to keep quiet till he was ready." Louis bowed his head. "Everyone thought he'd go to college, but that boy was conflicted. He seriously considered staying home, starting a family. He would have worked in the shop with me. When I retired, he'd take over. That store is the work of generations. You don't just give that up." He took Susan's hand. "Now Marie can move in with us. We can help raise our grandchild."

Dor asked Susan, "Marie says Keith never ate dairy?"

"That's right. It bothered him when he was little. I took him to the doctor. He said Keith was probably lactose intolerant.

Better safe than sorry. I switched to soy."

"Did anyone else know he didn't drink cow's milk?"

"I'm not sure, but it wasn't an issue. Keith was careful."

"Did you make Keith a smoothie for the Halloween Open?"

Susan looked bewildered. "Yes. I always make those, to give him a boost when he's competing. I had to work that morning, so I left it in the fridge."

"What were the ingredients?"

"Soy yogurt is the base. Let's see, that day it was blueberries—"

"The autopsy found dairy yogurt in his stomach."

Susan looked at him blankly. "No, no, I put in soy. I'm certain I—" She pressed a hand to her heart. Silent tears streamed down her face. Then Susan said, "Louis, how could you?"

"What are you talking about? Don't look at me like that, honey."

She raised her voice. "When I saw that dairy yogurt in the trash, I had a terrible feeling, but I *just couldn't believe it*. You still like your dairy, so I told myself it didn't matter. But you did it. *You killed my baby!*"

"No! I only wanted to stop him from going away. It was just a terrible accident. You have to believe me. All I wanted to do was slow him down. If he won that scholarship, he'd be gone. You said milk makes him sick, so I thought—I just made myself a smoothie, and switched it with his. I never meant to kill him. I loved Keith like my own son!"

A GUEST AT THE LAND HOUSE

BY JUDITH FOWLER

FROM THE AGE OF nine, John had taken orders from the Land family's cook. Mr. Land brought the boy to Bessie to help her in the kitchen, and she had run the child ragged in the years since. The Land's plantation house and Bessie's kitchen had become John's world, replacing the one he'd known where his mother had died of fever, and they both worked the fields.

At sixteen, his hand dwarfed the bone-handled knife used to clip herbs from the kitchen garden. Most of its fragrant plants, grown from seeds John had planted, were ordered by his master's wife from an English catalogue.

It was because of the mistress that he found himself in the garden at this hour. He'd just been handed his dinner service clothes by Bessie when Mrs. Land entered the kitchen and asked them to move up their baking day. The lady of the house wanted her son Francis Jr.'s guest, Mr. Connelly, to taste Bessie's herb bread.

John had retrieved his knife and a basket for the herbs while Bessie fumed. "She got us making dough all night by candlelight, if we want anything to rise by morning. Sourdough culture don't stretch because she tells it to," Bessie said. "That spoiled son of hers wants it, more like. She aiming to kill two birds with one bread," she said as she shoved John out the kitchen door.

The news sat poorly with him, too. He had the barn barrel to finish. Instead he'd spend tomorrow sitting in front of the beehive oven, tossing in handfuls of cornmeal to test the heat.

He'd felt proud of himself that morning, though.

"How you figured out one tool from the other, I don't

know," his master had said when John showed him how he had hammered hoop iron and riveted it securely to the barn barrel where its old wood binding had cracked.

"Those cooper's tools haven't been used since we grew tobacco here," the master told him. "My ancestors had two hundred slaves planting, drying, and making barrels for shipping the leaves to England."

In John's lifetime, he'd never seen more than twenty people in the wheat fields or working on the brick house.

"I could mill my grain locally if you made barrels, John," the master said. "I'd save some of that profit I'm losing now by sending the grain to Richmond to be milled and sold."

John's thoughts had raced all day about learning a trade. He'd already fixed leaks in some casks the master let him work on for a neighbor's family. The man threw him two coins that the master let John keep. He put the coins in a flattened tin from the pantry, so that it fit in his pants pocket. He touched his pocket whenever emptying chamber pots made him lose hope.

He had cut enough herbs to make Bessie happy. John placed the little knife in the basket and stood to stretch.

The kitchen garden lay near a brick path. On the path stood Mr. Connelly, the young gentleman visiting Francis Jr.

"Evening, sir." John twisted the sleeve of his shirt and looked down at his feet.

Each night of his visit, Mr. Connelly called for his glass to be refilled so often that John looked to his master for permission before he poured the wine out. Each time, the master nodded and looked away from the drunken guest at his table.

If Mr. Land launched into his favorite story about soil cultivation, the younger men stifled yawns. Francis Jr. tried to change the subject with a joke, but as soon as Mr. Land's daughters began giggling, the master excused himself and went off to the parlor to look at his Fry-Jefferson Map. The more Mr. Connelly drank, the louder he bragged about the idle week the two friends had spent fox hunting and gambling.

"Come look at the map, John," the master said one evening. "I rode over those mountains at your age."

John asked him to point to where Virginia became Maryland.

In Maryland, slaves had bought their freedom. John planned to run. Someday.

Right now, though, Mr. Connelly pointed a riding crop at him. "What's that you're carrying, boy?"

"Just herbs, sir," John said, and stomped down loose soil from his boots. He closed the gate to keep out deer and rabbits and waited for Mr. Connelly to let him pass so he could go in the house.

"I hear you're good with your hands," Mr. Connelly said.

"Yes, sir."

"It's John, isn't it?"

"Yes, sir."

"Well, John, I need your help," Mr. Connelly said.

The young master had treated John badly in front of Jacob Connelly. John chose words that couldn't be used against him. "No disrespect, Mr. Connelly. Cook be waiting on these. Master will surely let me help you in the morning, sir."

The young man moved toward John, grabbing the basket. Herbs spilled out when he set the basket on the back stoop. "Dinner's not for a while. Follow me."

With that, the guest marched off.

As John passed the stoop, he looked for the knife in the basket but didn't see it. He followed Mr. Connelly into the barn.

The straw on the dirt floor made the place humid. Connelly loosened the cravat he wore at his neck. "It's warm in here."

Then he pointed to his belt. "Undo this, boy."

John helped men off with their boots all the time. Nothing else.

"Don't be scared." Mr. Connelly took a step toward him. "Haven't you had carnal relations by now?"

The pretty shoulders of a field slave named Margarite came to John's mind.

Mr. Connelly touched John's rope belt with his crop.

"Sir, I—"

"I saw you watching me at dinner."

The man's face so close, his breath smelling of spirits, made John's thoughts go red. "Francis Jr. told you to do this, sir?"

Mr. Connelly put his hand on John's cheek.

The man leaned in to kiss him. John backed up so far it

knocked the bow saw off the wall. He bent to pick it up where it fell on the straw.

Mr. Connelly's riding crop fell next to it.

John looked up.

The white man had Bessie's knife raised.

John had sharpened that blade himself. He shouted for help. The man stabbed him in the throat.

John fell. He spit blood when he tried to rise and then lay motionless. A barrel rested on its side a few feet away. Connelly found a horse blanket and rolled John onto it.

A woman called John's name. Connelly pulled out the knife. The body was light enough to lift the short distance to the barrel. He pushed it inside as far as it would go.

He'd return when everyone was asleep and bury him. Placing a shovel behind the barn door, Connelly picked up his crop and the knife. The bloody straw could be freshened later.

Using the house's side entrance, he snuck up the stairs to change for dinner.

—— 👧 ——

"Fresh marjoram," Mrs. Land said. "Doesn't supper smell good?"

The aroma of collards and pork roast wafting out of the dining room had her nearly faint with hunger. But she made her family wait until Mr. Connelly joined them. When he did, he smelled of spirits.

And there was more confusion as John couldn't be found.

Bessie told Mrs. Land how she found her herb basket without her knife. Mrs. Land ordered her to calm down. She suspected Bessie knew more than she said. In any case, baking day would be put off until someone was found to mind the oven.

Mrs. Land wasn't sorry John had fled. She never approved of bringing him into the house, resembling her husband the way he did. If Mr. Land fathered John, he'd never admitted it to her.

It didn't impress her that Reverend Walkes baptized John at the same time as her son Francis. Heredity laws kept John in his place. And her husband wasn't foolish enough to consider manumission.

Runaway laws existed, though. Her husband would not be eager to punish what the law called an "obstinate Negro." But Francis Jr. stood to inherit John. She'd caught her son often enough at dinner, daggers in his eyes as he watched the slave carve their meat.

She worried about her son's temper.

Over dinner, Francis Jr. showed off for his guest. "By Virginia statute, Father won't be charged if he overcorrects John and kills his own property."

"That's enough, Francis," her husband snapped.

Jacob Connelly barely spoke. Maybe he wasn't suitable, after all. Life in the plantation house would be more peaceful if John never turned up. And the bile in Francis Jr.'s nature might come in handy in a courtroom, once he passed the bar.

The year 2020 found Jenine Walker guiding tours through the Francis Land House. Her appreciation for what the house represented had deepened in the three years she'd worked there.

The Land family's plantation paralleled the history of the earliest enslaved African people to arrive in Virginia four hundred years earlier. A 1654 land grant and the purchase of hundreds of enslaved laborers allowed the first Francis Land to develop a thriving tobacco industry. The family's accumulated wealth enabled a later heir, also named Francis, to build the 1804 house now maintained by the City of Virginia Beach.

Antiques enlivened the rooms of the home built in the Georgian-style so popular in the late 1700s and early 1800s. Jenine demonstrated clever inventions like the rope bed and a mending table with a hiding place for writing materials. In the formal dining room, simulated molded jellies and main courses on elegant china looked good enough to eat.

She'd grown to appreciate the famed Fry-Jefferson topology map from 1753, a copy of which hung in the Land House foyer. Thomas Jefferson's father had fought off wild animals to accurately survey and delineate Virginia's river systems and mountains.

The history of the house after it was sold by the last Land heir included other owners and, in the 1950s, Rose Hall had been a dress shop for women. When the city brought the house and its seven remaining acres under its protection, they made a walk by the river that guests could take after touring the house. Jenine had just suggested the walk to her two o'clock tour group when she heard something odd.

A Public Works bulldozer dredging silt from a stream beyond the parking lot had fallen silent. Usually, it groaned on until four o'clock. Jenine peeked out the parlor window. The dredging crew stood together on the bank of the stream, looking down.

Tom Barrett and his dad were on that job. Curiosity gave her an excuse to say hello to them. In a few minutes, her tour would end outdoors by the kitchen garden.

— 🎎 —

Francis Land stared out his parlor window. Everything but the sky belonged to him.

He'd have to report John as lost property. The magistrate who rode through the county seat had to be given a petition of grievance.

John must have run for Maryland. His only documentation was a certificate of baptism.

Mr. Land's cousin, John's father, had been run out of Princess Anne County by debt collectors. After Mr. Land heard about John's mother's death, he had prayed for guidance. Once he brought the boy to the house, he never regretted his decision.

His son's guest retired early, stumbling up the stairs after saying goodnight. The girls lacked restraint around Jacob Connelly, whose propensity for drink and gambling reminded Mr. Land of his ne'er-do-well cousin. Any hint of a marriage proposal would be discouraged, even over his wife's objections.

John's flight was a blow to Mr. Land. Just that morning they talked about the cooper's tools and shipping grain directly from here. The only other soul in the house who felt pained was old Bessie. The cook's inconsolable face—tears streaming down, herb basket in her shaking hands—told him she was as shocked as he was by John's action.

Francis Jr., on the other hand, made a joke of it at dinner.

With a bow to his wife, Mr. Land expressed his wish to take the river air before going to bed.

There were many days he wished he could leave the plantation behind. Duty compelled him to hold it for the next generation. Walking past the barn, he felt droplets hit his collar. The sky warned of a cloudburst, the type seen so often in Virginia. How far could John get, with rain coming, armed with nothing but Bessie's knife and a hope of reaching the border? He counted on John to keep watch with him over the changing landscape and to take care of things that needed fixing, like that water barrel.

Mr. Land ducked into the barn to wait out the sudden shower.

— 🐾 —

Jenine thanked her guests and walked over to where the dredging crew stood on the bank. She caught Tom's eye. At orientation three years ago, Tom had talked about his fiancée. Three years later, no ring. When he wasn't dredging, he volunteered with the city's ambulance service.

"We've never dredged up something like this," he said.

Muddy bones and half a skull lay dripping water on the bank.

"We pulled these bones out from that massive root bulb," Tom said. "There are other rib bones still in there, and something metal."

She moved closer to get a better look, but slipped on mud. Tom grabbed her arm.

"Better stay back, Jeannie," Tom said.

She felt her face redden. He always mispronounced her name. She hadn't cared.

"The bulldozer was working its way around a culvert when its teeth got stuck," Mr. Barrett said. "Somehow that body got raised into the air and trapped within the root system. Don't ask me how."

"I read that skulls popped out of the sandy banks of the Thames in England, when the water level changed drastically," Jenine said. The men seemed interested, so she continued. "And in Ireland, where the wet climate and erosion challenges are like ours, medieval skeletons barely covered by stones keep showing up."

Tom's father nodded. "I have an army buddy who works construction in Maryland, and he found a whole cemetery under the foundations of a house. That old footbridge under the sluice acted like a coffin. Most of our crews pulled up more than silt on these projects."

A member of the crew spoke up. "Maybe the guy died sitting under the tree."

"He was buried near it, that's for sure. Somehow the tree grew around his bones," Jenine said. "I wonder if he's related to the Land family?"

"If he was," Tom said, "wouldn't they have given him a decent burial?"

"Maybe he was enslaved." Jenine accepted Tom's hand to steady her while she bent low to get another look at their find.

"We're still on the clock, fellas." Tom's father looked at his team. "Tom can handle this. He's used to carting people around in ambulances."

Jenine watched Tom's face, as did the crew.

"I deal with people in the twenty-first century," Tom said.

"We can't leave him here and go back to work," one of the men said. "It's not right."

"How about this?" Jenine asked. "I'll ask my boss which city department I need to notify. Tom's influence with 9-1-1 will get police and a medical examiner here faster. "

As Jenine turned to go, Tom mouthed, "Thank you," and dialed his phone.

Her calls made, and the day's paperwork filed, Jenine retrieved her tour folder from under a sofa cushion in the parlor. Something tugged at her thoughts. She had a copy of the 1810 census because of its relevance to the 1804 house. Comparing it with an earlier census might reveal a name not on the later one. The metal Tom mentioned might be a clue to the age of the bones.

The office manager wanted to lock up. Jenine took her folder with her so she could write up the discovery of the bones to send to her supervisor in the morning.

Tom ran toward her in the parking lot. His crew had left, the area near the sluice was circled with crime-scene tape, and a forensic team had taken the remains.

"What a day, huh?" Tom said. "I'm not on call tonight. Want to catch an early dinner?"

"I think my cat can wait another hour. Where shall we eat?"

She wasn't dressed for a Town Center bistro, and neither was Tom.

"There's a good Mexican restaurant across the boulevard. Meet me there?"

Jenine's car idled at a red light on the boulevard. First date jitters took a back seat to the other event of the day. They had literally dredged up someone from the past. Today, the plantation below the asphalt had been as real as the late afternoon traffic she was navigating right now. A mile away, sleek high-rises and posh stores had taken root where there had once been tobacco fields.

As if offering a bridge to her two visions, a flock of gulls cawed and scattered when she parked in front of the restaurant.

Jenine opened the restaurant's large glass door. Smells of peppers and onions stirred her appetite. Glancing around the restaurant, she spotted Tom, who had already started on the chips and guacamole.

He handed her his phone. He'd taken pictures of the bones and the thin metal can.

"Look at that one, Jenine. They found coins in the rusted can. I asked if I could show one to you, since you're the historian. No luck. Probably thought I'd try to pay for your dinner with it."

He got her name right.

— 🎎 —

Mr. Land waited in the barn until the cloudburst ended.

The barrel John had worked on still lay on its side on the straw. He might as well pull it upright. John wouldn't be back to work on it tomorrow, if ever.

It was heavy. Someone had stuffed a blanket inside it. He tugged at it. Something was inside.

John.

So, Francis Jr. had finally taken revenge on John. That must have been why he quoted law at dinner about killing property.

Mr. Land could say he killed the slave himself. He could say John attacked his son, and he stepped in to save Francis Jr.

The slave's throat was cut. *Bessie's knife.*

He had blamed himself for forcing his son to live with John like a rival. Maybe Francis Jr. believed John to be his brother. Mr. Land had felt charitable all these years when he ought to have told his son the truth.

He couldn't find the shovel, but he found a pick that would do. He got the blanketed body into a haycart, then stood the barrel upright. He pushed the cart through the wet dark night until he reached the pine trees by the water. Everyone believed John had run away. He would wait until Francis spoke to him. No one else had to know his son was a murderer.

— 🎭 —

Jacob Connelly put up his hand to block the sun that glared in his eyes. His head throbbed. He must have passed out from drink when he went to bed.

The body.

Had he slept all night?

He heard the family talking down in the dining room.

Did I go back and bury the body? Connelly couldn't remember.

His hands were clean; probably he'd washed them after burying the body.

He wore the clothes he'd worn at dinner. Under his pillow was the knife.

Connelly held his boots so no one would hear him going down the back stairs.

He ran to the barn.

The barrel was upright. It was empty.

So, he had buried the body.

But the shovel was still behind the door.

Had someone found the body or had he, in his fright, mistaken John's wounding for death? If the slave had revived, did he reach the house? If he told them what happened, how could he speak?

The blanket was gone. A slave from the quarters might have found him. Or he'd staggered out and lay right now on the grass, dead.

Should he say anything when he went back in the house?

He could not face any of it. He saddled his ride and stopped for nothing except to water his horse until he arrived home at dusk and saw his mother at the front door.

In late spring, Mrs. Connelly wrote to Mrs. Land. She asked if she might trouble the family with a two-day visit.

From the moment her carriage crossed the footbridge, she tried to rise to the occasion for her hostess's sake. The ladies asked why her son left so suddenly without saying goodbye. They guessed he had quarreled with their brother. Once Mrs. Connelly told them Jacob had ridden north to practice law and might never return, they stopped trying to draw her out.

Mr. Land showed her his Fry-Jefferson Map. She teared up, thinking of Jacob on his travels. Mr. Land offered her his handkerchief and spoke of a runaway slave. No one accused her son of anything. Perhaps, somehow, the slave had lived and then escaped. Jacob couldn't tell her for certain what had happened to the man whose blood was on that knife.

On the day she took leave of the Land family, Mrs. Connelly said she wished to take a walk before her long carriage ride home. She carried her bonnet and concealed a metal box beneath it.

Beyond the footbridge, she found a patch of ivy under the pines. With the toe of her slipper, she made a hole in the soft dirt large enough for the box. She covered it with stones.

Whatever happened next, she hoped God would forgive her. "Lord, let his letters bring mercy, if not peace."

In his latest letter, her son sounded like a madman. Since swearing off drink, he believed he was trailed by a phantom. He had forged papers to help free a Negro woman. Mrs. Connelly would leave the situation in God's hands. If He desired the box to be found right away, let it be found. She'd placed Jacob's letters in it, plus the little knife with the blood dried on it. These would explain everything after she was gone.

Jenine waved at Tom when she saw him the next morning. Dinner had been fun. Writing until midnight had left her bleary-eyed. In five minutes, she'd attach her report to an email, enhanced by the photos Tom sent to her phone, now that he had her number.

She hoped she could stay awake for her tours.

Tom ran over to her car. "You'll never believe this, Jenine," he said, smiling broadly.

"What?" Jenine smiled through a yawn. "Another body?"

"I told them not to move it, but to wait for you."

"You mean there *is* another body?"

Tom laughed. "Nope. A moldy metal box with a little knife in it. And some letters."

Acknowledgments

The authors would like to thank Teresa Inge and Adele Gardner for their time and talent. We appreciate their attention to detail in proofreading and editing our manuscripts. We would also like to thank Koehler Books for publishing *Virginia is for Mysteries*.

Virginia is for Mysteries Authors

TERESA INGE

Teresa Inge grew up reading Nancy Drew mysteries. Combining her love of reading mysteries and writing professional articles led to writing short fiction and novellas.

Today, she doesn't carry a rod like her idol but she hot rods. She juggles assisting two busy executives at a financial firm and is president of the Sisters in Crime, Mystery by the Sea chapter. Teresa is the author of the *Virginia is for Mysteries Series, 50 Shades of Cabernet, Mutt Mysteries Series, Coastal Crimes-Mysteries by the Sea, and Murder by the Glass, Cocktail Mysteries.*

Teresa resides in Southeastern Virginia with her husband and two dogs. She can be reached on all social media or by posting a comment on her website.

Links:

Teresa Inge Website and Blog: http://www.teresainge.com
Twitter: https://twitter.com/@teresainge7
Facebook: https://www.facebook.com/teresa.h.inge
Instagram: https://www.instagram.com/teresa.h.inge/
Goodreads: https://www.goodreads.com/teresainge
Amazon Authors: https://www.amazon.com/Teresa-Inge/e/B06XGZ7RTG
Pinterest: https://www.pinterest.com/teresainge7/
LinkedIn: https://www.linkedin.com/in/teresa-inge-cap-07687820/
BookBub: https://www.blurb.com/user/teresainge?profile_preview=true
AllAuthor: https://allauthor.com/author/teresaingeauthor/

Kiss, Makeup, and Murder by Teresa Inge

When Connar Randolph, owner of the historic Cavalier in Virginia Beach discovers the dead body of a prominent hotel guest and is accused of murder, she uncovers a love triangle, a kiss with a wealthy playboy, and a suspicious family member when trying to solve the mystery.

Chalk it Up to Murder by Teresa Inge

When chalkboard artist, Jojo Bennington designs a chalkboard for a wedding guest in Virginia Beach, she becomes the prime suspect when the guest is murdered with the chalkboard since Jojo was the last to see her alive.

KRISTIN KISSKA

Kristin Kisska used to be a finance geek, complete with MBA and Wall Street pedigree, but now she is a self-proclaimed *fictionista*. Kristin contributed short stories of mystery and suspense to nine anthologies, including DEADLY SOUTHERN CHARM (2019). She is a member of International Thriller Writers, James River Writers, and is the Vice President of the Central Virginia chapter of Sisters in Crime. When not writing, she can be found on her website~ *KristinKisska.com*, on Facebook at *KristinKisskaAuthor,* Tweeting *@KKMHOO,* and on Instagram *@KristinKisskaAuthor*. Kristin lives in Virginia with her husband and three children.

Vendetta By the Sea by Kristin Kisska

When four high school friends meet to co-celebrate their fortieth birthdays, old wounds resurface. At least one won't leave their beach week reunion alive.

YVONNE SAXON

Yvonne Saxon is a former middle/high school English teacher and librarian who wants to be an art fraud investigator, a codebreaker, or a secret agent when she really grows up. Until then, she's writing her characters into trouble on the page. She lives in Chesapeake, Virginia, with her family, and enjoys cooking, creating, and reading mysteries and suspense thrillers.

Dirty Business by Yvonne Saxon

Val tries to salvage a family Thanksgiving going wrong, while at the same time attempting to keep history where it belongs!

FRANCES AYLOR

Frances Aylor (www.francesaylor.com) won the IngramSpark Rising Star Award for her first novel, *Money Grab.* A Chartered Financial Analyst, she is a past president of CFA Society of Virginia and gives presentations on money management. A member of International Thriller Writers and president of Sisters in Crime – Central Virginia, she is an avid traveler who has paraglided in Switzerland,  gone white-water rafting in Costa Rica, and fished for piranha in the Amazon. Her short stories appear in *Deadly Southern Charm* and several other anthologies.

Contact her at fjaylor@hastingsbaycapital.com.
Facebook: https://www.facebook.com/FrancesAylorAuthor/
Amazon Author Page: https://www.amazon.com/Frances-Aylor

Deidra the Dog Detective by Frances Aylor

Diane's dream summer job at Kings Dominion amusement park was dancing the fairy princess role on stage, with handsome college student Larry as her prince. Instead, beautiful blond Becky got both the princess role and the prince. Diane sweltered outside day after day in a fuzzy labradoodle costume, entertaining children as Deidra the Dog Detective, star of a hit movie. Then she stumbled over Becky's body in the woods. Besides Diane, who wanted to kill Becky?

JAYNE ORMEROD

Jayne Ormerod grew up in a small Ohio town then went on to a small-town Ohio college. Upon earning her degree in accountancy, she became a CIA (that's not a sexy spy thing, but a Certified Internal Auditor.) She married a naval officer and off they sailed to see the world. After nineteen moves, they, along with their two rescue dogs, have settled into a cozy cottage by the sea. Jayne's publishing  credits include more than a dozen mysteries of varying lengths. A complete list can be found on her website www.jayneormerod. com.

Sorry, Wrong Number by Jayne Ormerod

Margaret Gunderson and best friend Carolyn Prewitt of Roanoke, Virginia are up the creek without a paddle when they find a floater aka dead body while kayaking on the Assateague Channel to retrace the route of the annual pony swim between Assateague and Chincoteague Islands. But when Margaret accidently texts a picture of the dead floater to a wrong number instead of the police, she and Carolyn set out to solve the mysterious man's death.

HEATHER WEIDNER

Heather Weidner writes the Delanie Fitzgerald mystery series set in Virginia (*Secret Lives and Private Eyes, The Tulip Shirt Murders,* and *Glitter, Glam, and Contraband*). Her Jules Keene Glamping Mysteries launch October 2021. Heather's short stories appear in the *Virginia is for Mysteries* series, *50 Shades of Cabernet,* and *Deadly Southern Charm,* and her novellas appear in The Mutt Mysteries series.

She is a member of Sisters in Crime – Central Virginia, Sisters in Crime – Chessie, Guppies, International Thriller Writers, and James River Writers.

Originally from Virginia Beach, Heather has been a mystery fan since Scooby-Doo and Nancy Drew. She lives in Central Virginia with her husband and a pair of Jack Russell terriers. Through the years, she has been a cop's kid, technical writer, editor, college professor, software tester, and IT manager.

Links:

Website and Blog: http://www.heatherweidner.com
Twitter: https://twitter.com/HeatherWeidner1
Facebook: https://www.facebook.com/
HeatherWeidnerAuthor
Instagram: https://www.instagram.com/heather_
mystery_writer/
Goodreads: https://www.goodreads.com/author/
show/8121854.Heather_Weidner
Amazon Authors: http://www.amazon.com/-/e/
B00HOYR0MQ
Pinterest: https://www.pinterest.com/HeatherBWeidner/
LinkedIn: https://www.linkedin.com/in/heather-weidner-
0064b233?trk=hp-identity-name
BookBub: https://www.bookbub.com/authors/heather-
weidner-d6430278-c5c9-4b10-b911-340828fc7003

Derailed by Heather Weidner

Sassy private investigator, Delanie Fitzgerald, gets more than she bargains for when sleezy strip club owner and her best, cash-paying client, Chaz Smith, hires her to find out who's blackmailing him and his buddies. She and her partner, Duncan Reynolds, have to find out what happened one summer evening twenty years ago and what it has to do with the Church Hill Tunnel cave-in. While trying to figure out the connection to the spooky, abandoned site where the train and several victims lie buried beneath a busy Richmond neighborhood, Delanie discovers the origin of Chaz's mysterious teardrop face tattoo.

To read more of the sassy private investigator's adventures, check out Heather Weidner's Delanie Fitzgerald mysteries.

MICHAEL RIGG

Michael Rigg is a retired Navy Judge Advocate, plies his trade as a mild-mannered civil servant and attorney by day, then morphs into a nascent mystery and thriller writer by night. Mike is a member of Hampton Roads Writers, as well as the Sisters-in-Crime national organization and its Southeastern Virginia Chapter—Mystery by the Sea. He and his wife live in Virginia Beach. Visit him online at www.facebook.com/michael.rigg.author.

Ghosts of Sandbridge by Michael Rigg

Retired Navy Pilot turned Private Investigator Ryan Kensington accepts what should be a softball undercover assignment to act as a vacationer, while secretly looking into why prices are plummeting at *Pirate's Hideaway*, an oceanfront rental in the Sandbridge section of Virginia Beach. Soon, he learns that all is not is all at it seems in this idyllic community tucked between the Atlantic Ocean and Back Bay. Ryan must deal with greed, an unplanned romantic encounter, deceit, and betrayal as he determines who is behind an invidious, fraudulent scheme.

MAGGIE KING

Maggie King is the author of the Hazel Rose Book Group mysteries. Her short stories appear in the *Virginia is for Mysteries* series, *50 Shades of Cabernet, Deadly Southern Charm, Murder by the Glass,* and *Death by Cupcake*.

Maggie is a founding member of Sisters in Crime Central Virginia, where she manages the chapter's Instagram account. Maggie graduated from Rochester Institute of Technology with a degree in Business Administration, and has worked as a software developer and a retail sales manager. She lives in Richmond, Virginia with her husband, Glen, and two mischievous cats. http://www.maggieking.com

The Last Laugh by Maggie King

Emily Bates arrives at Julie Ruthers's home in Charlottesville, Virginia, expecting to enjoy a good meal and companionship with her new friend. Instead she walks into a crime scene and learns how too much betrayal can push one woman to exact revenge by unspeakable means.

By the time Emily realizes how much danger she faces, it may be too late!

SMITA HARISH JAIN

Smita Harish Jain has had several short stories published in anthologies for Mystery Writers of America, Sisters in Crime, and Akashic Noir, as well as in Ellery Queen Mystery Magazine. She has several more short stories coming out in the next year for Ellery Queen Mystery Magazine, Malice  Domestic's Mystery Most Diabolical, Chesapeake Crime's Magic is Murder and other publications. She was thrilled to have this opportunity to write a story set in one of her favorite cities and hopes readers come to enjoy Fredericksburg both in these pages and in person.

Unfinished Business by Smita Harish Jain

The Fredericksburg Specters and Spirits Tour takes a deadly turn, and the city's young mayor must catch the killer, before any more tourists become ghosts!

SHERYL JORDAN

Sheryl Jordan began reading all genres of books at a young age, her favorites being mysteries and true crime. As a child, she often read four to five books while vacationing with her family. Sheryl completed her bachelor's degree in Criminal Justice at Saint Leo College and completed a paralegal  certification at Old Dominion University. She is a member of Sisters in Crime National and the Mysteries by the Sea chapter. Sheryl is the author of *Manipulation, Money and Murder,* a fictitious novel based on true crimes and a short fiction in Coastal Crimes anthology. Born in Portugal, raised in Minnesota, she now resides in Virginia with her family. She loves spending time with her grandchildren, Nana's Angels.

The Lady Ginger by Sheryl Jordan

Eboni and Ember Snoe are excited to move into their new luxurious home with great views of Lake Smith in Virginia Beach. While moving in, strange things begin to happen that may turn their dream home into a house of horror.

VIVIAN LAWRY

Vivian Lawry has published short works in more than fifty literary journals and anthologies, and a selection of these stories are published in Different Drummer. She's also published three novels: Dark Harbor, Tiger Heart, and Nettie's Books. Appalachian by birth, she now lives and writes near Richmond, Virginia. Like Vivian Lawry on Facebook, and check out her twice-weekly blogs at vivianlawry.com.

A Dinner to Die For by Vivian Lawry

Clara, a prostitute during the Civil War, specializes in clients with peculiar pleasures. She's invited to a party with long-time client, Colonel Levereaux and six food fetishists. Only five of them survive the night.

MARIA HUDGINS

Maria Hudgins is the author of four Dotsy Lamb Travel Mysteries, Death of an Obnoxious Tourist, Death of a Lovable Geek, Death on the Aegean Queen, and Death of a Second Wife. These stories are set in Italy, Scotland, the Greek Islands, and Switzerland, respectively.

Before using a place as a setting, Hudgins visits and takes copious notes. Two mysteries in her new Lacy Glass Series are now available on Kindle and Kindle Prime.

Scorpion House centers around an expedition house in Luxor, Egypt. The Man on the Istanbul Train follows the young botanist from Istanbul to an archaeological dig in central Turkey. She lives in Hampton, Virginia.

She Simply Vanished by **Maria Hudgins**

"Standing atop the ramparts at Hampton's Fort Monroe, a local woman sees a couple talking at the seawall down below. Seconds later she looks again and sees the man but not his companion, a girl in a green dress. The girl has disappeared. The woman goes to the police with absolutely no evidence but with the certainty that something bad has happened."

ROSEMARY SHOMAKER

Rosemary Shomaker mulls story ideas and exercises her writing craft from Central Virginia. Her work features the mystery of seemingly everyday, banal surroundings, circumstances, and routines, and her stories often include dogs and trees.

Revelation by **Rosemary Shomaker**

Culpeper Virginia's Fairview Cemetery holds sadness, fear, and upset for Vickey Martin. As she looks west past her father's grave to the Blue Ridge Mountains, her Grandpa Lew's blank date-of-death beckons from the Grayson headstone where her grandmother rests, waiting for her husband. Grandpa Lew's in the hospital, but it's the acute need to dig another family grave that unhinges Vickey as this trip home from her city job rocks her world.

MAX JASON PETERSON

Max Jason Peterson is the mystery moniker of a professional member of Sisters in Crime, SFWA, and HWA. With mystery stories in *Mystery Weekly Magazine* (cover), *Seascape: The Best New England Crime Stories 2019*, and *A Study in Lavender: Queering Sherlock Holmes*, Max has over  440 stories, poems, art, and articles published all told (under bylines including C. A. Gardner, Lyn C. A. Gardner, Adele Gardner, and other variants). Max is a genderfluid individual who loves owls, cats, and intelligent shades of the color blue. Find Max shooting b&w film old-school in the noir nightscape.

The Halloween Open by Max Jason Peterson

Beneath the snarling wolf painted on his fencing mask, Keith Semper has big dreams. But when two talented young fencers square off at the Halloween Open, one ends up with a scholarship. The other one winds up dead.

JUDITH FOWLER

Judith Fowler's master's degree in forensic psychology and monthly meet-ups with SinC group Mystery by the Sea keep her hopelessly focused on courts, crimes, and deviance. You can enjoy her work in the SinC anthology *Coastal Crimes* and friend her on FB @ Judith Johonnot Fowler and @ Legal Rights in the  Courtroom. She has also won prizes for memoir and poetry with the support of Virginia Beach Writers, Hampton Roads Writers, and The Muse.

A Guest at the Land House by Judith Fowler

What is history? Maybe it comes down to what you think you know, in this re-imagining of life in a 19th century plantation house, and the ripple effect from one visitor's terrible behavior.